The
True Swing

by Tom Scheve

ISBN-10: 0-9638957-3-7
ISBN-13: 978-0-9638957-3-8

Requests to the Publisher for permission should be addressed to
Orange Publishing
P.O. Box 1987
230 North Bennett Street, Bldg. #1
Southern Pines, NC 28388-1987
tomequispirit@earthlink.net

For general information on other books written by this author contact
Tom Scheve
c/o Orange Publishing
P.O. Box 1987
230 North Bennett Street, Bldg. #1
Southern Pines, NC 28388-1987
tomequispirit@earthlink.net

Printed in the United States of America
10   9   8   7   6   5   4   3   2   1

Table of Contents

"If you let go of what you are, you'll become what you might be."

Lao Tzu

Student: "Is there such a thing as a true swing?"

Teacher: "Yes."

Student: "How can I learn it?"

Teacher: "It cannot be learned."

Student: "Then how can I attain it?"

Teacher: "It cannot be attained."

Student: "Then how can I know it?"

Teacher: "*Who* wants to know?"

June 1998

Chapter 1

I had just crossed a bridge, only to find myself lost. *Wait a minute — shouldn't there be a sign?* I reached for my directions, which were no more than ink scribbles on a used napkin, the words smeared and laced with mustard and hot dog grease. It said, "Turn right on *something* Bridge Road. Cross bridge. Look for sign on right, says...*Golden River*? Turn onto gravel road."

So where's the sign?

I shook my head, pitched the directions aside, and wondered why at age thirty, my male ego had me roaming a remote area of southwestern Ohio where there was nothing but endless rolling cornfields and long stretches of woods. I couldn't even find a radio station on my new Mustang GT. The radio had been spewing out nothing but static since the freeway.

"Damn that noise," I said out loud and punched a tuning button. More static. I started punching at all the buttons. A voice finally crackled in ***"Eleven o'clock, and it's another hot June morning,"*** but then crackled out.

I was reaching again for the tuning buttons when a bright light streaked through the passenger window and exploded inside the car "Holy Crap!" I shouted and jerked the wheel.

The light hung inside for a few seconds then flashed out, but the Mustang was out of control, careening off the road onto a gravel drive. I slammed the brakes, throwing the car into a spin, tossing dust and gravel everywhere. With my foot still hard on the brakes, the car abruptly slid to a stop, pitching my head forward into the steering wheel, and snapping it back against the seat. For a moment, bright sparkling lights flashed everywhere. A moment later, all went black.

Chapter 2

A loud chirp just outside my opened car window nudged me into semi-consciousness. I shook my head. *Where am I?* It was quiet, and still. Another chirp cut through the silence, hanging in the air for a moment, then slipping back into the stillness.

I was vaguely aware of being in a car, my car, but the engine wasn't running, the hissing static of my radio was gone. A moment passed or was it two, when I heard breathing — hard, deep breathing, coming from inside the car. I stiffened and looked over my shoulder. There was no one there. *Is that me, breathing?* I shook my head, trying to focus, trying to… *Gees! Are those my hands?* They looked strange and unfamiliar. So did the steering wheel, the gauges, the dashboard — so detailed, so vivid, as if I were seeing them for the first time.

Another breath, but this time I *felt* the breath heave my chest, and the air draw into my lungs. The breath I had heard, it was mine — a sense of my Self was returning. But something wasn't right.

I couldn't see through the windshield! *What the heck?* An eerie brown fog had engulfed the car. Suddenly the car felt small and constricting. I needed out. I grabbed the door handle. It was locked. I groped for the lock but couldn't reach it — my seat belt was holding me back. I twisted, trying to free myself, but it wouldn't release. Then something caught my eye. A shimmering glow beckoned in the swirling fog. It appeared suspended in a field of dancing, pulsating lights. I gripped the steering wheel and pulled myself forward.

HISSsssssss…POP!

"…NOW IS THE TIME! YOU'LL LOSE BIG IF YOU DON'T ACT NOW! IT ALL STARTS…" *Damn!*

The radio kicked on at full volume, blasting me back into my seat. I grabbed the knob, clicked it off, and fumbled for my seat belt. Finally, it released. I popped the door lock, swung the door open, and clambered to get out.

What the…?

The brown fog was fading. In fact, it wasn't fog at all. It was just a dust cloud that must have swirled up when my car slid across the gravel. *But what about the shimmering light?*

Using the steering wheel, I pulled myself forward and peered through the windshield. The dust was thinning and where there had been pulsating lights, now stood a small, square wood sign, partially obscured by the tall June grass. The border and letters were painted in rich gold. It said, "Golden River."

Sweat poured down my face as the heat dripped into the open windows. *Was I hallucinating? Maybe it was the sun reflecting off the gold lettering through the dust. But what about the flash of light on the road?* I glanced out the side window and caught the sun reflecting in my mirror. *Could that be what it was?*

The door was still ajar, so I pushed it open and swung my leg out. Squish.

Now, what? I tried to pull my leg back in but it wouldn't budge. The gravel road was dry and dusty except for a large patch of soft tar under my foot. With a fair amount of effort, I freed my shoe from the road, but not from the gravely mess. It came into my new Mustang with my foot. I slammed the door, slumped in my seat, and dropped my head on the steering wheel. *What the heck am I doing here?*

Chapter 3

How did I end up here, in the middle of nowhere? The question didn't warrant an answer. I knew how I got here; I just didn't know why, and I doubt if it could have happened any differently. It had all started about six weeks ago on a cloudy but warm day in early April. Everything on Mill Branch Golf Course was a gloomy gray, including my golf buddy, BJ. He was taking his sixth practice swing, struggling to fix something we all knew was unfixable.

WHOOSH!

My other golf partners, Larry and Tom, slouched on a bench next to me with their heads in their hands. The sounds of early spring were in the air, but they were fighting the sound of BJ's practice swings.

WHOOSH!

"We should have packed a lunch," Larry said under his breath.

"Maybe lunch and supper," Tom said and looked up. "You know, as bad as he's..."

"Don't say it," I warned.

He said it anyway. "As bad as BJ's playing, he's still got you by five holes on the back nine."

WHOOSH!

"I told you not to say it."

"Hey, no need to get upset. One of us is always taking your money — nothing new here."

"What I can't figure," Larry added, "is why you keep losing, given the amount of time you spend working on your game."

WHOOSH!

"He's got a point," Tom said. "You've studied and read more about golf than anyone I've ever known. Next to BJ's swing, yours looks great, yet you're always on the losing end."

WHOOSH!

I glanced back at BJ. It wasn't a pretty sight. At five feet ten, two hundred and fifteen pounds, he swung his club with all the power of a lumberjack, but with none of the grace. His idea of the perfect swing was to kill the ball, and he often admitted it. "Hey, if you don't swing at the ball with all you got, what's the point?"

Finally, he stepped up to his ball. We all held our breath.

WHOOSH!
WHIFF!
The ball sat untouched on the tee. As BJ tried to unscrew himself from his miss, Tom and I cringed in anticipation of Larry's usual wisecrack. But it didn't come.

What? No cynical remark? No merciless dig? I glanced at Larry. He was biting his lip hard, holding back, probably deciding whether BJ was beyond coping with sarcasm. He caught my eye and then Tom's while shaking his head. We understood. We were allowing him to pretend that his miss had been just another practice swing.

WHOOSH!
Another practice swing.
WHOOSH!
And another.

My patience was now wearing thin, but I kept quiet. BJ had a temper and the way he was approaching his ball — nostrils flared, eyes narrowed, mouth distorted, gripping his club so tightly his knuckles were white, was a bit scary. When he jerked his club to swing, I cringed.

WHOOSH! WHIFF!
Another miss, but the gale-force wind from his swing blew the ball off the tee and rolled it a yard. Larry could no longer restrain himself. "It went straight."

WHISH WHISH WHISH WHISH...
Oh, Crap! That horrifying swirling sound I knew all too well — a golf club in manic flight, let loose by a golfer with too much power and too little control. Larry and Tom ducked, but I was too late.

WHISH! WHOMP!
The club head swirled past me, but the handle whacked the side of my head and sent me straight to the ground.

Chapter 4

"Jo-o-oh-hn! Jo-o-oh-hn! Aaarrre yoouuu aallll rrrriiighhhtt?"

Through my flickering eyelids, I could see BJs face staring down at me from what seemed a great distance. Then, like air escaping from a balloon, I shot upwards over the trees and into the overcast sky. For an instant, nothing was visible, but then I burst through, into an infinite sea of cobalt blue, filled with billowing white clouds.

Where am I? What am I?

The questions startled me, but a moment later they dropped away, and I expanded into the entire space of the sky.

The overcast below me rolled back like a curtain in play, revealing a wondrous scene — a golf course, stretching from horizon to horizon. It was a spectacular sight. Luxuriant green fairways sifting through perfectly manicured sand traps. Lakes sparkling silver in the sunlight. Rolling greens accommodating candy-striped poles with large red flags.

Like a feather floating on a summer breeze, I drifted gently down and was gliding effortlessly, free and unhindered, until something in particular, drew my attention — a fox, darting across one of the tees where a woman was teeing off.

CRAAACK!

She connected with perfect timing sending the ball long and straight down the middle of the fairway. *What a great drive!* But she took her club and angrily jammed it into her bag, mumbling that it didn't go exactly where she wanted. *Such a beautiful setting — such a great shot. How can she not be happy?*

Another golfer across the fairway caught my attention just as he was about to chip his ball onto the green.

Clip!

The ball sailed to within a foot of the hole but instead of smiling, he tossed his club on the ground and shook his head. "Why in the hell couldn't I have done that on the last hole!"

Drifting to the next hole, another golfer was preparing to putt, but he backed away. I heard him say that if he didn't make this putt, it would ruin his best game ever.

And so it continued, from golfer to golfer, all lost in their thoughts while existing in such a spectacular setting. It made no sense — fretting about what had already passed, worrying about what might be.

Why can't they see? The game is not in the past or the future. It's right here, right now. I started shouting down at them, "Wake up! Wake up before it's too late!"

Chapter 5

"Too late for what?" BJ asked with some concern.

"Are you all right?" Tom asked.

Familiar voices. Vague images. I blinked a few times. Tom, BJ and Larry came into focus. "Yeah, I'm okay," I said, shaking my head. "'Just had a strange dream."

"When?" Larry asked. "You were only out for a few seconds."

BJ offered me his hand, but not an apology. Once he saw I was okay, the side bet took precedent over getting whacked with a club. We all understood that, so he asked, "Are you able to play the last hole?"

My groggy mind still had enough sense to take advantage of the situation, so I asked, "Are you going to give me extra strokes for getting knocked unconscious?"

"Right," BJ said with sarcasm. Larry and Tom hurried away, feigning that they hadn't heard me, which proves that when there's money on the game, nothing short of death will get you extra strokes.

By the time we reached the eighteenth green, BJ was gloating — staring at me with that "I got you by the ass" grin. With his ball resting only two feet from the hole, he said, "You know, even if I four-putt, I'd beat you."

"Is that so?" I said.

They all stopped in their tracks. Indifference was not something they expected from me when there's a wager on the game. But I had no idea what my strokes were. Throughout the last hole, my mind had slipped in and out of the clouds. One moment I had felt like my old self, the next like an observer, watching my buddies and myself as if we were all actors in a play or characters in a dream. As they stood there staring at me, I half smiled. *What if all of us are in a dream of some greater being? And what if that being were to wake up? Would we all disappear?*

A voice interrupted my thoughts and I looked at Larry. "What did you say?"

"I didn't say anything," Larry said as he shrugged at Tom and BJ.

"Now you're hearing things?" Tom asked.

"No, I didn't hear anything," I lied.

But I *had* heard something. A murmur, and it was still there. As we walked off the green, the murmuring persisted. It didn't sound like the usual voice inside my head. I strained to listen, but the words weren't quite intelligible, but I felt compelled to go to the clubhouse.

"Where are you going?" Tom asked. Beers always came first, and the snack bar was the other direction. I didn't answer. The voice was becoming louder, the words clearer. I clasped my hands over my ears as I entered the clubhouse. In response, the voice shouted, *"Sell your clubs and be done with this!"*

"What?" I said right out loud, startling the golf pro behind the counter. The voice shouted again, *"Sell your clubs and be done with this!"*

The pro eyed me suspiciously as I approached. *"Ask him to make you an offer. Take it and walk away before it's too late."* Just as I reached him, I recoiled, stopping dead in my tracks. *No! This is not the answer!*

"Can I help you?" the pro asked. I ran for the door and didn't look back. When I found my buddies, they were two pitchers of beer into alcohol-induced camaraderie.

"Well?" Tom asked.

"Well, what?"

"Are you going to tell us what's going on?"

"What makes you think something's going on?"

Tom shook his head at Larry and turned back towards me. "For one thing, not caring that BJ took your money. For another, hearing voices that aren't there. Walking into the clubhouse with your hands over your ears. Should I go on?"

Larry poured another round and included one for me. I gulped it down, grabbed the pitcher and poured another. I gulped it down just as quickly and looked at their staring faces. "What!" I said. No answer — just starring and waiting.

"Okay, okay, give me a minute to gather my thoughts." I poured another beer. It went down even quicker and my thoughts blurred.

"Well, it sort of goes like this. When-BJ's-club-knocked-me-out-I-became-the-sky-but-I-wasn't-really-the-sky-because-I-was-flying-through-the-clouds-until-I-noticed-the-earth-was-one-big-golf-course-and-there-were-birds-and-a-fox-and-I-swooped-down-and-got-inside-some-golfer's-heads-as-they-hit-some-great-shots-and-then-I-woke-up-and-we-played-the-last-hole-and-I-heard-this-strange-voice-telling-me-to-sell-my-golf-clubs-so-I-went-to-the-clubhouse-but-I-didn't-sell-them-and-I-ran-out-the-door-and-came here-to-find-you-guys-getting-sloshed."

Except for the final slurp of BJ's third beer, there was complete silence.

"Well?" I asked impatiently.

"You owe me ten bucks for the game, a buck for the beer," BJ stated matter-of-factly.

"Hell! Is that all you can think about?"

"Hey," Larry blurted out, "just because he took your money and tried to kill you doesn't mean you shouldn't be nice to him."

I tried not to smile.

"I think I know what happened to you?" Tom interjected.

"Is that so?" I said. "I can't wait to hear this."

"You had a near-quitting-the-game experience."

While they all bellowed, I couldn't help but smile. His beer-colored wisdom actually made some sense. Maybe not a near-quitting-the-game experience but perhaps a near-death experience, thanks to BJ's flying driver. While their laughter continued, my mind drifted. Something had changed, but I wasn't sure what.

"Hey, John. Are you still with us?" Tom asked.

"Yeah," I answered, but I wasn't really.

"You look a little lost."

Good choice of words. I did feel lost, perhaps for the first time in my life. Lost, and full of questions. *Is there more than just what appears to be? What kind of game are we really playing here? And...* My mind went blank. *There had been another question, wasn't there?* I struggled to recall it, but nothing came. Nothing that is, except for the conviction that the game as I had known it, was over.

Chapter 6

One might think I would have given up a playing partner that tried to kill me with his golf club, but for me, friendship trumped accidental assault and battery. So when BJ, Larry, and Tom talked me into playing a round a few days later, I accepted. But by the time we reached the fifth hole, they were probably wondering if taking my money was worth the risk of playing with a golfer who was self-destructing. The knock to my head, the experience of having that dream, constantly losing wagers, had catapulted me onto a desperate quest to fix my swing. And that desperate quest turned into a swinging frenzy that included slashing away at the ball and being oblivious to everything around me. On the sixth hole, a voice finally broke through my trance.

"Stand clear."

It was Larry's voice — not loud, but insistent enough to pull me back into sanity. I glanced up. Larry, BJ, and Tom were standing at least twenty-five feet behind me.

"What are you guys doing way back there?" I asked with controlled irritation.

They all looked at each other, surprised that I had even noticed them.

"Exercising caution," Larry finally said.

"What?"

"We're playing it safe. You've been swinging like a wild man."

I'm swinging like a wild man? In my mind's eye, I pictured the wild man of Borneo — a fiery-eyed, crazed creature, flailing a club. *I'm swinging like a wild man?* Right then and there, I knew it was time to seek help. All the wrist straps, training clubs, altered putters, and other golf gizmos I had purchased weren't doing their job. What I needed was something more. It was time to find an instructor.

Instructor #1

"Bend your legs. Stick your butt out. Straighten your back. Butt out. Get your head down. Left arm straight. Butt out."

My first instructor was simply not going to be happy with my swing unless my butt stuck out.

"Bend those legs a little more and stick that butt out!"

Never in any major golf publication had I read about a "sticking-your-butt-out" approach to a better swing.

"Surely you can stick it out a little more than that."

Was this a mental ploy? Was he trying to take my mind off my swing by making me self-conscious about how stupid I look? But he didn't let up. He really did believe my butt was the center of my swing. *What the hell are my golf buddies going to think when they see me swinging away with my butt hanging out?* It was time for a new instructor.

Instructor #2

"Take your driver and show me your grip. Good!" he said. "But move your right hand over just a bit to your left. Okay, now place your head slightly behind the ball but directly over your hands."

My new instructor thought the problem was in my grip and made no mention of my butt — maybe I'm getting somewhere.

"Now, without moving your head, spit."

"What?"

"Without moving your head, spit, and let it drop straight down."

"Spit?

"Yes."

"Straight down?"

"Yes."

I let go a wad of spit. It splattered on the back of my hands.

"Perfect!" he exclaimed.

From where I was standing, it didn't look so perfect.

"This shows that the relationship between your head and your hands is good."

If my hands have such a good relationship with my head, why did my head spit on them?

"Now Swing."

WHASK!

Uh-oh. The ball flew off to the right. He teed up a ball for me and I swung again.

WHASK!

The ball took an even greater bend to the right.

WHASK!

Oh, crap! Not the god-awful slice, the big "banana. This can't be happening.

WHASK! WHASK! WHASK!

The instructor stared at my grip, then stared out over the fairway, and then stared at me. "Try turning your hands a bit more towards the target."

WHASK!

And so it went for another hour before I finally paused, glaring at my instructor. He furrowed his brow and said, "Maybe try sticking your butt out just a little."

Instructor #3

"We can rid you of that slice," my new teacher said. I looked around to see who "we" were. "Turn your grip, so your hands are turned away from the target and your palms are parallel with each other. If you drew lines up from the base of your thumbs, they should hit the point of your collar on the right side of your shirt." He pulled a large dry marker from his shirt pocket.

"No need to draw a line up my shirt," I said. "I get it."

He put the marker back and said, "Now swing at the ball."

WHASK!

The ball sliced into some woods that lay just beyond the right side of the range.

"Hmm. Let's try that again, but drop your right foot back."

WHASK!

Again, the ball sliced into the woods — the sound of golf ball meeting trees echoing back as if mocking us. He stared out over the woods for a long moment.

"Swing again," he said meekly.

WHASK!

Again, in the woods. The instructor looked at my stance, looked back to the woods, then back to my stance.

"Perhaps even stronger on the grip and relax it a little."

WHASK!

Back into the woods.

Two kids, who must have been searching for balls in the woods shot out of the trees, running for their lives.

"That's....hmm. Let's see," my instructor said. "Try putting less strength in your right hand, keeping that left arm straight and turn your club head in a bit. Imagine yourself trying to hit the ball with the front head of your driver."

I felt all bent and twisted, like a pretzel.

WHASK!

We both stared at the ball as it sailed into the woods. He stood silent, in disbelief. It was near impossible to slice a ball from that position with that grip. He knew it and I knew it. I thought about my golf buddies. How were they going to react to my new butt and pretzel swing?

Instructor #4

"Your left brain is telling your right brain lies about yourself — that you're no good, that you can't swing a club correctly," my new instructor explained. This instructor came highly recommended by a psychologist friend, who felt that somehow my subconscious was getting in my way.

He placed a ball on the tee, and I swung.

WHAMP!

A new sound and a deep fear rose from my gut as I placed another ball on the tee.

WHAMP!

The ball sliced and fell short.

WHAMPF!

The ball sliced and fell even shorter. *Oh no!*

WHAMPF! WHAMPF! WHAMPF!

A full swing with my driver and the ball didn't even reach the hundred-and-seventy-yard marker. No way had I figured my swing could get worse, but now it was attacking my manhood.

"You've got to tell your right brain not to listen," he said.

I've come a long way. My butt to my brain.

"Your left brain is also telling your right brain that you're not capable. And your right brain believes it."

I was beginning to feel like I was in a group lesson. *Maybe I should ask him for group rates.*

"Believe me," he said. "We can fix this."

He just didn't understand. My golf buddies would put up with the wild man swing, the butt hanging out, the spitting on myself — and would probably even forgive the "pretzel" stance. But the loss of distance? Absolutely not. "Wimp" would be the underlying message of all future golf jibes.

The instructor placed a ball on the tee and while I stood over it, concentrating on not listening to my left brain, I realized I could no longer hear my right brain. In fact, I could no longer hear any brain. My butt started inching out, my right foot dropped back, my right hand moved over on the grip, and I was twisting into a pretzel position. I couldn't stop myself. I spit on my hands, jerked the club back, flailed at the ball, and watched it go a hundred and fifty yards to the right.

Later that afternoon, I shut myself in my den. Every golf book and magazine I had ever bought was there, waiting to be reread. And I attacked them all. But I already knew the mechanics of a correct swing — why couldn't I do it? I understood the concept of chipping from every angle and distance — why did my body fail to deliver. I had a keen eye for breaks and grains in greens — why did my stroke fail to get the ball on line?

No answers came, only silence. But the silence itself seemed to communicate something. I didn't so much hear it as felt it. Like it or not, I was on a path, and there was no turning back.

Chapter 7

With four lessons and four teachers behind me, it didn't seem possible that my swing could get worse. But after nine holes of ribbing, attacking my manhood, uncontrollable laughter at my butt and pretzel swing, and losing money on every hole, I had to admit that it was not only possible, it was true. As I stood next to BJ at the snack bar, I mumbled, "I'm about ready to cash in my swing."

Irma, the head cashier, ears perked up. "So your swing has unraveled, has it?"

It was not surprising that she had overheard me. Irma made it her business to overhear everyone, as well as to state her opinions — loudly. Usually, we ignored her. But my thoughts had me distracted and I answered.

"Yeah," I said with a sigh.

Tom's eyebrows shot up in surprise. He knew I knew that to answer any of Irma's question would engage her in a conversation — a conversation that would never end well.

"Uh-oh," I said, and quickly ordered a lemonade. My buddies hurriedly snuck over to a nearby table.

"Did you hear about Henry Smithson?" she asked with a twisted grin. Irma's only reason for working at the course was to be to make golfers miserable. Rumor had it that her husband had left one day to buy a set of golf clubs and never returned.

"Who's Henry Smithson?"

"He used to play golf with Jim Weller every Saturday. I *know* you know *him.*"

I *did* know Jim Weller, but how did she know?

"I don't know Jim Weller all *that* well," I said just to take the wind out of her sails.

"What are you talking about? He got you your belt selling job, didn't he?"

How she knew these things, I had no idea. She was right. Jim Weller had helped me get my job. It was shortly after my divorce when Jim and I had met by chance over a round of golf. A casual conversation between holes led to inquiries about each other's livelihoods. When I told him I was in sales and actively searching for a new job, he had grinned and said, "Waisting Away."

"I'm not wasting away yet," I had responded.

"No, no. Waisting Away is a belt company that has just been bought by the company I work for — American Credential."

Like everyone else in Cincinnati, I knew of American Credential. They were one of the fifty largest companies in the country and made a practice of buying and developing smaller businesses.

"Waist...w-a-i-s-t," he added. "Get it? Belt around the waist? Waisting Away?"

"I got it," I said. "I was just trying to ignore it."

He shared my lack of enthusiasm about the name but assured me they were a reputable company with a good employment package, and in need of good sales reps. His influence had gotten me an interview, and I'd been working there ever since.

"So what happened to Henry what's-his-name, and what's it got to do with me?"

"His swing fell apart, just like yours. I told him he should quit golf and go do something worthwhile, but he wouldn't listen. All you golfers are the same."

"So are you going to tell me what happened to him?"

"He was out here at the range almost every day, just swinging away. It was pitiful - nothing worked. Then he found this instructor way out in the boonies. Some range about forty miles west of here."

She paused to make sure her last sentence had the intended effect. It did, and I waited. Once she was sure I was hooked, she slowly strolled to the soda dispenser and idly filled my lemonade glass. She cleaned the soda dispenser while she was there. Finally, she shuffled back, handed me the lemonade, and asked, "You want some ice?"

It's ninety-five degrees out, and she's asking me if I want ice?

"SO WHAT HAPPENED TO HIM?" I demanded. Irma truly hated golfers.

"I never saw him again."

"What do you mean you never saw him again? You mean he disappeared out there? What kind of story is that?"

"No. What I mean is; he never came back here." She paused and raised her eyebrows which pulled her lips up into a crooked grin. "I hear rumors, though, that he's playing pretty well."

I sighed in frustration. "Do you know the name of the guy who helped him?"

"I don't think I ever overheard it."

That's a laugh. "Does he still give lessons?"

"How would I know?"

"Do you at least remember the name of the range?"

"Wait a minute." Irma reached under the counter and pulled out a stained white napkin. I could see black scribbling on it.

"The Golden River is what it says here."

"Where did you get that?"

"What do you care?" she taunted, holding it out like bait.

"How about a phone number?" I asked, tugging at the napkin.

She shook her head slowly. If she had any more information, she wasn't going to give it up.

"I heard about your 'big banana' slice," she said, twisting the knife. "I think you ought to check this guy out."

Despite my ego not wanting to take Irma's bait, I had to admit to myself if not to her, that she had me, hook, line, and sinker. I folded the napkin carefully and stuffed it in my pocket. If this mysterious instructor did exist, I had to find him. He could be my last hope.

Chapter 8

So here I was, spun out on a gravel road in Nowhere, Ohio, searching for who-knows-what. Before turning the ignition key, I glanced into my rearview mirror to see if the Golden River sign was still there and to make sure it wasn't glowing. It was still there, and it wasn't glowing. As the engine rumbled to life, I shifted into drive and slowly rolled forward.

CLANK. CLUNK. CHING.

Now, what? I sped up a bit.

CLUNK!

Damn. The back tire had rolled through the soft tar and was kicking gravel against the sides of my Mustang. I sped up, slowed down, and sped up again.

CLINK! "Ouch!"

A stone flew up and hit my elbow. It served me right for hanging it out the window. Anyone else would have had the windows up and the air-conditioning running. But I was in the minority — one of those few who loved the hot summer days.

"Ouch!"

Another direct hit. I stopped the car, thinking I'd take a look, but thought better of it. The hits to my arm were probably a lot less painful than seeing what the gravel was doing to the sides of my car. Instead, I stared blankly out the window. Endless rows of young corn stalks crowded right up to both sides of the road. I half laughed. What would Larry, Tom, and BJ think if they saw me parked in a cornfield, tracking down some golf instructor who might not even exist?

Hell, what could they say? It's not my fault. If it's anyone's fault, it's theirs. Or at least, BJ's. His flying club had certainly done a number on my life. It had been fine until then. At the age of thirty, I was healthy, made friends easily, had a great-paying job with lots of free time, and money always found its way into my pocket when it was needed. My ex-wife had once said, "John, you could fall down a toilet and come up wearing a three-piece suit." She was probably right.

But that whack to the head had jolted me right out of whatever contentment there was in my neat little life. Now, something was missing. *But what? Is there more going on than what there appears to be? And...and... and what?* That other question was still there, lingering just outside of my consciousness, unwilling to show itself.

At least I was certain about one thing: golf. No matter how well or how badly I played, I loved the game. Perhaps the real question was: Why can't I find a consistent, true swing that won't break down under pressure? After all, it's the question that got me here. Perhaps the answer lay right in front of me. With that thought to spur me on, I eased my foot on the accelerator.

The gravel road widened a bit as it left the cornfield, then swerved and followed alongside a small scenic river. The river flowed gently beneath massive Oak and spreading Maple trees. The setting had to be one of Mother Nature's most picturesque, but my mind was somewhere else — maybe a good thing since the gravel was still pummeling my car.

Wait a minute! A thought hit me like a thunderbolt, and I slammed on the brakes. *Why would anyone in their right mind put a driving range out here in the middle of nowhere? Have I been duped? Has Irma gotten her final revenge?*

"Crap!" I said right out loud. *I've been sent on a wild goose chase.* I punched the gas but quickly slowed as the road curved away from the river and wound through an array of plush green foliage and majestic old trees, all vying for my attention. But I stayed focused on my anger and pushed forward.

A bit further, the road widened, and the gravel turned to blacktop. My anger dissipated as a feeling of uneasiness had me wondering where this road might be taking me. My apprehension increased as I entered a grove of towering sycamores that lined both sides of the road. The tops were swaying, throwing luminous spears of sunlight at the ground, at the hood of my car, at my windshield. It was mesmerizing, the play of light, and my head spun. But a glimpse of something ahead quickly sobered me up: a white cinder block building.

The road abruptly ended, delivering me into a small paved lot. There were no marked parking spaces, but there were no cars either, except one: a new '97 VW Jetta. I pulled directly in front of the building and parked. The white block structure was framed in various shades of green from the bushes and trees that surrounded it.

It would have made a perfect June photo in an Ohio Valley calendar. Maybe it already had.

Just beyond the building lay a meadow of rich green grass, interspersed with dandelions, assorted wildflowers, and…and…*what?* It took a moment to grasp what I was seeing.

Yardage markers. Round white yardage markers. They blended so naturally into the setting that only a golfer would have noticed them, if at all. "Well, how about that?" I said, right out loud. "Looks like Irma was telling the truth after all."

As I opened the car door, I spied a late 70's Chevy pick-up partially hidden by a small shed. I also noticed a massive clump of gravel, intermixed with bits of cornstalks and weeds, tarred to the side of my car. "Crap," I said, shaking my head, but found myself smiling. *Why on earth am I smiling?* It wasn't natural, me not being mad. *Could this place have something to do with it?*

I scanned the surroundings until my attention settled on the building. My eyes were drawn to the entrance, a slightly bowed wooden screen door above a single concrete step. My breath quickened, but I didn't know why. It was just an old door, with a step, yet I took some comfort staring at it. It was the kind of door you'd find on an old country farmhouse — warped frame, rusting hinges, ancient spring. I could almost hear the "creak" of its opening, and the familiar "slap" when it shut, ushering in friends and strangers alike.

I moved slowly towards the entrance, but when I reached the step, I hesitated. Not because of the door — it was the darkness beyond the screen that gave me pause. It was as if I'd been given notice: Once you enter, there's no turning back.

I drew in a long, deep breath and reached for the handle.

Chapter 9

CREAK.

SLAP.

The inside was quite dark, mostly from my eyes trying to adjust. A wash of sunlight pouring in through a large rectangular glassless window on the far back wall didn't help. As my eyes continued to adjust, a counter lined with wired buckets appeared in front of the window, and ominous shapes around the floor transformed into freestanding display cases and racks of golf clubs. The mixture of the darks and lights reminded me of a neighborhood bar on a sunny afternoon; where some things are easily seen while others lie hidden in the dark. As the room continued to reveal itself, I saw that it was no more than a sparsely stocked golf shop at best, appearing to contain nothing of much importance.

"Hi."

I jumped and spun in the direction of the voice, and hit a large rack. Golf clubs went flying.

"I'm sorry," a female voice said. "I didn't mean to startle you."

I was staring into large, limpid blue eyes, the color of a Colorado sky. She was quite beautiful, and I was caught completely off guard. I didn't know what to say, so I dove into the scattered clubs and scrambled around the floor, picking them up. She started to help but backed away from my frantic activity.

"Here," I said, thrusting the shafts towards her. I was a bit surprised she hadn't run for the door. Instead, she gave me a long, searching look, and smiled as if she recognized something about me.

"I apologize for all this," was all I could think of to say.

"Oh, no need," she said, taking the clubs and putting them back on display.

I watched her as she headed for the counter. Her legs were long and slender, slightly muscled, and tan. The light from the window shone on her bare, slim waist, where her short white top didn't quite reach her khaki shorts. Once behind the counter, she turned towards me.

"Would you like a bucket?"

"Sure," I said. She handed me one, leaned over the counter, and peered down at the mess on my shoe.

"Don't ask," I said.

She smiled and gave me a slight nod as if asking me for something.

"What?" I finally said.

"That'll be a dollar fifty."

"Oh," I said.

"And three hundred for the damaged clubs."

"What?"

I saw from her wide-eyed expression and engaging smile that she was kidding, and I relaxed, slipping into my normal joking banter.

"Hey, if you think my moves in here were entertaining, wait till you see me on the range."

"Well, you've got a lot more room to maneuver out there," she said, gesturing towards the view from the back window.

Through the opening, I could see that the range was empty, except for a fellow sitting on one of the benches behind the tees. I started to ask if there was an instructor around but decided to hit some balls first and check the place out. I grabbed the bucket and headed to the door. Just as I opened it, I snuck a quick peek in her direction. Somehow she smiled at my stolen glance without ever looking up.

Chapter 10

CREAK.

SLAP.

As I walked out of the building, a wall of heat hit me. Not even a breath of air moved in the hot, sticky mid-morning air. But I wasn't complaining. I loved the Ohio Valley summers — the heat, the humidity, the long hazy days, the hot steamy nights. I shivered. *Hah! Only I could shiver in ninety-degree heat.* But my shiver may have been more a tingle of eager anticipation of what was to come.

I opened my trunk, retrieved my golf shoes and after putting them on, grabbed my clubs. As I headed for the range, a flurry of questions took hold of my mind. *Why would any decent instructor be way out here? Why isn't anyone else here? I wonder what the story is on the girl in the shop.*

When I rounded the building, I abruptly halted as a flurry of yellow butterflies lifted from the dandelions. The twitter of birds, the buzzing of locusts, and the drone of a prop plane high overhead instantly grabbed all my questions and threw them away. As I stood there, looking out over the meadow aka golf range, it felt as if I was staring at one of those picturesque scenes you'd find in a jigsaw puzzle, and I was holding the last piece. A smile effortlessly appeared on my face, and when I moved again, my hurried walk turned into a leisurely stroll.

As I approached the tee area, I glanced at the man on the bench. His khaki shorts and loud yellow golf shirt strongly suggested that he was a golfer — a worn-out golfer, given that his head hung down on his chest as if he were asleep. He must have been practicing — he had a driver and a half-empty bucket of balls by his side.

Just as I was turning away from him, a glint of light shimmered across my field of vision, and I blinked. My eyes shifted to a hardbound book with a pebbled black cover lying by his side.

A flash of light and a book appears? No. Surely, that book was there already. Wasn't it? Of course. The flash was probably a reflection, maybe from his watch, or a ring.

It was time to stop imagining things and get down to business. I dropped my bag and bucket of balls on the nearest tee and teed up.

Okay. Left elbow pointed in toward left hip. Right arm loose and closer to body than left. Now, take club head past right knee. Break wrists while left arm is still traveling straight back. Right arm close to body. Bring hips around. Sixty percent weight on left side. Turn left heel towards right. Hands high on top. Pull left arm down. Uncock wrists. Transfer weight. Follow through.

WHAMPF!

The ball popped off the club head and landed ten feet in front of me. *It figures.*

I placed another ball on the tee.

WHUMPF!

My club hit the ground, and then the ball, rolling it about twenty-five yards.

THWOMPF!

The ball pulled left from my hitting it off the heel. *Well, at least it went fifty yards.*

WHAMPF!

Finally, contact with the ball, even though it was my wimpy, hundred-and-seventy-yard slice. After exhaling a frustrated laugh, I stepped back from the tee area. My incredible performance must have awakened the fellow on the bench — he was now watching me. Embarrassed, I said, "Some swing I've got, huh?"

There was a momentary pause in which I was expecting a conversational nicety — something that might make me feel better. Instead, I got a smile — a broad, unassuming smile that for some reason, commanded my attention. *Was this the same person I saw a minute ago?* I studied him more closely. With thick, silver-gray hair curling over a rugged but youthful face, it was hard to tell his age. He could have been 65 or 45. Suddenly realizing that I was staring, I picked up the conversation.

"I wish I could find a good, true swing — one that I could count on."

He stood up. Such an ordinary thing to do, standing up, but there was a natural, effortless flow to his movement that gave me pause. When he faced me, I was surprised that his height was about the same as mine. He appeared much taller.

"Where have you been looking?" He asked. His voice was kind and clear, and I detected a hint of playfulness.

"For what?" I asked.

"For your True Swing."

"Oh," I said. "'You mean, where have I taken lessons?" He smiled but didn't answer. "Well, let me see. Maybe the question should be, 'where haven't I taken lessons.' The Great Oak Golf Club for one, the Grey Ash Country Club, Whitewater Range, The Mill course, Sharon Woods..."

"And did you find it?"

"Find what?"

"Your true swing."

"Oh. Well no, obviously."

"Do you think you'll find it here?" he asked.

There was a stillness in his eyes such as I'd never seen before. His gaze penetrated deep within me. I felt helpless to look away, so I surrendered. At that instant, I was staring into — well, nothing. Then suddenly, out of that nothingness, my reflection appeared. I blinked and shook my head. He grinned, his eyes twinkling, as if he had seen what I saw, and knew something I didn't.

"I don't know," I finally answered. It took a moment to regain some composure, but finally, in true salesman form, I answered his question with a question. "Do you think I will?"

He chuckled at my response, but his gaze stayed fixed on me. "Nope," he said. You won't find it here."

His words stung. I was sure this was the teacher for whom I'd been searching. "Are you an instructor?" I asked.

He grinned. "Are you a student?"

"Yes, and a frustrated one. I've been looking everywhere for help. If I can't find it here, then where?"

"This is the end of our first lesson," he said as he picked up a ball and tossed it to me in one fluid motion.

I sighed with relief. *He wants to see my swing again. Don't blow it.* I dutifully placed the ball on the tee and began my setup.

Okay. Left arm, no, left elbow pointed in toward left hip. Is that right? He's watching you, John, do it right. Take club head past right knee. Make sure he sees you're no duffer. Break wrists. Left arm, no, right arm close to body. Bring hips around. No, I turned too soon. Pull club down with left arm, swing as hard as you can, show him you're no wimp.

THWOMPF!

The ball flopped about twenty yards into the range. I stared at the ball, slumped, and searched for an excuse. Slowly, I turned to face him. "Listen, I really do know how to…" *Where did he go?*

A cranking engine and a roar interrupted the quiet of the meadow. I spun just in time to see a puff of smoke blow out the upright exhaust of a John Deere. My would-be instructor was heading into the range, dragging a ball collector behind. I stared blankly at him. *This was a lesson?*

Absently, I placed another ball on the tee. With my left elbow pointed in toward my left hip, I set up again.

Who is this fellow, anyway? My club head started past my right knee. *I wonder if my swing scared him off.* My club reached the top of my back swing. *Maybe he didn't even* see *my swing.* My weight shifted to my left side. *Why did he call this a lesson?* The club started downward in a forward thrust.

WHAAAAACK!

The sound was deafening. The ball shot out low and straight and then began to rise. It seemed to pick up energy, soaring upwards and out, way out, past the two hundred eighty yard marker. Only then did it begin its descent. When it hit the ground, it rolled another thirty yards. For just an instant, I was aware of nothing but that vision. Then came disbelief, and confusion. *Where the hell did* that *swing come from?*

I spun around, looking, hoping, even praying that someone had witnessed it. But the tractor was chugging in the other direction, and the girl was apparently still inside the shop. Although disheartened, I immediately teed up another ball and swung.

THWOMPF.

I teed up another.

THWOMPF.

Then another.

THWOMPF. THWOMPF. THWOMPF.

I slammed my driver down, snatched up the remaining balls, and started throwing them into the meadow. Suddenly I felt stupid; especially since each one went further and straighter than the ones I had just hit. Dropping back off the tee, I plopped down onto the bench and leaned forward with my elbows on my knees, and sighed.

It was ten minutes, maybe twenty that I sat there staring blankly out at the range. *What is going on? A teacher who says I won't find what I'm looking for here, then says this is a lesson? A lesson that ends before it starts??* But then I thought about that incredible drive. *Perhaps another illusion that needs to be explained away.*

As I sat there feeling sorry for myself, one thing seemed certain. My would-be instructor wasn't coming back. Maybe it was time to add another failed instructor/student relationship to my experience.

I stood up and grabbed my bag, noticing that my clubs hung heavier on my shoulder than they had when I arrived. At the back window of the building, I set them down and gazed across the meadow.

"Here," a voice said from behind. The girl from the shop was leaning over the window ledge, smiling, holding out a folded white index card.

"What's this?" I asked, taking the card.

She ducked back inside without answering. *Didn't she hear me?* I glanced down at the note. *Maybe the note is some version of 'Sorry I can't help you ' and she didn't want to stick around to see me suffer.* I left it folded, and walked to the car.

By the time I put my gear away, the note had become moist and sticky in my hand. Before unfolding it, I took one last look at the cinderblock building in its near-perfect setting and wondered if I'd ever get back here. Surely the note held the answer. Slowly I peeled it open.

YOUR SWING IS YOUR TEACHER

NEXT LESSON TUESDAY, 11:00

JOSH

Chapter 11

The setting sun flashed orange across my windshield. The glare made me swing a bit too sharply into the Silver Tee Center parking lot, and Josh's note went flying across the dash. I lunged for it with such determination that it scared me. When I got my car back under control, I felt my hand clutching the note tightly, as if I were afraid of losing it. Perhaps I was afraid — afraid of losing the only real, tangible thing that proved yesterday had really happened. *After all, I hit a three hundred yard drive, didn't I?* I stared at the crumpled note in my hand. *Your swing is your teacher.*

As I circled the lot for the third time, a multitude of giant floodlights clicked on. Endless rows of cars instantly snapped into artificial daylight making me question my sanity for being here in this architectural atrocity of blacktop, concrete, AstroTurf, and rubber tees.

After finding a parking space a full half-mile from the range, I was certain that no real golfer in his right mind would consider practicing here, even if it was close to his house and stayed open late. But it *was* close to my house, and it *did* stay open late, so I paid my buck fifty at the shop, grabbed a bucket of balls, and headed to the lower level of the boxed-in tees.

All the tee boxes were filled with golfers, each occupying his own little cubicle, each trying to fix his swing. *What a pathetic sight.* Nevertheless, I took the last open cubicle and completed the picture. After doing a bit of stretching and taking a deep breath, I teed up my ball. *Your swing is your teacher.*

THWOMPF!

Two golfers to my right gave me a "watch it buddy look" after seeing my ball sail across their spaces. I shrugged my shoulders and put on a pitiful face.

Now, what did that teach me? Was my grip loose at the top of my swing? Was my swing outside in? Did my body turn too much?

THWOMPF!

Okay. What did that swing teach me? Was my right foot too far forward? Was my grip too strong?

THWOMPF!

Damn. Was my left arm straight? Did I follow through? Maybe my hands weren't having a good relationship with my head.

I let go a wad of spit.

SPLAT.

THWOMPF!

With my hands sticky from spit, my butt sticking out, my grip turned away from the target, I swung, and swung again, analyzing, dissecting, and scrutinizing every detail of my swing. Still, every shot was the same — short, wimpy, and to the right.

My swinging frenzy would have lasted the night if I hadn't sensed the feeling of being watched. *Oh, Crap. I've been swinging like a wild man again, and I must have drawn a crowd. What kind of sadists would take pleasure in watching a fellow golfer self-destruct?*

"Hey, Arbor."

I slowly turned. No crowd, thank goodness — just Tom and Larry sitting on the bench. Each had a tall mug of beer, with an extra one sitting between them. As I eyed both of them, I realized that they gave validity to my earlier thoughts — no real golfer in their right mind would practice here.

"Look at this," Tom said to Larry. "There must be a thousand golfers here and the tee boxes are empty on both sides of him. What do you think? Did they shut them down for safety reasons, or do you think John scared them off?"

"I think the 'butt and pretzel' swing grossed them out," Larry said.

"How long have you guys been back there?" I asked, half scowling as I stepped off the tee. Assuming the untouched beer was for me, I chugged most of it in one gulp.

"Long enough to know you don't need to practice that swing anymore," Larry said.

"Thanks for the support," I responded.

"Hey," Larry said. "No need to be sarcastic. You should be grateful you have friends like us."

"Yeah, I supposed you're right. I appreciate the beer."

"I'm not talking about the beer," Larry said. "I'm talking about letting someone play golf with us who drools on himself with his ass hanging out."

Tom choked out a laugh in the middle of a swallow and sprayed beer all over me.

"Thanks a lot for *both* beers," I said and picked up my clubs. "But I think I'll head home before you offer another."

Chapter 12

The next day, after finishing my appointments, I headed out mid-afternoon to my favorite range: Whitewater. It was hot, humid, and hazy — one of those typical Ohio Valley days where the sun was up, but was hard to find in the milky white sky. Of course, for me, it was perfect weather and would have been a great afternoon for a leisurely drive if it weren't for the not-so-good thoughts of last night's practice at the Silver Tee. But as I pulled into the Whitewater lot where there was real grass, real trees, and real golfers, my mind began to clear. As I headed toward the golf shop, which was little more than an open-air shed, the attendant Harvey rose sluggishly from his favorite sagging lawn chair.

"Hi, John," he said as he handed me a bucket. "How's that wimpy slice of yours doing?"

"How'd you know about that?" I asked, but then said, "Never mind. I don't want to know."

"So?" he said.

"So, what?" I asked.

"So how's that wimpy slice of yours doing?"

"If you must know, I believe I've mastered it," I answered, handing him a buck fifty.

"Then what are you doing back here?"

"Your swing is your teacher," I said and walked to the tees.

My muscles ached from last night causing me to wonder why I wasn't at the local neighborhood bar. *Your swing is your teacher; that's why.* Somewhere inside me was a three-hundred-yard drive itching to show itself, and I was determined to find it before my lesson with Josh. With my driver in hand, I bravely stepped onto the tee and searched my brain for everything I ever knew about swinging a club.

Maybe it's in my grip.

I moved my left hand onto the grip, adjusting my hold so that the club rested in my index finger and palm. My right hand slid into place.

THWOMPF!

Maybe it's in my legs.

I flexed my knees, lowering myself about two inches but keeping my weight on the inside of my right foot.

THWOMPF!

Maybe it's in my arms.

I pulled my club back and fully extended my left arm, keeping it relaxed and straight, with my right arm close to my body.

THWOMPF!

Maybe it's in my head.

I steadied my head, careful not to move it, keeping my eye on the ball.

THWOMPF!

Maybe it's in my clothes.

I tightened my shoes and adjusted my underwear.

"John Arbor?" a voice said behind me.

The voice was familiar which is why I hesitated to turn around. But I did and found myself facing teacher #3, the one who had taught me the "butt and pretzel" stance. We stared at each other for a long, painful moment, no doubt simultaneously visualizing the amount my swing had deteriorated. He wanted to say something encouraging, but nothing was forthcoming. When the silence grew too awkward, I let him off the hook by asking a question.

"So what do you think of my swing since you last saw it?"

He broke eye contact, dropped his head, and I instantly regretted asking the question. There was another long, awkward pause, but this time the salesman in me said: "You've asked him the 'closing' question now shut up and wait for his answer."

"Well, actually…ah…your slice doesn't seem all that bad, now that you've, ah… taken all the distance off."

I thanked him, gathered my gear, and headed home.

* * *

"Two days in a row?" Harvey asked, reaching for a large bucket.

"Make it two buckets," I said. "If I don't get it today, I promise you I'll spend the next three nights thinking about it over a case a beer."

"Don't get what?" Harvey asked.

I gave him a hard stare.

"Oh yeah," he said. "Your club is at your teacher's."

"Your swing is your teacher," I growled and walked out the door.

It was time to get serious. Whatever it took, today was it. I wasn't leaving until I analyzed every last detail of my swing. *Your swing is your teacher.*

Both buckets emptied quickly as I inspected every nuance of my grip, my stance, my back swing, my follow-through, my alignment. Shot after shot, no part of my swing escaped my inspection.

Harvey kept the buckets coming. But as the afternoon slipped into evening and evening into night, the sound of golf clubs hitting balls melded with the chatter of insects and distant frogs. An overwhelming tiredness descended upon me, and my mind started to drift.

WHAAACK!

The ball flew straight off the tee and sailed out to the two hundred and fifty-yard marker before descending. *Damn! I wasn't paying attention. How did I do that?*

Your swing is your teacher. Immediately, I teed up another ball and swung.

THWOMPF!

My "perfect" wimpy, slice.

I teed up again.

THWOMPF!

Again and again.

THWOMPF! THWOMPF!

Another hour passed. Two more empty buckets lay by my side, and I was no closer to that swing. It took all the will I had left just to tee up the last ball. *I've got to hit this one well before I leave.*

With my last remaining bit of faith and determination, I directed my focus on the back of that ball. After checking every part of my body, I moved into the back swing. I shifted my weight as the club started into a forward thrust. But somewhere before the club hit the ball, doubt struck, and I knew it was going to slice and fall short.

THWOMPF!

It sliced. It fell short.

"Wait a minute. Did I know where that ball was going before I hit it?" I asked myself right out loud.

"I have no idea, buddy," a golfer walking behind me answered.

I didn't acknowledge him — I was too busy turning this question over in my mind. *Could this be important, knowing where the ball is going before I hit it?* Suddenly, something seemed very right about that thought. Quickly, I placed the last ball on the tee, visualized a perfect three hundred yard drive, and swung.

THWOMPF!

"Well, that worked well," I said to myself while watching the ball slice short and disappear off the side of the range.

My club slid from my grip and dropped to the ground as I slumped in exhaustion. For a long time, I just stood there, staring blankly into the night, until a voice startled me out of my reverie. Harvey was standing beside me.

"Did you say something, Harvey?"

"Yeah. I said if your club is at your teacher's why don't you just go get it?"

I shook my head, gathered my clubs, and dragged myself to the car. On the way home, I passed a corner food mart and remembered my promise to Harvey. I pulled in.

"You drinking that whole case yourself?" the clerk asked.

"Yeah, but I've got three days to do it."

Chapter 13

It surprised me that the Golden River sign was so easily visible after crossing the bridge, especially after last week's debacle. As I turned onto the gravel road I gave it an askance look, half expecting it to flash, sparkle, or float away.

As my eyes shifted back to the road, a sizeable patch of tar appeared — the one I had driven through last week, and it was right in my path. No way was I going to clean that mess off my car again. I hit the brakes and jerked the wheel hard, pulling my car into a half spin. The wheels locked, the car slid sideways to the edge of the tar, and the engine died. Reality struck. Here I was again, sitting in a stalled car in the middle of nowhere, searching for who knows what.

But I chuckled and had no idea why.

As I stared at the tire tracks embedded in the gooey tar, I recalled those globs plastered to the sides of my car. It should have made me angry, having spent a day washing my car and having to throw away a perfectly good pair of shoes, but it struck me funny.

After starting the engine, I backed up and skirted around the tar. *How can I be in a good mood after spending a week of slicing balls all over the county?* Easing back in my seat, I drove through the cornfield, inhaled deeply as I took in the full beauty of the river, and smiled wide when I entered the grove of sycamores. By the time I reached the driving range parking lot, I had found myself excited, almost giddy.

The lot was empty except for the same pick-up truck that was there last week parked near the shed. *Just my luck, they've gone out of business.* I searched for signs of life as I pulled close to the building, and parked. There was none, but the screen door was slightly ajar, and the door behind it was open.

While fiddling with my keys I caught my reflection in the rearview mirror. Without thinking, I dabbed at my hair, checked my breath, and glanced at my watch. It was 8:30. *8:30?* My lesson was at 11.

As I stepped from the car and headed toward the building, a face suddenly appeared in my mind, and it wasn't Josh's. It belonged to the girl with the wide blue eyes and the friendly smile. My good mood, coupled with my early arrival and fussing with my appearance, was starting to make sense.

CREAK!

SLAP.

A tingle of excitement ran up my spine as I stood in the dark, listening for the sound of her voice. But no greeting came.

"Hello?"

No one answered. I inched my way to the counter and looked out the back window.

"Hello-oo."

No one was on the range.

Intense sunlight angled through the back window, casting part of the countertop and floor in a brilliant light but leaving the rest of the room that much darker. Blinking didn't help, so I just waited until my eyes adjusted. When the furnishings and fixtures began showing themselves, I noticed a framed photograph hanging on the wall near the back window. I walked over for a closer look. It was a faded photo of an old man with thick white hair and a full beard, holding a driver as if it were a staff. He wore such a happy expression; I found myself smiling back. At the bottom of the photo was a poem, handwritten in a flowing script. "Sitting quietly doing nothing — spring comes, and the grass grows." *A poem about doing nothing — my kind of poem.*

The room was now more visible, so I took the opportunity to scan the contents. It was a strange golf shop, with its half-empty display cases and sparsely stocked shelves. Missing was all the golf paraphernalia that most golf shops carry — golf "gizmos" that touted to fix your swing, pitching absurd promises like, "Pick up 30 more yards on your drives or your money back."

At least there were sets of golf clubs displayed throughout the room. But on closer inspection, I found the sets incomplete and mismatched. Many were used. I smiled, remembering how the girl in the shop wanted to charge me three hundred dollars for the clubs I scattered across the floor last week and then felt disappointed that she wasn't here.

"What was that?" I said right out loud. A flash of light had shot across the room from the far dark corner of the shop.

"Hello? Anyone there?"

I walked cautiously toward the corner where some darkened images loomed up from the floor. To my relief, the shapes took on the form of a floor lamp and a tall wooden chest. I examined the lamp, wondering if maybe a short might have caused the light flash. A chain hung down from beneath a small laced shade. Just as I reached for it, a faint glow flickered in the corner of my eye, emanating from the direction of the chest. When I turned to look, it vanished.

"What the...?"

I pulled the lamp chain, and a soft amber glow fell on the chest, revealing that it wasn't a chest at all. It was a small, antique bookcase stuffed with books. Next to it was a small wood bench. I leaned in to examine the titles. *Five Lessons: The Modern Fundamentals of Golf* by Ben Hogan. *The Lectures of Huang Po. Selected Essays* by Ralph Waldo Emerson. Bob Toski's *The Touch System for Better Golf. Thus Spoke Zarathustra. The Square-to-Square Golf Swing. The Lotus Sutra. Hsin-Hsin Ming. Play of Consciousness. The Three Pillars of...*

A tiny thread of light formed a halo around one of the books on the second shelf. *That's strange.* Tenuously, I touched the cover, and the book immediately slid out and dropped into my hands. The title was written in gold leaf script on a black cover: "Handbook of a Master Instructor."

Handbook of a Master Instructor? There was something odd about the book — the way it felt — as if it belonged in my presence — as if something drew me to it and then handed it over. But that made no sense and being one who always had to seek logical explanations for the unexplainable; I took a closer look at the shelf. Stooping over, I peered through the vacant slot where the book had been and saw that the bookcase had no back. *Ah, ha!* Behind it was the cinderblock wall where a tiny beam of sunlight had managed to shine through a small hole in the grout. *Well, that explains the light, but what about the book jumping into my hands?* Upon closer inspection, I discovered that the second shelf was tilted downward. *Plain old gravity. It probably just slid out when I touched it.*

The black pebbly surface of the cover was familiar. *Of course. It's the same book I saw last week, laying on the bench next to Josh. Strange that a light flash has drawn my attention to it again.*

For reasons I can't explain, I was reluctant to put the book back. As I stood there holding it, trying to decide what to do, a tingling sensation swept through my hands and spread up through my arms.

My eyes unfocused, and my head spun as I fell backward onto the bench. The book followed, dropping into my lap and through fuzzy eyes, it looked to be open, but the page appeared awash in light — the words shimmering. I drew in a deep breath and while shaking my head to dispel the dizziness, it finally ebbed, and the words on the page came into focus.

The Mastery of the Fox
Part I. The Fall

Some part of me was afraid to look any further into its pages, but another part of me wouldn't let it go. I turned the page. A moment later I was in another place.

Chapter 14

The Mastery of the Fox
The Fall

*I*n a large stretch of woods that lay among landscaped fields of closely cut grass lived a beautiful and very quick red fox named Golda. She was quite a stunning fox — her glowing coat and long fluffy white-tipped tail turned many a creature's heads as she scurried through the woods.

But what was most striking about Golda was not her physical appearance — it was how delightfully carefree and happy she was. But of course, Golda couldn't be other than happy and free for she lived in a very special place. She lived in the Here and Now.

"Ah, she lives in the present" you might say. But if you believe the present to be a point between past and future, you would not be right. The Here and Now is outside time itself, where the past doesn't exist, and the future never arrives. Imagine! A place with no past to regret, nor future to cause worry. Where things are seen as they are, not as they might be - where one can be free to experience the wonder of every moment.

For instance, once a slithering snake sprang from under a bush and lunged at Golda with fangs fully exposed. Had she not been in the Here and Now, she might have hesitated, trying to decide what to do, or she might have frozen in fear, imagining the consequences of such an attack. Instead, she simply reacted, springing away quickly from the snake's grasp. Of course, Golda had momentarily felt instinctive fear, but the next instant she was laughing at the snake's acrobatics as it did a double flip into a stream.

Such a wonderful place, the Here and Now! It's where Golda would have spent all the rest of her days had it not been for that one fateful moment that changed her life forever.

It happened one sunny afternoon when Golda was meandering along the far edges of the woods. She came across what looked like a shiny, perfectly round, white dimpled nut lying on the forest floor. She had heard stories about these strange white nuts — that they had never been seen growing on a tree or a bush, but would just mysteriously appear on the ground or in the bushes. She recalled old stories about the white nuts such as a squirrel that tried to crack one open and eat it. An endless rubbery worm hiding inside had attacked the poor squirrel, sending both the worm and the squirrel into a wild frenzy. None of the woods creatures had ever tried to eat one again.

Whether it was the past stories or the way the white nut glistened in the sun, or whether it was just life adhering to its own plan, it caught Golda's attention, and her path shifted — she was now heading in the direction of this strange white object.

She crouched down directly in front of it and laid perfectly still. It was like nothing she had ever seen before. As she stared at the white object, something stirred deep inside — something she had not experienced before, and it made her shiver. At the same moment, a quietness had settled over the forest as if it all it was holding its breath, waiting to see what Golda might do next. Her instinct was to bid goodbye to this strange white nut and head her merry way, but whatever that *was* that had stirred within her had attached itself to that shiny, white nut and wouldn't let go.

How beautiful it is! A voice said.

Golda jumped and spun at the same time, but no one was there. She was quite surprised, and very confused, but seeing no danger; her attention quickly returned to the white nut.

The voice spoke again.

How beautiful it is!

Golda jumped and spun once more. Again, she saw nothing but heard a twig crack in the distance. And then the voice shouted.

Grab it!

She instantly sprang at the white nut and snatched it in her teeth. Her eyes narrowed as she whirled to see what creature might be lurking nearby. But it was only a passing deer. It suddenly felt very strange standing there with the nut clenched tightly in her mouth, glaring at a deer. Again she heard the voice.

That deer might also think this nut is beautiful.

Golda didn't jump this time. She was now more confused than afraid. She had never experienced anything quite like this before — a voice talking to her from nowhere? And that strange sensation that she had felt earlier was getting stronger. It wasn't a pleasant feeling, but more like what she would have experienced had she stepped on a thorn. But the feeling wasn't located in particular part of her body. With a sudden shiver, she dropped the nut, lowered her head, and stepped back.

This nut could be the reason for these unpleasant goings on, the voice said.

Now becoming more curious than afraid, she carefully approached the nut, sniffed it, and nudged it with her nose. As she did so, the voice spoke again.

But it *is* so very beautiful.

Golda agreed, and even though she wasn't sure who she was agreeing with, she was starting to like the voice — the way it offered opinions about things. Yet Golda's instincts were suggesting something different, telling her to turn away and move on. But the more she stared at the stunning white nut glistening in the sunlight, the more it fascinated her.

Had she not been so absorbed, she might have noticed that the Here and Now, the place where she had always lived, was slipping away. Strange indeed, for the woods and her surroundings were still there, just as they were. A moment later, a tremble rippled through the universe as the voice spoke for the first time from inside Golda's head.

I have to keep it!

* * *

The next page was blank, and I found myself back on the bench under the dim light of the lamp. It suddenly occurred to me that I was in a strange place, reading a strange book, without permission. With caution and a certain amount of guilt, I glanced around the room. All was quiet, and everything seemed as it should be. Since my watch said 9:05 and my lesson was at 11:00, I wasn't sure what I'd do for the next two hours. I glanced back down at the book. The page was no longer blank. Did I turn it?

* * *

As the end of summer drew near, the once happy and carefree Golda had become noticeably different from the other forest animals, and they didn't quite know how to react. Seeing one of their fellow creatures, sitting in the middle of a white patch of nuts, eyes narrowed, looking this way and that, was quite unusual, to say the least.

The first time Golda suspected that something was not quite right was a morning when the sneaky, slithering snake that had lunged at her once before struck again. Golda hesitated for a moment before leaping out of its way, just barely eluding its attack. When the snake did another double flip into the stream, Golda was not amused. Her instinctive fear didn't come and go as it should. Instead, the voice screamed inside her head. **WHAT WOULD HAVE HAPPENED IF YOU HAD BITTEN ME, YOU MEAN SNAKE?!**

As the days slipped by, Golda sensed that the newfound voice had its drawbacks, such as creating drama in her formerly untroubled life, but still, she felt the voice was important. It allowed her to reflect on what she had done and enabled her to plan what to do next. So it became extremely helpful in her search for more white nuts. The white nuts now gave purpose to her existence and having them made her happy.

As the days turned to weeks, her newfound voice increased, working incessantly, acquiring new information, sorting it, and then offering it up for consideration. **Where do these nuts come from? Why are none growing on trees or bushes?** It pressed on and on until one day the voice did something quite remarkable. It took all the questions, thoughts and ideas that had accumulated since her first encounter with the white nut and combined them into one large thought. That large thought then merged into a possibility, and from possibility, a theory emerged that stopped her in her tracks. **The nuts can't just suddenly appear from nowhere. There must be a source!**

This was quite a revelation for Golda. She now had a belief and faith that there was a source! From that moment on, she focused all her energies on finding that source, believing it would lead to an unending supply of her precious white nuts. And then, of course, she would be forever happy. But as the weeks passed, and with only a few more white nuts to show for her efforts, Golda was getting wary. Her faith in the source began to waiver. She might have begun to question it had she not come across two strange looking upright creatures standing in a small, flat grassy area just beyond the woods. She would normally have given them a quick glance and been on her way, but this was the area where she had found most of the nuts. Being perfectly still and well hidden behind some dense thickets, she crouched down and watched.

Slung over their shoulders were large bags. The bags contained a bunch of sticks, which puzzled her, as did the small area of short grass. It was so different from the woods and thickets that bordered it on all sides.

Golda slid deeper behind the thickets as one of the creatures walked to the front of the grassy space and stood between two gold stones. From where she crouched, she saw that the short grassy area gave way to a long beautiful field of grass. It stretched out and downward as far as she could see.

Just when she had decided she had seen enough and started to leave, one of the creatures reached inside the bag and pulled out a small round object. A flash of white caught her eye, and her heart jumped. It was one of her precious white nuts!

Golda's heart raced as she crept carefully to the edge of the thickets, and watched as the creature pulled a long stick from the bag. A large shiny wood knob was attached to one end and a black covering on the other. Golda continued staring in wonderment as the creature took a small white twig, stuck it in the ground and proceeded to balance the white nut on top of it.

Quite strange, the voice said. But then things got even stranger.

The creature stepped up to the nut and started to dance. His body swayed back and forth, his feet started to wiggle, his shoulders bounced up and down, and all the while, he waved his stick all over the place. Golda forgot herself for a moment and giggled. Abruptly, the creature stopped and stood perfectly still. Golda held her breath, thinking he might have heard her. But suddenly, and without warning, he pulled the stick up over his shoulder and flailed it at the white nut.

WHACK!

Golda jumped back. The stick struck the nut so hard it went flying high into the air and out of her sight. She was flabbergasted, then angry. **How could he strike such a wonderful thing and send it away!**

But her confusion abruptly switched to excitement upon realizing what she had just discovered. **I have found the source! I have found the source!**

* * *

As I turned the page, a folded piece of paper jumped out of the book and drifted to the floor, yanking me out of the land of foxes and squirrels. Or perhaps it just slid from the page when I turned it. I quickly snatched it up and was about to unfold it when the previous guilt of handling someone's personal property without permission raised an objection.

Chapter 15

Staring at the folded note wasn't getting me anywhere so I slipped it back between the pages. But as I reached over to place the book on the shelf, I couldn't let go, or maybe *it* wouldn't let go. *It's probably the folded paper and my curiosity getting the better of me.* Being that it was only 9:50 and that I was still alone in the building, I dropped the book back in my lap and started anxiously flipping through the pages. But the note decided it didn't want to be found. Exasperated, I stopped shuffling the book, looked down at the open page and gulped as the words jumped off the page.

The Mastery of the Fox
Part II. The Master Instructor and the True Swing

The Master Instructor? The True Swing? At that moment, nothing could have pried me from that book.

* * *

Somewhere in the Midwest, hidden deep within miles of spreading woods lay what some have claimed to be the finest golf course in the land. Those who have *made* the claim are among the very few who actually know of the course's existence and perhaps the only ones who have ever played it. Those same few are also no doubt responsible for the bizarre and mysterious stories about the course and the woods surrounding it.

Some have claimed that golf balls miss-hit into the woods just disappear. Others have gone so far as to insist that on a particular hole, golf balls would vanish right off the tee. Whether the tales are true or not, those who have heard them agree that there must be more out there than meets the eye.

Perhaps the stories are why a certain Master Instructor had chosen it to be the place for his yearly golf challenge. Each summer, he would openly invite his students to a particular course to participate in specific events. Although not all would come, those who did believed they might finally answer the question as to whether the True Swing did truly exist.

The problem is, the answer as to whether the True Swing exists lies somewhere within the wisdom of a Master Instructor. But it seems that Master Instructors like to talk in riddles: "If I were to say I have realized the True Swing it would not be true. If I were to say I haven't, it would be a lie."

So the only alternative for the students would be to partake in the challenges set forth by the Master Instructor. A unique "twist" to these events is that the students would not know what the challenge would be until it began. Since the goal of those who participated was to be deemed a Master Instructor by realizing the True Swing, they would accept the guidelines without question. So each morning, they would arrive at the course and patiently await instructions.

So the question remains: Can the True Swing be obtained, learned, or realized? Perhaps the best way to answer that question is by telling a tale of three student golfers who were chosen to participate in a challenge held on hole number nine. Each student was asked to choose one golf ball, one tee, a driver of his or her choice, and walk alone to the ninth hole. Once there, the ball was to be teed up in the center of the gold markers and driven down the fairway. What could be simpler than that?

1

Golfer number one took a driver, ball, and tee and walked briskly towards the ninth fairway. His gaze fixed straight ahead, but his eyes were unfocused as if his mind was working overtime, most probably concentrating on executing the challenge correctly, perhaps even visualizing the event to come.

With continued deliberation, he approached the tee at the ninth hole and carefully scrutinized the small level tee area, noting the location of the two gold markers just short of the woods. Using his feet as a measure, he carefully stepped off the distance between the markers. Once satisfied with the placement, he teed up his ball and examined every aspect of his swing including his grip, backswing, forward swing, and follow through.

"Well, this is it," he said right out loud. "My chance to realize the True Swing. My chance to become a Master."

With the ball lined up with his right heel, he shifted back and forth, waggling his club, and cocking his head from the fairway to the ball.

Suddenly out of nowhere, a sudden flash of reddish-brown appeared at his tee and just as quickly vanished. Golfer number one jumped back in surprise, thinking he imagined seeing a white tipped tail of a fox disappear into the thickets. When he looked back down at his tee, his ball was gone.

He stood there, stunned, unsure of what just happened. Then reality struck. A fox had stolen his golf ball. A freak event and his chance of being a Master and realizing the True Swing was snatched right out from under him.

It was a very slow walk for golfer number one, heading back to the clubhouse and he berated himself all the way. If one could have overheard him, they would have learned that this was not the first time his efforts had been thwarted. It seemed that every time he had come close to getting something he wanted, something else would always get in his way.

2

If you would have seen golfer number two steadily sauntering down the cart path towards the ninth hole, you would most likely describe him as alert and present. Unlike the concentrated focus of golfer number one, number two saw much more of that which was unfolding around him. In his years of training, he had learned to focus his awareness to where it was needed and to prepare for the unexpected. Perhaps this state of mind would be what was needed to perform well such a simple task.

When golfer number two reached the ninth tee, he inhaled deeply and exhaled slowly while gazing out over the rolling slope of the fairway. His eyes were quick and alert, and they took note of the trees to the right, the sand bunkers to the left, and the lake in the distance.

Satisfied, he turned his attention to the small grassy tee area, discerning the gold markers and the woods and thickets that bordered the three sides. After sighting the distance between the markers, he felt confident where his tee and ball should be placed and inserted them in the center. With relaxed purpose, he slid his hands onto the grip of the club and stepped up into his stance. After a few waggles, he allowed himself to relax and settle into a comfortable state of mind.

Just then, his eyes shifted. Something had caught his attention at the far edges of his peripheral vision. With lightning speed, he snatched up his ball just before a blur of red fur flew over his empty tee and vanished into the woods.

It took a moment for Golfer number two to realize what had just happened. But when he did, a grin grew from ear to ear, and he shouted, "My God! I have just outwitted a fox!"

Still grinning, he placed his ball back on the tee, settled into a composed position behind his ball, and swung. With a smooth, powerful release, the ball was struck perfectly, sending it over three hundred yards down the center of the fairway. As he picked up his tee, he exulted at his performance. "I did it!" he said under his breath. "I hit a perfect drive and outwitted a fox to boot."

Believing without a doubt that he had beat the challenge and achieved the True Swing, golfer number two brimmed with pride as he headed back to the clubhouse. He could hardly wait to disclose his remarkable story to the Master Instructor and receive his validation.

3

If golfer number three was concerned about how to execute the challenge on the ninth hole, he showed no sign of it. His pace along the path was neither slow, nor fast, nor deliberate, or with purpose. His eyes were relaxed and untroubled as if they were naturally absorbing everything around him. It was if he was not separate from the surroundings or perhaps his surroundings were not separate from him. If one had tried to guess what was on the mind of Golfer number three, the guess might have been "nothing at all."

When he arrived at the ninth tee, he paused and smiled. Unlike golfer number one and two, he was not inspecting or scanning the area — it was more as if he was just appreciating the moment of seeing such beauty of all that lay around him. After lingering a few moments, he strolled across the grassy area with no indication of marking off the distance. When he neared the center of the gold tees, he stopped, reached into his pocket, and pulled out a golf ball. Just as he was about to place the ball on the tee, he abruptly straightened and stood perfectly still.

With childlike curiosity, he turned towards the thickets behind him. There, in the dense foliage, were two intently focused eyes staring out at his ball. The penetrating stare from the eyes in the brush shifted from the ball and locked eyes with the golfer. Within that momentary reflection, everything stilled.

"So you want my golf ball today, sly fox?" golfer three asked in a clear, kind voice. The sound of his voice must have startled the fox, for she cautiously drew back.

"You may be very smart, sly fox, but be on guard. Your intelligence may not get you what you want."

The fox's eyes stayed fixed upon the golfer as she backed deeper into the thicket, then she turned and scurried off.

Golfer number three grinned with delight at being a part of such a wonderful and unique encounter. Without a moment's hesitation, he tossed the ball into the thicket and hollered after the fox, "I hope you find what you seek."

With that, Golfer number three wandered back to the clubhouse unconcerned that he was no longer on the path.

* * *

The story stopped in the middle of the page. The rest of the page was blank as were the following pages. *What the hell?* My feeling of being uncomfortable was shifting to anger, and knowing the folded note had to be somewhere still within the pages, I turned the book over and shook it. The elusive folded note fell into my lap. Without hesitation, I opened it.

LIBERALLY TRANSLATED FROM THE BLUE ROCK COLLECTION CASE #19

Josh asked, "What is the True Swing?"

Reply: "Everyday life is the True Swing."

Josh: "Can it be mastered?"

Reply: "The more you try to master it, the more it will evade you."

Josh: "If I do not try to master it, how can I know...?"

The faint sound of an engine interrupted the quiet of the room. I stopped reading and listened. It was growing louder. I hastily folded the note and put it back just as the engine quit outside the building. After placing the book back onto the shelf, I jumped to my feet and turned off the light. As I was heading towards the door, the girl who worked in the shop walked in.

"Hi," I said sheepishly, hoping I didn't look as guilty as I felt.

"Hi," she said. "I'm glad you came back." Her smile was so warm and genuine that I trembled slightly, and my anxiousness dropped away.

"My name is John Arbor," I said. "'Sorry I didn't introduce myself last week."

"That's all right, John," she said, still smiling. "My name's Bobbie, Bobbie Atkinson. 'Looks like you got here a little early." She glanced at her watch at the same time I looked at mine: 10:45. *If she thinks 10:45 is a little early, I wonder what she'd think if she knew I was here at 8:30.*

"If you're looking for some clubs to knock across the floor, there are some over in the corner."

Her quit wit took me by surprise, and I laughed right out loud. "Maybe next week," I said with a chuckle, "if you move them closer to the middle of the room."

"Fair enough," she answered.

"Will Josh be here?" I asked, suddenly wondering if I should have called to confirm.

"Oh, he's already here — probably down by the river." She pointed off to the right side of the range. "You'll see a dirt path at the end of the last tee."

Chapter 16

As I walked the path, my thoughts were jumbled, drifting from Bobbie to the story of the fox, to the folded note and then to last week's conversation with Josh. When I had told him I was looking for a decent, true swing, it hadn't occurred to me that there actually might be such a thing; much less that it could be mastered. The more these thoughts about the note, the book, the true swing, and this off-the-beaten-track-driving-range spun in my mind, the more it felt as if I were in some sort of dream. *If I am, whose dream is it?*

My thoughts abruptly stopped when I came upon Josh. He was sitting on the ground, legs folded, gazing out at the river. His hands, which were resting on his knees, faced slightly upwards, with his thumbs and index fingers touching. His golf shirt, a concoction of royal blue and hunter green, was loosely tucked into a pair of gray sweat pants. The scene should have seemed strange to me, but strangeness in this place was becoming the norm.

"Josh?"

He looked up and smiled that same ingenuous smile I remembered from last week. "Hello, John," he said.

It startled me that he knew my name.

"I saw your name tag on your golf bag last week," he explained as if he had read my mind. I gave him a searching look, thinking there was more to his knowing than he was letting on.

He returned his gaze to the river, and I watched him, anxiously waiting to see how this lesson might begin. He said nothing — just continued to stare out over the river. After a few long moments, the silence became awkward, at least for me, so I crouched down and initiated the conversation. "I hit balls all last week." He still didn't respond, so I continued.

"I took your advice to heart about learning from my swing. I examined my forward and back swing, stance, grip, everything. But nothing worked. I just couldn't find a comfortable rhythm."

Still, he offered no reply and I was running out of things to say when, suddenly, that one decent hit I had a few nights ago popped into my mind. Didn't seem important, but somehow I felt compelled to mention it. "You know, I did have one good hit last week." Josh turned and fixed his clear, steady gaze on me.

"Tell me more about that," he said.

"Not much to tell, really Except it was the only drive that went straight all week, and actually, it went a fair distance. I'm not even sure how it happened. I was tired and frustrated — wasn't even paying attention when it happened."

He laughed as if that made sense. "So what did it feel like?"

I had to think about that for a moment before I answered. "It felt great but elusive. Sort of like finding something that was lost after you had given up looking for it."

His eyes widened a bit as if he were pleased with my answer.

"What happened after that?"

"Well, I tried to do it again, but the harder I tried, the worse I did."

"Come with me," he said as he got up and walked to the river. I couldn't help but marvel at his movement — fluid and free.

At the river's edge, he stooped down, cupped his hand and scooped up some water. As he looked out over the river, the water sifted through his fingers. Finally, he turned to me and said, "Do you see the river?"

Of course, I could see the river, but I figured it must be a trick question. I hesitated before answering and then tenuously said, "Sure I can see it."

"Not everyone can, you know."

"They can't?"

"Often, people's minds are too cluttered to allow them to see what's right in front of them. Look again and tell me quickly what you see."

Again I hesitated, trying to figure out what he might be up to. It had to be some sort of test, so I carefully contemplated how to respond.

"Well, I guess if you think about it, a river contains a multiplicity of things." *Now that sounded good.* "And I suspect this river generates a lot of power downstream — perhaps enough power to light a whole town." *I'm on a roll.* "And also, if you look closer you can see that it sustains endless varieties of life, and provides vast supplies of drinking water. I guess it is quite incredible when you think about it."

"Perhaps not as incredible as simply seeing the river as a river," he said.

"Huh?"

"John, when you *think* about what you're seeing, you miss seeing it." He looked back towards the river. "Look. Do you see the flow of the river?"

"Yes," I said sheepishly.

"Can you point it out to me?"

I pointed. "There. It's the moving water that creates the flow."

"Can you go get it and bring it here?"

"What?"

"Can you go get the flow and bring it here so we can take a closer look?"

"Of course not," I said. "You can't take the flow out of the river."

"So how do you know it's there?"

"Well, it's…The river is… It's the direction…" My mind was spinning from the strange questioning. I was getting frustrated. "I don't know. I guess I just know it because I know it."

"Exactly," he exclaimed. "John, be careful of your intellect. It can get in the way. Words, concepts, definitions — they can all get in the way."

"In the way of what?" I asked.

"What do you think?"

"The true swing?" I asked awkwardly.

Josh faced me, and I felt the full force of his presence. His eyes locked into mine with such penetration that I felt dizzy and had to turn away. I walked over to the river's edge. *What is going on here? Could there actually be such a thing as a true swing?*

Suddenly, my thoughts stopped, and the sound of trickling water and the twitter of birds emerged out of nowhere. A slight breeze brushed my face, and I felt the sensation of moist ground under my feet. Leaning over a large limb of a willow tree, I stared down into a small pool at the river's edge. The water gently swirled, then settled for a moment, revealing my reflection. It stared at me, and I stared back as new thoughts arose and drifted through my mind. *Who is this guy? And what's the deal with the river? You can't separate the flow from the river? You need to see the river as a river? Words and concepts get in the way? Maybe he's telling me something about my swing — that the flow, the energy, can't be separated into parts. Am I separating something that can't be separated — looking at the parts without seeing the whole?*

The water swirled again, and my reflection vanished, taking all my thoughts with it. A strange quietness arose all around me, and I became instantly aware of sounds — a distant crow caw, rustling of leaves, the buzzing of a nearby bee. But it didn't seem like I was doing the listening. There was just hearing, and a sense of drifting, as if I were in the middle of the river, being swept away. And then I was, and for an instant, there was an urge to swim to shore, but the urge vanished, and somehow I became the river itself.

It's flowing without effort, filling up deep holes, passing lightly over the shallows, maneuvering around boulders, taking on whatever shape it occupies, all the while heading for its final destination. How free, just floating, drifting with the current.

A thought arose. *This seems familiar. Yes. The same feeling came over me when I got whacked with BJ's club.* More thoughts arose, and I remembered where I was. *I'm supposed to be having a lesson.* Instantly, I was back on shore, dazed.

"What the hell is going on Josh?" I asked as I turned in his direction, but he was gone. Just then, a distant but familiar sound came to my ears — the cranking of a diesel tractor engine. *Oh, no. Not again.*

I hiked back up the path. Sure enough, Josh was on the tractor out in the meadow collecting balls. I made my way along the back of the range to the rear of the building, trying to get his attention. It was no use.

"John," a lovely voice said from behind me.

I spun around. Bobbie was leaning out the window, waving a folded white card. As I took it from her, she said, "See you next week, I hope."

It took a moment for her words to register, and when they did, I realized that the folded card was my ticket to come back. "I'm sure you will," I answered with my best smile.

When I reached the car, I leaned back on the trunk and looked up with a sigh of relief. Clusters of rich green leaves from the tall sycamores were dancing in the breeze, creating haphazard patches of blue sky and shafts of bright sunlight. One of the beams struck the note as I unfolded it, giving it a strange glow.

WHEN YOUR THOUGHTS
VANISH,
THE TRUE SWING WILL
APPEAR.
NEXT LESSON TUESDAY, 11:00.
JOSH

Chapter 17

Harvey was asleep in his lawn chair with his ball cap pulled down over his eyes. His feet were propped up on a row of wire buckets. I had to laugh. Only Harvey could nap in ninety-degree heat, not to mention the humidity that hung in the summer air like a steamed towel.

"Hey Harvey, I see you found another use for the wire buckets."

He pulled his cap up and grinned. "Hey, John," he said as he straightened in his chair. "You're not seriously going to hit balls in this heat, are you?"

"What do you think?" I asked, standing there in my golf shoes, with my golf bag slung over my shoulder.

"By the way, did you ever get your club back from your teacher?"

I stared at him and shook my head.

"Forget about the club," I said. "I'm working on something new."

"Oh yeah? What's that?"

I hesitated. *What the hell.* "When your thoughts vanish, your true swing will appear."

"Ah, a good piece of advice."

"What?" His response surprised me.

"Now let me think," he said as he took off his cap and scratched his head. "Who was it that said that?"

"You've heard this before?" I asked.

"I think so, but I can't remember where."

Could it be possible that he knows Josh? Where else could he have heard it? Sweat started seeping through my shirt, so I left him to wrestle with his thoughts and headed toward the tees. The range was nearly empty — only one other poor soul had braved the heat.

"When your thoughts vanish, the true swing will appear," I murmured while pulling my driver from my bag. *Now, what could this mean? Should I quit thinking about my swing while I'm swinging?*

I gripped the club lightly and settled into my stance. *Now don't think about your back swing.* I drew my driver back. *Don't think about putting sixty percent of your weight on your right foot.* I shifted my weight onto my right foot. *Don't think about the club having to be parallel to the ground.* I stopped the club parallel to the ground. *I'm not thinking about shifting my weight back to my left side.* I shifted my weight to my left side. *I'm not thinking about how I'm losing my balance.*

As I fell backward, the club slipped from my sweaty hands and flew into the range. The other golfer gave me a sharp look. I pretended not to notice and reached into my pocket for Josh's note. *When your thoughts vanish, the true swing will appear.* It should have said, "When your mind goes, so will your club." *How can someone have no thoughts?*

A speaker crackled somewhere in back of me, and Harvey's voice filled the range. **"Would everyone please stop hitting golf balls so that John can get his club?"**

My face turned red. Sure, there was only one other golfer on the range, but I felt his stare as I retrieved my club. Even worse, Harvey had forgotten to turn off the microphone. His sidesplitting laughter was being broadcast across the range and probably into the next county.

I admitted defeat. Not because of the heat, or the humidity, or even Harvey's laughter. I did not know how to practice Josh's new axiom: *When your thoughts vanish, the true swing will appear.* I grabbed my club, threw it into the bag and headed directly to the car, hoping to avoid Harvey. No such luck. When I neared the clubhouse, he stuck his head out and yelled.

"Yogi Berra."

"What?"

"Yogi Berra."

"What are you talking about?"

"What you said before. It was Yogi Berra. He said, 'You can't think and hit at the same time.'"

Tuesday morning arrived, and I felt strangely guilty having worked at my job all week rather than practicing Josh's instruction. Most people would feel guilty playing golf all week rather than working, but as I stared at the old screen door, I felt as if I had let Josh down.

CREAK.

SLAP.

"Hi, John."

Hearing Bobbie's voice, my spirits immediately lifted. With the sunlight streaming through the back window, all I could see was her silhouette — but what a silhouette it was, and I couldn't help but stare. When my eyes finally adjusted, I said, "There you are," and she smiled.

I walked toward her, trying to decide what to say next when a light flickered in my peripheral vision. It drew my gaze to a book lying further down on the counter. It was the *Handbook of a Master Instructor. Here we go again.* I glanced at Bobbie to see if she had noticed anything. If she had, she didn't show it. She was counting money. *Money?*

"Oh, geez," I said. "I never even thought about paying for my lessons." She stopped counting, and her blue eyes looked directly into mine. I almost melted.

"Don't worry, John. Your lessons haven't officially started yet."

"They haven't? When do they officially start?"

"They officially start when Josh lets me know," she said with a chuckle. "He charges thirty-five dollars per lesson."

I was about to say, "Only thirty-five dollars?" but thought better of it — best to wait and see if I'll ever get an official lesson.

"Where is Josh?" I asked while casually reaching for the book. Her face gave no sign of disapproval, so I picked it up. That same tingly feeling shot up my arms and washed through my body as it had last week. I shuddered and glanced at Bobbie. She was preoccupied, scanning some papers. As my gaze lingered on her, I wondered if it was the book, or her, that was causing the tingles.

"He's out back on the range," she answered and glanced at her watch. She looked at me sideways. "You seem a little early again."

I checked my watch. 9:30. *Damn. I'm an hour and a half early.*

"Well, better early than late," I said while inspecting the book's cover. "Hmm…*Handbook of a Master Instructor.* Interesting title."

"Oh," she said, somewhat surprised at seeing the book. "Now, how'd that get there? You know, sometimes I think that book just appears out of nowhere. I guess Josh must have left it out."

"May I look through it?"

"I don't see why not," she said. "There's a lamp over there next to the bench if you'd like."

I have permission.

I slid into a position where I could flip through the pages without attracting Bobbie's attention. My goal was to find that note. I had to see the rest of what it said. While keeping an eye on Bobbie, I flipped the book upside down, and I fanned the pages until the note dropped out. Using the book as a shield, I unfolded it and read.

LIBERALLY TRANSLATED FROM THE BLUE ROCK COLLECTION
CASE #19
Josh asked: "What is the True Swing?"
Reply: "Everyday life is the True Swing."
Josh: "Can it be mastered?"
Reply: "The more you try to master it, the more it will evade you."
Josh: "If I do not try to master it, how can I know it is the True Swing?"
Reply: "The True Swing does not belong to the world of the senses. Neither does it belong to the world absent of the senses. Knowledge is a delusion and ignorance is senseless. If you want to realize the True Swing, make yourself as vast and free as the sky. Name it neither good nor not good as you like."
With these words, Josh realized the True Swing.

Josh realized the True Swing? What the heck does that mean?
Carefully, I returned the note to the book and leaned back. The book fell open on my lap, and I looked down.

The Mastery of the Fox
Part III. The Path

This can't be happening!

Chapter 18

The Mastery of the Fox
Part III. The Path

*T*hat night, Golda couldn't sleep. The day's events had her baffled. After months of snatching precious white nuts from those strange creatures, she had been foiled twice in one day. And the voice in her head was asking questions she couldn't answer.

Finally, she got up and climbed from her den. One might think she would have been pleased, seeing her precious collection of white nuts glowing in the moonlight. But her mood was halfhearted at best. Something wasn't right and hadn't been right since the day she had first encountered the voice. Of course, she knew that this powerful voice with all its reasoning was very useful. After all, it had helped her acquire her treasure. But it never let up, catapulting her from one emotion to the next with its incessant talking.

Suddenly a breeze stirred the treetops, and a ray of moonlight struck one white nut set apart from the rest. She looked at it with a sigh of pleasure, remembering earlier that morning when she had taken that nut from the first unsuspecting creature.

It would have interested Golda to know that at that very moment, the same creature was thinking about her.

1

*W*ho would have expected that a fox would steal my golf ball?" golfer number one said to himself. He was sitting alone in his den. "A fox steals my golf ball! It's just my rotten luck."

A warm night breeze ruffled his curtains, inviting him to look out into the starry night. But he could only see one thing. "A fox steals my golf ball. All the years of instruction and practice, trying to master the True Swing and a fox steals my golf ball. Why is it that something in my life always happens that gets in the way of my goals?"

Unlike many previous nights, when he sat berating himself over some unforeseen mishap, tonight the weariness was just too heavy. Years of struggling with the game, trying to master the True Swing was finally taking its toll. His eyes half closed, as he continued to mumble "Why is it that something in my life always happens that gets in the way of my goals?" Then utter exhaustion descended on him like a heavy blanket, and he dropped into a dream.

He continued muttering in his sleep about missed putts, shank shots, hooks into woods, and the slyness of foxes. But as he tossed in his chair, something odd happened. The curtain fluttered, and the moon's pale light streamed through the window, soaking everything in a glistening white glow. At that same moment, golfer number one's body relaxed into the light, and he mumbled, "Why is it that my goals always get in the way of things that happen to me in my life?"

"Huh?" he said out loud. He jumped up in his chair. "What did I just say? My goals getting in the way of the things that happen to me in my life?"

As he awakened more, he grew excited. "Could it be that my life hasn't been getting in the way of my goals; that my goals have been interfering with my life? All those missed putts and bungled shots — could they all be a part of what makes the game worth playing?"

In a flash, he saw. His life was not the problem; it was how his mind looked at it. He shouted right out loud. "A fox stole my golf ball! How incredible! A fox stole my golf ball right off my tee.

Maybe I didn't fail today after all.

* * *

Meanwhile, back in the woods, Golda's voice had finished with the first creature and moved on to the second — the one that had snatched the ball right out from under her. She was somewhat shocked that such a quick, sly fox as she had been outsmarted. **How could that creature have been so keen as to see me coming, since I am the quickest of foxes?** Said the voice.

Golda waited for some reasoning that might make sense, but instead, the voice just kept suggesting one thing after another, and kept on suggesting so quickly that she could no longer keep up. Finally, she stopped trying, and a strange thing happened. The voice gave her a startling answer. **He must have a voice like mine — a voice inside his head, with ideas and theories, that offers opinions and tells him what to do.**

Little did she know that at the very moment in which the voice gave her an answer, the creature that had snatched her ball was asking questions of his own.

2

Golfer number two was sitting alone on his front porch. The night was bathed in moonlight — the air thick with the sounds of crickets and katydids — something golfer number two usually found wonderfully soothing. But tonight, these sounds were intrusive and irritating.

Just a few hours earlier he had learned he was not to become a Master Instructor nor did he realize the True Swing. It made no sense to him at all. Everything he had done on the ninth hole had been perfect — saving the ball from the Fox, teeing it up in the right place, hitting it long and straight down the fairway. He was so sure that the Master Instructor was wrong that he continued going over and over it in his mind.

After entering the room where the Master Instructor waited, he made it a point to take in the surroundings. The room was dimly lit by candlelight and a faint smell of incense wafted through the air. The Master Instructor was sitting on a cushion near the back wall. An empty cushion sat at his feet, inviting visitors to sit directly in front of him.

Golfer number two slowly made his way to his teacher, took his place on the cushion, and proudly relayed his story, articulating every detail of how he outwitted the fox and how well he hit a long straight drive right down the middle of the fairway. After he had finished, the Master Instructor looked deeply into his eyes and said, "Tell me, who is it that claims to have witnessed such a strange happening?"

Golfer number two paused at the question because the Master Instructor already knew who he was.

"What do you mean?" asked golfer number two.

"Who is it that just asked, 'what do you mean?'"

Again, golfer number two paused, and said, "It was I who said it."

"And who is 'I'?" the master asked.

"What do you mean, 'who is I?'"

"Who is it who is asking, 'who is I?'" asked the Master Instructor, again.

"I do not understand."

"How can you be a Master if you do not know who you are?"

And that was it, the end of the meeting.

The more golfer number two thought about this, the more he thought the Master Instructor had to be wrong. "Perhaps there is another Master Instructor who will truly see that I have mastered the True Swing," he said to himself. "And I'll keep searching until I find one that will."

* * *

Meanwhile, Golda had become pleased with her voice's assessment of how the second creature had outwitted her. She even felt respect for the creature for being so cunning — for being like her.

However, her being pleased with herself was short lived. The voice brought up creature number three, and she shivered. *That* **creature knew I was hiding in the thickets. Yet, I was so still. This could not be possible.**

3

The moon was exceptionally bright in the hazy night sky when golfer number three approached the clubhouse. Had anyone noticed his effortless walk through the moonlit night, they might have thought him a spirit.

Inside the door, the flickering candlelight reflected in golfer number three's eyes, and the Master Instructor caught sight of him. From across the room, they both respectfully nodded, and golfer three approached his teacher and sat down on the cushion. Once settled, the Master Instructor gazed deeply into his student's eyes, and then grinned, "How are you?" the Master Instructor asked.

"I am quite well, thank you," said golfer number three, returning the gaze. An eternal smile emerged from both faces at the same time, and they laughed.

The Master Instructor picked up a book that lay beside him. On the black pebbled cover, inscribed in gold leaf script, were the words *Handbook of a Master Instructor.* He handed the book to golfer number three and said, "I give this to you with great joy."

As golfer number three graciously accepted it, the candle flames burst to twice their size and the flickering light danced about the room.

* * *

"John?" Bobbie said.

"Huh?"

"John, it's about time for your lesson."

"Oh," I said, and the book slammed shut. Bobbie jumped slightly, and I was about to say that the book slammed on its own. But it was getting tiring, trying to explain these occurrences away.

As she turned her attention back to her work, I shuffled the pages, checking to make sure that the note was still there. It was, but as I was about to close the book, I noticed that the note looked different — smaller. *Now, what?* I slid the note from the book and unfolded it.

The True Swing

There is no True Swing outside the mind. There is no True Swing inside the mind. Where there is nothing and everything, no right or wrong, good or bad, where there just is, the True Swing is. To recognize the True Swing, let go of desire and be as you are. Awaken to the True Swing by recognizing That which does the swinging. When the True Swing is recognized, the essence of all that is taught is recognized and suddenly there is seeing, not by the one, and yet there is not two; never was.

What!? Where did this note come!? I started shaking but still managed to put the note back in the book and replace it on the shelf. It was a struggle making it to the screen door, and when I reached it, Bobbie gave me a curious look and asked, "Are you all right?"

"Yes," I lied.

Chapter 19

CREAK.

SLAP.

As I stepped outside the door, the morning sun struck me with such intensity I staggered. The leaves of the sycamores appeared luminous in the sunlight, their edges a fiery silver. Tiny sunlit jewels seemed to be bouncing off the tree trunks, darting through the branches, and dancing around the parking lot. The red color of my car was so vivid I had to shade my eyes.

What the hell is happening?

When I reached my car, I thought it best to keep moving so I popped the trunk, grabbed my clubs and headed towards the range. As I rounded the building, the hairs on my arm stood up, as if an electrical storm were approaching. *This is crazy. Keep moving, John.* When I neared the back of the building, Josh was on the range with driver in hand. *I'll bet he knows what's happening.* Just as I was about to approach him, he initiated his swing, and I stopped dead in my tracks.

My God! His arms and upper body are turning in slow motion!

When the club finally reached the top of his backswing, it appeared to hang in midair as if in suspended animation. *This can't be real. My eyes must be playing tricks on me.* It seemed an eternity before his hips finally moved into the ball, followed by his shoulders and arms. Then everything accelerated with such intensity and speed that his body dissolved into a blur. Yet his head was motionless, hanging just above his body as if it were a separate entity. The ball vanished from the tee with a distinct *"CRAAACK"* that echoed through the meadow.

I rubbed my eyes in disbelief. When I looked again, Josh was bent like a reed in the wind, his club at his back, his weight resting on the outside of his left foot, looking like a statue of a golfer you'd find in the Golf Hall of Fame. I scanned the meadow for his ball. It wasn't there.

That had to be an optical illusion or a figment of my imagination. Whatever it was, anger was starting to boil through me. I had had enough. I dropped my bag and walked straight towards him. He saw me, but before he could even offer a greeting, I spat out a question.

"Was *that* the True Swing?"

His eyebrows lifted as if he were surprised by my question. *Yeah, right.* I had a feeling he knew I was watching him, so I stated boldly "I've been reading your *Handbook of a Master Instructor,*" but then I backpedaled. "Bobbie gave me permission. It was lying out on the counter."

Josh looked at me, and our eyes locked. I was again taken aback by the force of his gaze. The next moment, he smiled, his eyes gleaming with a sort of playfulness. "If I told you it was the True Swing, it would not be true. However, if I told you that it wasn't, it would be a lie."

Here we go again with the riddles. But I didn't back off.

"So there is such a thing as a True Swing?"

"Yes."

"Yes?"

"Yes."

A direct answer? It threw me, and it took me a minute to respond. "Can I learn it?"

"It cannot be learned."

So much for the simple answers.

"But it is simple," he added.

I stared at him, stunned. *Now he's responding to my thoughts?*

"Then how can I attain it?" I asked.

"It cannot be attained."

"Then how can I master it?"

"It cannot be mastered."

"Then how can I know it?"

"Who wants to know?"

What does he mean, "Who *wants to know?"*

"I want to know!" I practically shouted.

"And who is this 'I' that wants to know?" Josh said with a flicker in his eye.

Abruptly, the story of golfer number two flooded into my mind. As my brain searched for the connection between what I had read and what Josh had just asked me, he continued. "The True Swing does not rest in the mind, John, the mind rests in the True Swing." His eyes bore intently into me, causing a tingling sensation to shoot up from the base of my spine and once again I felt disoriented.

"John, why don't you grab your driver and let's see you hit some balls."

"What?"

"Let's see you hit some balls."

Abruptly, I snapped out of it. *At last! A lesson!* My confusion was quickly replaced by excitement as I considered the prospect of learning that swing. I grabbed my driver and hastened to the tee.

"Now John, before you swing at the ball, tell me what you know about the golf swing."

Without hesitation, I launched into a detailed description of swing angles, hand positions, weight shifts and how each related to the other. By the time I finished, I had given him a synopsis of every lesson, article, and book I had ever read, ending with a short summary in modern physics. (I left out the "butt and pretzel" part.) My admiration for him grew for listening so patiently — my dissertation had lasted a full ten minutes.

"John, your mind holds more knowledge about the golf swing than anyone I've ever known."

"You're kidding?" I was truly surprised.

"Let's have you hit some balls."

As I placed the first ball on the tee, Josh asked, "Now, before you swing at the ball, are you going to review all you know about the swing?"

"Yes."

"Then you're going to stand there for ten minutes?"

"Well, actually it's a condensed review. I just pick out certain things to focus on before I swing."

"Like what?"

"Well, they change each time, depending on how I'm hitting the ball."

"Why don't you just go ahead and hit this first ball away, then do the review on the next drive?"

"Okay. I said."

I instantly pulled the club back and took a full swing at the ball.

WHAAAAACK!

The ball flew straight out to the two hundred and seventy-yard marker before it dropped.

"Nothing wrong with that swing," Josh said, then turned and walked off.

I stood there, stunned. *What the hell? Where did that swing come from?*

I hurriedly placed another ball on the tee while trying to recall what I had just done.

WHAMPF!

It wimped out to the right. I swung again.

WHAMPF!

And again.

WHAMPF!

The bucket quickly emptied with no improvement until I was down to the last ball. It was sitting on the tee, taunting me, so I backed off, walked around to the back of the ball and gazed out over the meadow. A mental picture was forming in my mind. *This ball is going to fly straight and long.* With more determination and desire than I thought possible, I stepped into my stance behind the ball. But something didn't feel right. *This isn't going to work, and I don't have to swing at the ball to find it out.* The ball remained sitting on the tee, as I packed my bag, and headed to my car. As I rounded the building, the screen door opened, and there was Bobbie, waving a folded white note at me.

Geez. Is this really happening?

"Hang in there," she said as she handed me the folded card.

Between what I had just experienced and what my heart was feeling, I could think of nothing to say. She smiled as if she understood and as I unfolded the card, she ducked back inside.

YOU ARE THE TRUE
SWING.
RELY ON YOUR SELF.
NEXT TUESDAY, 11:00.
             JOSH

Chapter 20

"You had a forty-eight," Tom said while walking off the ninth hole of the Great Oak golf course. "And you're down five dollars for the nine." Our normal Saturday golf wager went from one dollar to two when my swing fell apart.

The Great Oak course was nothing special — we just liked the fact that the ninth hole ended at the clubhouse. We could pause, refresh, and have a beer before heading out on the back nine.

Given my overripe "banana" slice, it was no surprise I was the big loser. To add insult to injury, Larry, BJ and Tom made me wait at the tenth tee while they grabbed the beers. My job? — to defend our position in line against anyone trying to jump ahead of us.

The foursome that was legitimately in front of us was preparing to tee off, so I sat down on the nearby bench. While absentmindedly watching them, my mind flashed on my last lesson with Josh. It had been four days since I had witnessed his swing, but I could still see it as clear as day. And yet it was all so unreal. *Did I imagine seeing his swing? Did I imagine mine? You are the True Swing. Rely on yourself.* Whatever those words meant, they had had no effect on me. Today's game proved it. But I was hanging on, looking forward to the next lesson. *Why?*

Even harder to explain was the feeling that I *was* on the right path, yet without having chosen it. It was as if everything was already set in motion. All that was needed was to get out of the way. *You are the True Swing, rely on yourself.*

"Hi John," a familiar voice said from behind me.

Could it be?

"Bobbie!"

My eyes widened as I turned. Never having seen her outside of Josh's shop, I hadn't realized just how strikingly beautiful she was. Her outfit was simple, tan shorts and a white cotton shirt, but she wore it well. When her blue eyes locked onto mine, they caught the sun and shone liquid in the light.

"What are you doing out this way?" I asked while trying not to look over zealous.

She sat down next to me, quite close, and said. "I just finished playing eighteen holes."

Immediately, I looked around to see who might be with her. She smiled at my obviousness. "Some girlfriends of mine had an opening for a fourth this morning. They've already left."

"Oh, yeah? That's great. Really," I said, groping for words. "It's just that, well, I don't know why, but it never occurred to me that you played golf. I mean, I don't know many women who play golf. Not that women shouldn't play golf. I mean, more women *should* play…"

"It's okay, John. I know what you mean."

"I'm glad you know what I mean because I have no idea what I'm saying."

She laughed.

"So how'd you shoot?" I asked.

"Weeelllll…I was doing all right until the eighth hole — you know the one with the huge oak sitting out in the middle of the fairway? I hit that tree straight on and my ball ricochet into the lake."

"Oh yeah, I know that tree. A lot of golfers don't think it should be there, but nobody has the heart to tear it down."

"It's already kind of split from the middle up," she said motioning with her hands, "as if it had been struck by lightning. I guess with enough confidence, one could fly a ball right through the split and have a rather easy shot to the green."

For a moment, I was at a loss for words, not remembering if I ever had a real golf discussion with a woman.

"Actually," I said, "the story is that lightning struck it. The bolt struck the tree, split off, then struck a golfer on the other side."

"Oh no," she said.

"Yeah. Supposedly, it knocked the guy ten feet into the air, singeing his whole body. He fractured his wrist and sprained his ankle. And that wasn't the worse of it."

"Oh my goodness!" she said. "What could have been worse?"

"He took a nine on the hole."

Her laugh was instantaneous and infectious, and I found myself laughing with her. Not everyone appreciated my sense of humor.

"Okay, John — you got me on that one," she said, shaking her head. "So seriously, did someone really get hit by lightning?"

"Well, the *real* story is that after the guy got struck by lightning, he just lay there in a daze. He had no idea what hit him, or where he was. And even though he was lying flat on his back, he was holding onto his golf club for dear life. The foursome behind him saw it happen and ran to him right away."

"What did they do?" she asked with concern.

"They asked him if they could play through."

This time her instantaneous laugh came with a friendly shove. I shifted, and slid off the bench. Grinning, I looked up, only to see BJ, Tom and Larry standing over me.

"Hey look, Tom," Larry teased. "John gets along with women as well as he plays golf."

BJ extended a hand and pulled me up. They all gave Bobbie a slow once over and then looked at me, waiting.

"I'm sorry," I said. "This is Bobbie." As I watched them checking her out, I grabbed a quick glance at Bobbie. She was smiling at me, so I relaxed.

"Bobbie, these are my golf buddies, BJ, Tom, and Larry."

"Glad to meet you guys," she offered, then put her hand on my shoulder. A tremble rose up through my body, and I wondered if she felt it. "I'd best be going, John. Oh, and I didn't mean to knock you off the bench."

"That's okay," I said blushing. "I deserved it."

"No, you didn't. I love a good laugh. I'll see you Tuesday."

After she had walked off, Tom said, "Wow. Where have you been keeping her? She's one good-looking babe. Who is she?"

As I gawked after her, I said, "She's a golfer. Isn't that great? She's a golfer."

Chapter 21

It was nothing new, me losing to Tom, BJ, and Larry. And after we finished the back nine of the Great Oak golf course, I forked over my money. But at least I had the semblance of an excuse. Thoughts of Bobbie had seized my mind — Bobbie sitting down right next to me, Bobbie gently shoving me off the bench, Bobbie laughing at my jokes.

Perhaps that's why, when Tuesday morning rolled around, I awoke feeling anxious and impatient to get to the Golden River range and why I again arrived two hours early.

When I pulled into the lot, my thoughts were cut short by the scent of honeysuckle and freshly cut grass. I couldn't help but draw in the peace and magic that permeated this place. By the time I reached the screen door, my anxiety and impatience had melted away.

CREAK.

SLAP.

"Hi, John." Bobbie's familiar voice greeted me from somewhere inside the shop. I squinted, searching for her in the dark. She stepped from the shadows into the light behind the counter. The sunlight streaming through the window backlit her head, giving the appearance of a halo.

"Ah, there you are," I said, and felt that familiar rush through my body.

"John, you know that…"

I cut her off. "I know, I'm two hours early again."

"Oh, no. It's not that. I'm glad you're here."

She's glad I'm here? She's glad I'm here!

"I was just going to remind you that you never did tell me the true story about the oak tree and the lightning. That is, if there truly is one."

"Are you kidding? Me tell you a third lightning story? That would be strike three. I'd be out."

As she laughed, a flickering light caught the corner of my eye, drawing my attention to the far side of the counter. It didn't surprise me to see the *Handbook of a Master Instructor* lying out. You would think I'd be used to the "flickering lights and there's the book" phenomenon, but I wasn't. There had to be an explanation. Quickly, I looked away, then back again. No flickering light. I glanced away again and quickly looked back. Still nothing.

"Is something wrong with your neck?" Bobbie asked.

"Oh, no. Just trying to get the kinks out," I answered while cocking my head from side to side, feigning stiffness. "Since I've got some time to kill, would you mind if I browsed some more through the *Handbook of a Master Instructor?"*

"Sure, except I'm not sure where it is."

"It's right over there on the counter," I said, pointing.

She looked back over her shoulder. "That's strange; I don't remember seeing it there earlier."

"Maybe Josh left it there," I offered as I walked over and picked it up. *Damn.* That same electric tingling shot up my arm, and the book dropped out of my hands hitting the counter with a thud.

Bobbie gave me a "what was that noise" look then shook her head. "He's been out of town all week."

"Who?" I said absently.

"Josh. He called about an hour ago and said he'd be here around eleven."

"That's good," I said as my gaze shifted from the book to Bobbie. She had resumed studying some papers.

The energy that keeps flowing out from the book when I pick it up left me with a feeling of trepidation. With apprehension, I reached out, touched it with one finger, and jerked my hand back. No shock. I touched it again and jerked back. Nothing. The energy seemed only to flow from the book if I hadn't picked it up in a while. Bobbie, sensing something bizarre going on at the end of the counter, glanced in my direction. I snapped to attention with an overly exaggerated grin.

"What are you doing over there?" she asked with a suspicious smile. "You look like the cat that ate the canary."

"I'm just curious about this book."

"Well, if you want to look it over some more, go ahead." She said, and glanced at her watch. "You've got a couple of hours, you know." The smile in her eyes all but told me that she knew she was the reason I was here early. *Damn. How could I be so obvious?*

Shock or no shock, nothing was going to keep me from this book now that I've been sanctioned again to read it, so I grabbed it up and walked to the bench. When I sat down the book opened on its own and in the next instant, all thoughts of Bobbie disappeared.

The Mastery of the Fox
Part IV. The Discovery

Golda paced back and forth in front of her den, oblivious to her precious collection of white nuts. She was fretting about that third creature that had been so keen as to see her hiding in the thickets. As she continued to pace, the night grew late, and the moon rose high overhead, illuminating all the white nuts around her den. Golda stopped and stared out over her vast treasure. The voice exclaimed, **How wonderful they look in the moonlight!** But just as quickly the voice returned to its most troubling problem, the incident with the third golfer. **This pacing is not helping. Maybe if I sit and contemplate this matter, I will understand how that creature so smartly outwitted me.**

And so Golda settled down among the white nuts and sat perfectly still to allow the voice to figure it out. Not even her tail flickered as she sat well into the night. When the morning sun threw streaks of orange over the horizon, she still didn't stir. She just sat, eyes closed, listening deeply to the voice, hoping that it would explain what had happened.

One by one, the forest dwellers emerged from their habitats, only to be greeted by the strange sight of Golda, sitting like a stone statue in the middle of a field of white nuts. It appeared odd to them that such a quick, sly fox would be sitting so still, instead of gathering food or scampering through the woods. So a few of the creatures gathered up some nuts and berries and left them by her side.

Golda didn't notice, for, despite her physical stillness, her mind was anything but calm. The voice was working hard, asking questions, formulating ideas, making suggestions. **How did that strange creature find me hiding in such a great hiding place? Did I make a sound that gave me away? Surely I did not.**

As Golda continued to sit, she discovered that the voice had other powers besides asking questions and formulating theories. It could recall something that happened from the past and replay it over and over, highlighting different aspects of the event. In fact, the voice replayed the scene with the third creature several times. On one replay, she was reminded of something familiar she had glimpsed in the creature's eyes. She also recalled a sound that was coming from his lips. **Perhaps he was trying to speak to me.** She remembered that the sound was soothing and gentle. She also recalled that he had thrown the precious white nut into the woods behind her as she ran away. **Why would he do such a thing? Are these precious nuts not important to this creature?**

As the last rays of the sun fell below the horizon and the forest dwellers returned to their lairs, they saw that Golda was still sitting perfectly still in exactly same place. As the night deepened, the full moon created quite an eerie scene — a stone-like fox haloed in light sitting among hundreds of round glowing white objects. Golda had no idea what a bizarre picture she was creating for she was listening ever more intently to this voice. It was working harder than ever. Its questions were coming faster and faster, each one leading to another and another and another. It was remarkable that Golda could sit so still with so much activity going on inside her head.

But just as the horizon was showing shades of pink from the first rays of the sun, she started to fidget. She was getting hot. **This is strange.** The air was cool, but heat was rising through her body, growing hotter by the second. She felt like she was going to explode. **This voice: Maybe it's pushing itself beyond its limits.**

SNAP! Without warning, the voice abruptly vanished.

After days and weeks of constant chatter, suddenly she was plunged into complete silence. She strained to listen. Nothing — just her breath — in, out, in, out.

With the voice gone, Golda suddenly felt afraid and alone. Feelings such as these were still new to her, and she didn't understand what they were. But being a brave fox, and curious by nature, she decided to delve deep into these feelings. Perhaps to understand how they came to be.

Instantly after making this decision, a vision of a white dimpled nut appeared before her. At the same time, the voice popped back into her head. **How beautiful it is.** Pain fell over her — the now-familiar pain that arose somewhere from deep inside — not the kind that came from a thorn or a bruise. This was terribly confusing. **How can I feel pain while envisioning something so precious? Could it be that the pain and the vision are related?** Golda decided to rid herself of the vision and see if the pain would go away.

But the vision wouldn't leave. **Well, if it's not going to leave, perhaps I should look at it more closely.** With all the effort she could muster, Golda, with her eyes still closed, focused on just the white nut. When she did, it vanished. Golda jumped at the abruptness. There was now nothing there. She was not even sure she was still there. But there was something familiar to the nothingness, and the earlier pain she felt was gone. It was only for an instant, but Golda was reminded of a place where she had once lived — where she was once free.

The very next moment, the voice burst forth, louder and more insistent than ever. **These white nuts *are* important. They bring happiness. But they also bring this pain. How can they do both?** Golda was fascinated that the voice was now arguing with itself.

On and on the voice went. **It seems that when I want more of these nuts and can't find them, I feel bad. When I find some, the pain leaves, and I'm happy. But the happiness soon fades, and I want more. Then it starts all again.**

The voice finally paused for a moment, but then shouted something that took her breath away. **Maybe the happiness isn't coming from finding the white nuts and maybe the pain isn't coming from not finding them.**

Golda tensed at hearing these words, and the voice went silent for a long moment. When it spoke again, it seemed less sure of itself. **If this happiness, or pain, is not coming from the white dimpled nuts, then where is it coming from?** The answer instantly appeared. **It has to be coming from the voice!**

Golda was appalled. Had the voice been tricking her — giving her the idea that the white nuts were the source of her happiness? Could it be that she could just let go of her attachment to these precious things, and everything would be as it had been?

Perhaps this revelation should have excited her, or given her hope, but for Golda, there was only discouragement. If the voice had been playing tricks on her all along, then it couldn't be trusted, to tell the truth about what made her happy.

With this realization came exhaustion. The ordeal of being awake for two days, wrestling with the voice, had taken all of her energy. As she looked around, she noticed the nuts and berries that her friends had left. Overcome with gratitude, she ate their offerings.

After having a drink from a nearby pool, she crawled wearily into her den and sank into a deep sleep.

The entire day and night had passed before Golda finally stirred from her slumber. She awoke to slivers of golden sunlight that had filtered into her den. Such dazzling beauty got her up and outside where she gazed in awe at the pinkish clouds mixing it up with the blue morning sky. She stretched luxuriantly, and glance at her collection of white nuts. They appeared different somehow, and she realized she felt better than she had remembered feeling in quite some time.

Just then, a squirrel came up the road with a white nut it must have found in the woods. When the squirrel got close, it tossed it into her yard. The voice said. **Just what I need. Another white nut.** This struck Golda funny, and she started giggling. It must have been a contagious laugh, for the squirrel started chuckling as well. Soon, other curious forest dwellers came around and joined in. What a sight! All these woodland creatures laughing away, and nobody knowing why, including Golda.

The rest of that day was wonderful for Golda. Every tree, every flower, and every creature she met was delightful. She felt lighter as if an invisible weight had lifted from her body. Still, Golda noticed that there was still traces of that "not so good" feeling, lingering. But now it felt more like the pain from a thorn that had been removed, and the wound was starting to heal.

Chapter 22

"Good morning, Bobbie."

"Hi, Josh," Bobbie answered.

Their voices jolted me from the book. It surprised me, not hearing a car drive up or the familiar "creak" and "slap" of the spring door. *Is it eleven already?*

"Good morning, John," Josh said as he looked my way. "I see you've taken quite an interest in the *Handbook.*" For a moment, I felt guilty, but he quickly smiled my guilt away.

"It seems that John has taken more of an interest in your Handbook than he has in me," Bobbie said, with an exaggerated look of being hurt.

Is she flirting?

"By the way," Bobbie continued, "when John arrived, the book was lying on the counter, but I don't recall seeing it all week. Am I going loony?"

Yeah, and what about those flickering lights?

Josh looked at me as if he had read my thoughts and heard my question.

"Well," he said playfully, "there are three possibilities. Either it was there all week, or it appeared suddenly out of nowhere, or..." Josh glanced at me, then at Bobbie.

"Or what?" Bobbie said impatiently.

"Or you *are* going loony," Josh said, and laughed. Bobbie playfully slapped Josh's arm with her notepad, and I laughed wholeheartedly. Then she pointed the notepad at me, laughed and said, "Don't encourage him!"

Right then, my emotions found themselves on that fine line between laughter and tears, and an overwhelming sense of joy engulfed my entire body. Perhaps it was love. Bobbie was simply beautiful and Josh's way of seeing things was pulling me in. There was an easiness in his relationship with life that was hard to explain. Nothing was forced or strained. It was as if he had given himself to it completely. *I wonder if he sees golf the same way.* Josh glanced at me and nodded, pleased at what I had just thought. I nodded back.

Wait a minute. I snapped back to reality. *He can't be reading my thoughts. He's probably just... just what?* There was no category in which he could be placed. No one I'd ever known was quite like him.

After setting the book back on the counter, I was about to ask Josh to explain the electrical tingling, the strange flickering lights, the book seeming to open by itself, but what came out was, "I think I'll go get my clubs."

When I came around the outside corner of the building, Josh was sitting on a bench, gazing at the meadow. He didn't acknowledge me, which was not surprising, so I set my bag down and sat beside him. His face was serene as if he were deeply absorbed in some tranquil scene. I scanned the meadow, hoping to see what he saw. I didn't, so I leaned forward and rested my head in my hands. *Should I interrupt him? Should I ask him if he's ever going to give me a lesson? What on earth is he staring at?*

It was strange how our "not talking" and "sitting in silence" routine had no longer made me uncomfortable. In fact, the silence was becoming more welcome, and as I sat there, I felt my thoughts dropping away. As they did, a yellow butterfly appeared that I hadn't noticed a moment ago, darting aimlessly across the meadow. Another butterfly lifted from a bright yellow dandelion, and both flitted about together, dancing over the short green grass. A bird called out, and there was the buzzing of some nearby locusts. Where ever I was, it would have been nice to have stayed, but my thoughts brought me back to the bench, and I blurted out a question.

"Josh, why is this True Swing so difficult for me, yet so simple for you?" *Why did I ask that? I don't even know what the True Swing is.*

He turned his head towards me, his clear blue eyes catching mine, the piercing gaze again catching me off guard. For an instant, I glimpsed something both wonderful and yet maybe terrifying. Then he let go, and his eyes wrinkled into a smile.

"That's funny," Josh said. "I was going to ask you the same question."

"What?"

"Why is the True Swing so difficult for you, yet so simple for me?"

I laughed right out loud and he raised eyebrows. "Well?"

"I have no idea how to answer such a question."

"That's a good answer," Josh said.

I grinned. It was the first time he had given me a compliment.

"No beaming now or that old ego will get in the way."

"Ego? What do you mean?"

"By ego, I mean your personal identity — that voice inside your head which has spent a lifetime conjuring up an image of who you think you are and then pressuring you to live up to that image."

"But a 'personal identity' — isn't that who we are?"

"Is it?"

With that question, it dawned on me that Josh didn't have a personal identity — or if he did, he didn't seem to get caught up in it.

"I'm still not sure what you mean, Josh. What does the ego get in the way of?"

"Well, for one thing, it gets in the way of the True Swing."

"And what is this…this thing that you call the True Swing?" I asked, wincing, knowing that I had again asked that unanswerable question.

"Since you've been reading the *Handbook,* you already know that if I were to tell you…"

"I know. It wouldn't be true. But could you try answering it anyway?"

"John, I've got to tell you, your golf swing could be the worst swing I've ever seen."

"What?!" A series of thoughts, each more painful than the one before, flooded my head. *It can't be, can it? Well, of course, it can. How else to explain all the hours I've practiced without getting better?* Suddenly I felt hurt, then anger. Why had he not told me the truth sooner? *Wait a minute. What did he say? That it* could *be the worst. He didn't say that it* was *the worst.*

"John, don't you find it amazing what my seventeen words just did to your ego? And you want me to use words to explain the Truth?"

I breathed a sigh of relief realizing he didn't mean what he said. He was just making a point.

"I see what you mean, Josh."

Hold on. Did he say "Truth" instead of "True Swing"?

Once again, he seemed to read my thoughts. "Words are not the same as Truth, John. They're just labels, which come from one's programming and beliefs, all of which makes up the ego," he continued. "If you are going to seek the True Swing, know that the "you" that you believe yourself to be, will not find it. Nonetheless, it's there, always waiting."

"Waiting for what?"

"Waiting for you to quit searching."

His words, constantly contradicting, made no sense. *But didn't he also say that words can't be trusted?*

"If I am not who I think I am — if I am not this ego, then who am I?"

"Exactly," he said with wider grin than I thought possible.

A smile crept onto my face along with a lightness of being that I'm sure wasn't there a moment ago. *Maybe I am on the right track. Maybe I can realize this mysterious phenomenon he calls the True Swing.*

"So Josh, what do you *really* think of my swing?"

Without hesitation, Josh said, "Actually John, it could be the best golf swing I've ever seen."

"No kidding?" I said, grinning from ear to ear.

He looked at me, eyebrows raised, as if waiting for me to figure something out.

Oh, Crap. "Okay, okay. I get it. I definitely get it. Words, ego, they can't be trusted."

Josh dropped back into his state of "whatever" while I sat there sorting through his words. But after a few moments, restlessness set in, so I picked up my bag and walked forward onto a tee area. Not being sure whether an actual lesson would happen, I pulled out my driver and asked, "Should I hit some balls and warm up?"

No answer.

I looked back over my shoulder and Josh was gone. I swung around, but he was nowhere in sight. *How could he disappear so quickly?* Thinking it was only about eleven thirty, I glanced at my watch. It was a little after two. *I've been out here for three hours?*

There was no sense in trying to figure this one out since nothing here was the norm. But one thing I knew for sure, the lesson was over so I headed for my car. When I rounded the front of the building, Bobbie was standing there waiting, holding another folded white index card and I couldn't help but laugh. "I take it this is for me?"

"Of course."

I accepted it and asked, "By the way, is Josh inside with you?"

She looked puzzled. "I thought he was with you."

"No," I answered.

"Don't worry. Sometimes he just disappears for a while."

"Just disappears?" I said, startled.

She took in my confused look, then laughed. "'Just a figure of speech, John."

"Oh, I know," I said with some embarrassment.

I expected her to duck back inside the building as she usually did, but she just stood there with an expectant smile, staring at the note as if waiting for something. *Perhaps she wants me to ask her out. Yeah, right. As if someone like her isn't already taken. More likely, she just wants to see how I react to Josh's note.*

YOU ARE THE TRUE

SWING,

SO WHO ARE YOU?

NEXT LESSON, TUESDAY,

11:00.

JOSH

(OVER)

My head reeled at Josh's question. Not because we had just talked about it. It just dawned on me that it was the final question that had been flirting on the edge of my consciousness ever since BJ's club had knocked me out. *So what kind of game are we playing here? How do I fit in? And who is it that wants to know?*

I looked at Josh's note, again. That's when I saw the word "over." *Over? That's a new twist.* I flipped the card.

> *Would you like to play golf Saturday afternoon at 2:00?*
>
> *Bobbie*

What's this? I read it again, glanced up, and disappeared into her smiling blue eyes.

Oh my gosh! Is she kidding!?

"Sure," I said casually.

Chapter 23

By the time I got home, the euphoria I felt from Bobbie having asked me to spend the afternoon with her, dissolved into worry and doubt. *What if it rains? Would she give me a rain check? What if I get sick? What if I make a fool of myself on the course?*

But Saturday finally arrived, and the weather was perfect — for me, anyway — hot, a slight breeze, high cirrus clouds, and sky that was uncommonly blue for Cincinnati. But still, I was nervous. *I really need to date more.* Hell, I wasn't even sure it *was* a date.

After arriving at the course, I checked in and paid for both of us. Bobbie hadn't yet arrived, so I walked directly to the putting green. With *my* swing, the driving range was out of the question. No need scaring my fellow golfers. Besides, how does one practice, *You are the True Swing, so who are you?"*

After a few missed putts, I realized I still had the jitters. But then I caught sight of Bobbie pulling her two-wheeled golf cart up the walkway, and I understood. She looked incredible, strolling along on those long slender legs, her hair pulled into a neat little ponytail. And her outfit — pale green shorts, white sleeveless top and matching visor — how could I help but stare? When the other guys on the putting green noticed her, they couldn't help but stare either — their heads all turned in unison.

"Hi, Johnny," she called out. The other guys' heads all turned in unison again, only this time it was towards me. I shrugged my shoulders and grinned. What could I say? She was with me.

"You called me Johnny," I said.

"You *look* like a Johnny. I hope that was okay."

"Absolutely," I answered, without telling her that I loved it. Being called Johnny always brought out the little kid in me. Only those closest to me used it.

"Have you checked in?" she asked.

"Yep, and it's my treat."

"Nothing doing." She reached into her purse and pulled out forty dollars. "I insist you take it," she said. "You might need it if we do any betting." She lightly punched my arm playfully and stuck the money in my hand.

"By the way, are we walking or riding?"

"Walking, if that's okay."

"Sure."

As we approached the first tee, my jitters worsened as fear took hold of my thoughts. *God help me. What if I miss the ball? What if my butt starts to stick out? What if I drool on myself?* Bobbie must have sensed my panic. When I pulled my driver from my bag, she said, "Now, Johnny, don't go trying to impress me, I know you're working on your swing."

Listen to her, John. Just hit the ball. Forget about whether you look like an idiot. I swung.

WHAMPF!

Alleluia! Sure, it sliced. Sure, it only went a hundred and seventy yards. But I hit it!

"Great slice, John," she said teasing as she walked onto the tee.

"You're playing from the men's tees?" I asked, surprised. The markers for the women's tees were usually placed a fair distance in front of the men's.

"Sure. No sense in taking advantage of you on our first date."

Did she say date?

When she stooped down to place her ball on the tee, I watched her every movement. It was a wonderful advantage I had, our being on a golf course. I was allowed to stare — that's what you do with your golf partners — watch them, and comment on their shots.

CRAAACK!

Her swing was a surprise. It was good, really good — head still, left arm straight, head down, good weight shift, great follow-through. The ball sailed low, straight off the tee, and landed in the middle of the fairway at least fifty yards past mine.

"I concede."

"Good," she said while picking up her tee. "Then we can just play and enjoy ourselves."

Right then, my jitters disappeared. And even though her final score was seventy-six to my ninety-five, it proved to be the most enjoyable round I had played in a long time. But the time had passed far too quickly, and I wasn't ready to let go of the day. As we walked off the eighteenth green, I said, "I don't know about you, but a beer and a burger would certainly hit the spot."

"A burger and lemonade would work for me," she responded.

We parked our clubs at the foot of a wood deck that extended out from the snack bar. The deck overlooked the eighteenth green and offered a sweeping view of the course — a perfect setting for the end of a perfect day.

"Bobbie, why don't you grab a table and allow me to get the food and drinks? After all, you beat me by nineteen strokes."

"Then perhaps you might change my order to lobster and wine. After all, nineteen strokes…" she said playfully.

Bobbie was staring out over the course as I set the burgers and drinks on the table. "They were out of lobster and wine."

She smiled and nodded towards the sun that was slowly sinking into the horizon. The sky had turned a powder blue in the fading orange light, painting the nearby clouds in purple and pink.

"A penny for your thoughts?" I asked.

"Oh, I was just thinking how much I love these hot summer days and nights," she answered.

"Me too," I said, amazed that we had "heat" in common.

I reached into my pocket, pulled out a penny, and put it in her hand. She laughed. Looking at those high cheekbones, her wide smile, and blue eyes, and the way the light of the setting sun caught her face, I trembled. Being with her seemed almost too good to be real.

"So Miss Bobbie Atkinson, where did you learn to play golf so well? Did Josh teach you, or do you have a golfer boyfriend somewhere?"

Do you have a golfer boyfriend somewhere? God. How can I be so obvious?

"You know, I was just trying to figure out how to ask you the same question."

"Really?" *She wants to know if I'm attached.*

"No one at the moment," I answered, perhaps a little too eagerly. "I've not been serious with anyone since my divorce."

"You were married?"

"Yeah, we divorced about two years ago." A sudden pain punched the pit of my stomach as those memories abruptly surfaced. Bobbie must have noticed. She apologized for bringing it up.

"Oh, don't apologize. It's just that I hadn't thought about her for a while — or the dogs."

"Dogs?"

"Yeah, she trained dogs professionally." I paused, then looked directly at her. "You're not a dog trainer, are you?"

"I once trained a friend of mine's dog to sit up. Does that count?"

She made me laugh, really laugh — not many people could do that.

"No. She was a professional trainer. But between her training, showing and caring for them, she had little time for anything else, including me. The whole dog training thing is more a lifestyle than a hobby — time-consuming and expensive. I love dogs, and most all animals, but I just wasn't into it."

"Did she have a lot of dogs?"

"About 400."

"What?"

"I'm kidding, but it seemed like that many. Perhaps twenty at the most."

"That still sounds like a lot."

"Devoted dog trainers never think they have a lot of dogs, even if they have a hundred."

"So is that what came between you?"

"I thought it did, but now I'm not so sure. It was probably just the culmination of a lot of things that weren't working between us."

"Did you love her?"

Her question startled me. It was so direct. *Did I love her? I must have. I married her. We stayed together for five years. Why did she ask me that?*

"Why do you ask?"

"Sometimes things happen, and the reasons appear complicated, but often they are very simple. If there's no love, there's no real basis for the relationship."

"Well," I said. "Perhaps the real question is 'what is love?' And I'm not sure I know how to answer that. It seems to me that love can't be defined or explained." I paused, and without thinking, blurted out, "Like the True Swing."

Even in the fading light, I saw the look of surprise on her face. But then she smiled. "Yes, John. I think you're right. I'm sure there's a connection." *So she knows about the True Swing.*

"Johnny, do you think that each person in a relationship can be independent and free, but at the same time, want what's best for the other — each respecting the other without being submissive or demanding?"

She struck a nerve. "You know, Bobbie, I think so. What I remember is always feeling guilty — guilty for not being interested in her lifestyle, guilty for not having enough money to help support it. I felt I was always giving more than I received. But that wasn't all her fault. Maybe what happened is that we lost respect for each other."

"It's difficult," Bobbie said, "to look back and come up with answers. Perhaps what happened was just life taking its course. No one to blame; no one at fault."

"Shit happens?"

She laughed. "Exactly."

It was twilight now — that magical place between daylight and darkness where thoughts often linger longer than they should. I took a deep breath, and as I breathed out, my shoulders relaxed, and I felt lighter as if I had exhaled all those old hurt feelings into the warm night air.

"So, Bobbie, have you ever been married?"

"No, not yet."

Not yet? Does that mean she's getting married soon? Didn't I ask her if she had a boyfriend? Did she ever answer me?

"So, are you seeing anyone at the moment?"

"You," she said, catching me completely off guard.

Is she teasing me? The moon's pale light wasn't enough for me to read her expression, so I pursued another line of questioning. "Do you think it's possible for two people to be happy together forever?"

"Sure, but I think only if each can love and take care of themselves first. If both are truly doing what they love, giving themselves fully to their lives individually and together, then everyone is happy, and the possibilities are endless, don't you think?"

"Wow," I said, "you must have had a unique upbringing."

"I did. My stepfather, who raised me, had a wonderful outlook on life."

"Your stepfather?"

"Yes, my real father died when I was one."

"I'm sorry. What about your mother?" I asked, but then backpedaled. "Unless you think I'm prying."

"Oh, no." But she hesitated for a moment, and her next words came slower and more deliberate. "As far back as I can remember, my mother didn't care for me much. I suppose after my father died, I became a burden. She probably married my stepfather because of me, rather than for love. She was often quite abusive to my stepfather and me as well."

"It must have been awful."

"Perhaps more for him than for me. He was very loving and compassionate to her and me, and he did pretty much whatever she wanted. *She* decided where we lived, what we did, what we spent, how we spent it. It was that way until he finally divorced her."

"But he did divorce her? That's interesting — that he would let her take advantage of him like that, yet find the courage to act on a divorce."

"I don't think he saw it as her taking advantage of him. He always loved life and always accepted people for who they were. It was his concern for me that made him decide to leave her. One night, while in a rage, she went after me with a broom handle. Right then and there, he snatched me up and left. Soon after, they got divorced."

"Is your mother still around?"

"The last I heard, she was living in California."

The moon had risen high above us and its pale light revealed her pained expression. *I need to end this conversation about her mother.*

"So your stepfather was pretty unique, huh?"

"I can't even begin to tell you," she answered with enthusiasm. "He showed me a world that was full of wonder and excitement rather than evil and cruelty. When I started walking, he let me roam the house, the backyard, all over. He encouraged me to explore, to see things from all sides and to question everything. But all the while I always knew he was there, watching and protecting. As I got older and went to high school and college, his only requirement was that I follow my aspirations and talents. He said he would always support me, emotionally and financially, no matter what my vocation, even if I wanted to be a driving range attendant."

"And I guess that's what you wanted?"

"And I never needed his financial support."

Thank you, stepfather, wherever you are!

Multitudes of fireflies had risen from the grass bringing the night alive with dancing lights.

"Look," I said and pointed.

"And listen," she added. Several tree frogs were singing a melody over a full chorus of katydids. We sat there quietly. *If only this night could last forever.*

"What do you do when you're not golfing, Johnny?" Bobbie asked, interrupting my thoughts.

"I'm a manufacturer's rep for a belt company called Waisting Away."

"Really?" she said, sounding somewhat surprised.

Uh oh. She doesn't like salesmen? But then again, maybe she just doesn't like the name.

"Get it? Waist…w-a-i-s-t. Waisting Away?" She didn't wince at the pun the way most people did.

"How did you get the job?" she asked.

"How did I get the job?" Her question seemed odd. "A fellow I had met on a golf course, Jim Weller, got me the job."

"Jim Weller?"

"Yeah, as a matter of fact, a lady that knew Jim is how I found out about the Golden River Driving Range."

"Is Jim Weller a close friend of yours?" Another odd question, I thought.

"I wouldn't say close. He works for the company that owns our company, American Credential. He's often invited me to play golf at some of the company outings."

"Have you ever played at any of them?"

"No, I've never taken him up on his offer. American Credential, you know, is a mega-million-dollar company — the twenty-fifth largest in the country, I think. And a lot of those guys are pretty good golfers, including Jim. I've heard that even the president of the company is a scratch golfer."

"Carl Lindstrom." she offered.

"Yeah, that's right." It didn't surprise me that she knew of him. He was a pretty flamboyant character and was in the news all the time. "In fact, Jim Weller had told me that Carl Lindstrom, together with the CEO of American Credential…"

"R.J. Richards," she interrupted.

"Yeah," I said, somewhat fascinated that she kept up with the financial side of town. But then again, everyone in Cincinnati had heard of R.J. Richards and his son Robert — the eccentric major stockholders and brains behind American Credential. Not many people knew much about them, except that they were purportedly worth about four hundred million dollars each. However, because of Jim Weller, I knew more about R.J. Richards than most. It was time to impress her a little.

"Not many know this, but R.J. Richards and his son Robert once set up a golf match against two touring pros, Hale Irwin and Freddy Couples. R.J. and his son beat them hands down."

"Where did you hear that?" she asked as if she doubted the story.

"Jim Weller told me. Of course, you probably wouldn't have heard about it because the match was kept very secret. Richards and his son are known for being incredibly private. Very few people, if anybody, even know what they look like."

A light flashed off in the clubhouse, and someone stepped outside and locked the door.

"Gee, I didn't realize it had gotten so late," I said, looking at my watch. It was ten thirty.

"Yes, "she said. "I should be going. I have to be at the range early tomorrow. I hope we can do this again."

When? Where? Just name the time! "Sure, perhaps we could do dinner?"

"I'd like that."

Yes! A second date!

"Do you live near here?" I asked.

"Not too far — about a twenty-five-minute drive."

After picking up our clubs, we walked quietly to her car, enjoying the sultry night air. She opened her trunk while I folded her cart. Sadly, I put her cart and clubs put away. *This evening can't end. What else can I ask her? Did she say she lived alone? Does she live with her stepfather?*

"Is your stepfather still around?" I finally asked.

She hesitated as if considering her answer.

Oh no. Bad question. He must have passed away.

But then she smiled and said, "Yes." We walked around to the driver's side, and she unlocked the door.

"Do you still see him much?" I asked, as she climbed into the car and rolled down the window. I crouched down next to the door to say good night, and our faces were suddenly close, very close. She affectionately put her hand on mine and gave me a quick kiss. "At the moment, I work for him, or I should say, with him, so I see him every day."

Her touch, her kiss — my mind was entranced. Then the significance of her words sunk in. *She works with him? Sees him every day?*

"Josh?" I asked. "He's your stepfather?"

"Yep."

"No kidding," was all I could think to say.

Chapter 24

Josh is Bobbie's stepfather? Between Bobbie's kiss and her startling news, driving home was quite a task. After missing one turnoff, I sat lost in thought at an intersection as the light changed from red to green, and back to red. No telling how long I would have been there had a driver not pulled behind me and honked.

Josh is Bobbie's stepfather? It wasn't clear why this new revelation was bothering me. *Does being his stepdaughter change anything? If so, what does it change?* Not only did I have no answer to this question, I had no idea why I was asking it.

Josh is Bobbie's stepfather. Well, that at least explains why she's a near-scratch golfer, and why she knows about the True Swing. I wonder if she's realized the True Swing. But then how would I know? I have no idea what the True Swing is. How on earth did I end up on such a strange path and where is it all leading?

By the time I turned into my driveway, I knew sleep was out of the question until I figured some of this out. And my front porch was the place to do it. It was deep and wide, stretching along the entire length of the two-story home. A cushioned rocker sat under a large ceiling fan, and when things needed to be sorted out, that's where I went. After grabbing a six-pack of beer from the fridge, I settled into my rocker and kicked my feet up on the porch railing.

HISSS...POP.

Beer foamed out of the can, and I jumped trying to slurp it up, but it slopped all over my pants anyway. *What the hell.* I blew off the rest of the foam, settled back, and took a big swig.

Now, let me see if I can sort this out. Josh is Bobbie's stepfather, and she works with him at the range. Is she helping him out? Or is he helping her out? No, she said she didn't need his financial support and liked working there. So how much could she possibly make? It can't be much; they don't appear to have any customers but me. Why do I even care what she makes?

HISSS...POP.

Maybe I should start from the beginning. When was the beginning? It has to be when I got clobbered by BJ's club. That's when my life changed somehow as if there's been something missing. So what do I do? I pursue golf. Why golf? Because I love the game.

But look where it's taken me — to a series of instructors who put me through contortions that might scare a seasoned yoga instructor. To top that off, my swing gets worse.

HISSS...POP.

So then I end up in the Outback of the Midwest with a teacher who gives lessons that aren't lessons and talks about a True Swing that can't be learned. To top it off, I meet a wonderful, beautiful woman working there who turns out to be his stepdaughter, and who just might be interested in me. Could it be that she truly is interested in me?

My thoughts grabbed hold of Bobbie, and my mind replayed my entire day with her, savoring every moment.

HISSS...POP.

So how does Bobbie fit into all this? And what is "all this?" What is it that I'm searching for?

My focus shifted to Josh, and the "Handbook" and the story of the three golfers and the Master Instructor. *Maybe my real question is: What is the True Swing? And what is Josh up to with his cryptic notes and so-called lessons?* "Your swing is your teacher." "When your thoughts vanish your true swing will appear." "You are the True Swing, so rely on your self." "You are the True Swing, so who are you?"

HISSS...POP.

Whatever the True Swing is, I'm no closer to it than I was when I first met Josh. But despite that, I'm still intrigued by him. On the one hand, he's like a regular guy. On the other hand, there's a lot more there than meets the eye. So maybe the real question is: Who is Josh?

HISSS...POP.

The soft hum of the ceiling fan, together with the five beers I'd drunk, had me struggling to follow my reasoning. Sinking deeper into the rocker, I drifted into that vacant zone somewhere between consciousness and sleep.

In the distance, a dog barked. A nearby cricket chirped loudly and a whippoorwill called out. A faraway voice spoke, and someone laughed in response. Sounds were there, but not there. Things were heard, but who was hearing? A stillness seemed to rise up around me that was between sounds — or was it between thoughts? Did any of it really matter? Can one change what already is, and will be? Could this story already be written?

Something incredible was churning up my insides when a passing mosquito landed on my arm, licked its lips, and decided on a late night snack. It jolted me awake, and I trembled. A mixture of both fear and excitement were playing havoc with my emotions, and at that moment, nothing made sense. Whatever was happening to me, I had no idea, but I felt certain that Josh held the key.

Chapter 25

CREAK.

SLAP.

"Two hours early again?" Bobbie asked from somewhere in the dark. "Am I that irresistible?"

"Now, how can I answer that if I can't even see you?" I asked, playfully.

Her voice came from the far side of the counter. Once my eyes adjusted, the first thing I saw was her smile, which was hard to resist. But still, my eyes darted about the room searching for the leather-bound book while half expecting a flash of light.

Bobbie must have noticed my inattention. "Is there something in here more important to you than me?" she teased. "Don't tell me: *The Handbook of a Master Instructor.*"

"Now how could that possibly be more important to me than you?" I said. "It's just that...there's something about that book. Something just draws me to it."

Her forehead wrinkled in thought. "You know, you're not the first person who has said that."

"Really? How so? I know the book belongs to Josh, but do you know where he got it?"

"Josh told me his teacher gave it to him. It's been around as long as I can remember." She paused for a moment. "Yet not around — like last week. Sometimes I swear it's not here, and then it just sort of shows up."

"And you see flickering lights when it appears?"

"What?" she asked. Then she smiled. "Oh, you're kidding, right?"

"Yeah," I lied, and quickly changed the subject. "I take it you've read it?"

"Well, now that's a strange thing. I've never really sat down and read it cover to cover or even went looking for it to read. But it always pops up when I've needed advice or help with an important decision. And what I *have* read in that book has always seemed to relate. Weird, huh?"

"Yeah," I said, and this time I meant it. "So what do you think about the land of foxes, and squirrels, and white dimpled nuts?"

"What?"

She has no idea what I'm talking about.

"Oh, never mind," I said quickly. "So, have you seen the book around?"

She lifted some papers off the counter and glanced underneath. At the same, there it was, a light flash in my peripheral vision. It came from the direction of the bookcase. Bobbie gave no indication that she saw it so I didn't say anything. But there was no doubt in my mind that the book was nearby as I wandered over to the bench. It was sitting by itself on the bottom shelf of the bookcase.

"Oh, there it is," I said and walked toward the corner as casually as possible.

"You have better eyes than I do," Bobbie said as she strained to see. "Be my guest."

Before she had finished her sentence, I was already seated and leafing through the first few pages. It had occurred to me that if I could find the author or publisher, it would reveal the book's origin. But no such luck. The first two pages were blank, but the third had a line of text, which only served to deepen the mystery: It read, "Many who visit these pages may later question this book's existence. Be assured that it is as real as you are." *What the heck does that mean?*

Leaning back on the bench, I peered over at Bobbie, checking for some sign that perhaps she knew what was going on. But she was absorbed in her paperwork. After rereading the words and realizing they made even less sense the second time, I sighed and turned the page. To my amazement, but not to my surprise, the story of the Fox continued.

Mastery of the Fox
Part V. The Awakening

*O*ne bright sunny morning Golda wandered off to the far edge of the woods, a place she had not visited for quite some time. She was delighting in her jaunt through the wiry bushes and the towering trees when she noticed that the place was familiar — the bushes and thickets, the short grass, the two golden rocks. **Of course,** said the voice. **This is where I used to hide, waiting to snatch up the white dimpled nuts from those unsuspecting creatures.**

Golda smiled, remembering how cunning she had been, grabbing those white nuts right out from under their noses. But then the voice interrupted with a question so disturbing that her smile instantly vanished. **Was I wrong to have taken the white nuts from those creatures?** This was something she had never before considered. **Would they have felt sad, having such beautiful things taken from them? My goodness! What have I done? But then, didn't they, themselves, hit them away?**

Just then, Golda noticed movement on the grassy expanse. She crept behind one of the bushes and cautiously stared out from the foliage. In the short grass, one of those upright creatures was standing over a white dimpled nut and wagging the long stick with the shiny knob. The sight of the precious white nut sitting on the small twig brought those old feelings of desire rushing back, clamping hold of her like a spring-loaded trap. But the creature abruptly stopped what he was doing, turned, and looked directly at her. Golda jumped back.

Oh! It's the very same creature that had seen me hiding before! He's spotted me again!

Golda's instinct was to run, but something stopped her. The creature didn't appear dangerous. In fact, his mouth widened across his face, and he made some curious sounds that tickled Golda and she wondered if he might be laughing.

Just then, Golda's voice decided to speak, giving her an intriguing idea. **If I can get a closer look at this creature, perhaps I will discover how he can find me so easily hiding in these bushes.** So she mustered up as much courage as she could and bravely stepped out into the open.

As the beautiful red fox with the white-tipped tail emerged from the bushes, the creature moved towards her. When they reached each other, their eyes locked. In that instant, time seemed to stand still, and the woods quieted as if the entire universe were attending to the moment.

"Well, Mrs. Fox, I see in your eyes that you may have discovered something more valuable than golf balls."

The sound of his voice was so soothing that Golda relaxed a bit. Still, she kept a watchful eye — after all, the creature did have a big stick. But her worries eased when the creature set it aside, put his palms together in front of his chest, and bowed to her. The gesture was done with such grace that Golda was sure it was a kind of greeting, and she bowed as well.

The creature then did something that struck Golda as both odd and amusing. He sat down and folded his legs, one over the other. Next, he took a deep breath, looked into her eyes, and uttered some more sounds. "But I see you still have questions that have no answers."

Golda couldn't understand what he was saying, but there was something calming in the tone of his voice, and comforting in his eyes that seemed wise beyond sounds. **Perhaps,** her voice suggested, **if I sit with this strange creature for a while, I will understand how he can see things that are so well hidden.**

And so Golda cautiously moved closer, settled into an upright sitting position and watched the creature keenly. The creature's eyes closed and his breathing slowed considerably. The only movement in his body was the gentle rise and fall of his belly. Golda began studying the creature carefully, but the rhythm of his breathing was mesmerizing, and it wasn't long before her eyes closed, and she became absorbed in the rhythm of her breath.

Both fell into a quiet stillness, nary moving a muscle as the sun rose high overhead and then traveled westward towards the horizon. As the time slipped away, some other upright creatures and a few of the woods dwellers that had passed by, paused to marvel at such a sight — two very different beings, so very still, sitting across from each other in the short grass. But they let them be.

Golda was drifting in a very peaceful place for what could have been minutes or could have been hours. No telling how long she might have stayed there had the voice not so rudely interrupted. **Who is this strange being who has the power to outwit me?**

Golda was startled and slightly annoyed by the sudden intrusion of the voice. Still, the question made sense — after all, it was the very reason she had sat down with this creature in the first place. If the voice felt this question was so important that it had to command her attention, perhaps she should give it some serious attention.

She shifted her focus to the question and waited diligently for an answer. None came, but she wasn't all that surprised. The voice, which was very good at asking questions, was not so good at giving answers. Besides that, the voice had deceived her in the past and even if it did offer an answer, how could she know it was the truth? So she let the question dissolve away.

Instantly, she felt something shift. When the question fell away, the desire for an answer fell away with it. **Well,** said the voice. **Perhaps the answer is not to need to ask the question.** The voice was different somehow and she wondered if the creature knew something she didn't. She opened her eyes and studied the creature from head to toe.

Who is this strange creature with such an odd way about him? The voice asked. The question caused Golda to giggle.

Who is this strange creature that likes sitting with foxes in the short green grass? Golda chuckled some more.

For that matter, who is this strange fox that listens to this strange voice that sits with strange creatures in the short green grass?

SNAP!

The last question shot through her like a lightning bolt. Golda was startled, but the voice continued.

Who **is this fox with this odd voice that keeps asking all these questions?**

It was *that* question that jolted something deep within. An intense heat slowly rose up Golda's spine and spread through her body. At first, she was afraid, but as it continued she felt herself expand, and then expand more until she filled the entire universe. It was both unimaginable yet wondrous at the same time. Golda waited for a comment from the voice telling her what was happening. When none came, she became angry, and suddenly she was drawn back into her small self.

What just happened? The voice now said.

There was a long pause, and again, no answer, just questions. It was as if the voice was now unsure of itself. She waited, and waited until it finally burst forth. **Just who are you, anyway?**

The question sent Golda reeling into incredible visions that spun wildly in front of her. The sun flew across the sky to the horizon, disappeared, and arose on her other side. Again and again, it darted across the sky rising and setting countless times. As it continued, her collection of beautiful white nuts appeared before her and turned from white to a faded yellow and began to crack and decay, finally dissolving to dust. She gasped, seeing that her precious white nuts would not last, no matter how many she collected.

Then she saw the leaves on the trees surrounding her den explode into fall colors, quickly shrivel, and drop to the ground. Rains came, then snow, then more leaves blossomed, withered, and decayed until the trees themselves fell and vanished into the dirt. She watched in horror as her fellow wood dwellers appeared, grew old, and faded away. Young foxes, squirrels, deer, all sorts of other creatures appeared and disappeared the same way. Even her beautiful fur turned dull and thin and dropped from her bones like an old coat.

Golda trembled in fear. Not only would her precious white nuts not last, but nothing will last. She watched the cycle speed along faster and faster, gaining on itself until she could no longer distinguish where things began and where they ended. The vision sped up so fast that it blurred with everything running together, merging into one, until…

FLASH! A blaze of light, then nothing.

Where Golda was now, she wasn't sure. It was a vast nothingness, but it was alive with energy, and the energy was familiar. Somehow she knew she was not separate from it, that it was a part of her, or rather she was a part of it, as was everything.

This can't be real, the voice suddenly challenged.

The voice put Golda instantly on guard, and she felt divided as to what to do as if she were on a threshold, standing half in and half out of an entryway, but an entryway to where? **Step back!** The voice shouted, but she couldn't move. Fear struck. She couldn't go back — knowing how life had been since she found the white nuts. But how could she go forward not knowing what lay ahead? She began shaking violently, hoping for an answer when the voice came roaring back, blurting out question after question.

Where is this fear coming from? Who is it that's afraid? What is it that is afraid? Is it the voice? For no reason that she could explain, she suddenly knew what she had to do. Even if it meant never seeing her home or her friends again, even if it meant ceasing to exist, she couldn't go back. So she did the bravest thing she had done in her life. She jumped through the doorway.

* * *

How much time passed after she jumped? Golda didn't know, nor did she care. When she made the decision, all her fears immediately vanished, along with her desires, and attachments. The barrier that separated Golda from the Truth — the one that kept her from seeing things as they truly were rather than as the voice said they should be — shattered into pieces. She was resting freely in an all-knowing Consciousness. It was pure and whole, and it breathed life into her, into everything. She saw that nothing existed outside of it. And this Consciousness was not just a part of her; it *was* her — had always been her, even when the voice had led her into believing that she was something other than her Self.

When Golda finally opened her eyes, there was the creature, and there were the bushes, and the thickets, and the stick with the shiny knob, and the white nut — yet there was no Golda seeing these things, no voice commenting on them. There was just seeing, and things being seen. And although the surroundings were the same as they had been, she was awestruck by the miracle of their existence. Tears welled and overflowed from her eyes — tears of such joy and abounding love that she could hardly contain herself.

"Welcome home, my fine furry friend," said the strange creature. And though she didn't comprehend his words, Golda understood completely. She had found her way back to the Here and Now.

Chapter 26

CREAK.

SLAP.

The slap of the screen door made me jump and the book shut in my lap. A quick glance told me no one entered, and that Bobbie must have stepped outside. It was good that she had, my eyes were watery, and I wasn't sure why. After laying the book on the shelf, I rushed to the door and swung it open, only to catch Bobbie coming in. When she looked at me, she said, "John, are you all right?"

"Yeah," I said, but my voice cracked. "My summer allergies are acting up — thought I'd get some air and grab my clubs."

The sun, the heat, and the stroll to my car helped to clear my head, but there was no doubt the Golda story had affected some part of me — more questions needing answers. Perhaps Josh will be more forthcoming in our lesson.

As I rounded the building, I saw the range was empty. Josh was nowhere in sight. Then it struck me — except for Josh and me, it was always empty. *Am I his only customer?* Couldn't be, considering the amount of golf balls in the meadow. The only cars I'd ever seen in the lot were mine, Bobbie's, and the Chevy truck, which I figured must be Josh's.

"This is nuts," I blurted out. "A ten on the Weirdness Scale. Why aren't there other golfers here? Why hasn't anyone besides Irma ever even mentioned this place to me?"

The more I thought about it, the stranger the Golden River Driving Range got. If the things that had happened to me here weren't so weird, I'd be tempted to talk to Tom, or Larry, or even BJ about it. But they'd never believe my stories about the mysterious book and the even more mysterious instructor. The urge to run suddenly sounded like a good idea, to put the Golden River far behind me. But I didn't — I couldn't. This place had a hold on me. And of course, there was Bobbie.

About ten restless minutes had passed and no Josh. I spied a bucket of balls sitting on one of the tees. *What the hell.* I grabbed my driver and went to work.

WHASK! The ball sliced to the right. *You are the swing. When your thoughts vanish, your True Swing will appear.*

WHASK! Sliced again. *You are the True Swing. Rely on your self.*
WHASK! Sliced again. *You are the True Swing, so who are you?*
WHASK! Sliced again. I glanced at the clubhouse to make sure
Bobbie wasn't watching, and stuck my butt out.
WHAMPF! Oh, no. Not loss of distance again.
WHAMPF!

Josh came up behind me, or so I thought. I felt his presence. *Oh,
crap. He probably thinks I'm a complete moron.* My face reddened,
and I turned, wondering what to say.

No one was there. *That's strange.* After teeing up the next ball, I
glanced back over my shoulder. Still, no one in sight. After scanning
the entire range to make sure no one was watching, I bravely
dropped my foot back, stuck my butt out, spit on my hands, and
swung.

WHAMPF!

Damn! My swing was deteriorating even more than I thought
possible. *Where the hell is Josh when I need him?* My anger and
frustration were reaching their limits. After placing the next ball on
the tee, my urge was to beat it into submission. How could I have
worked so hard, spent so much time practicing, and still fail so
completely?

John, back off, relax. Don't swing at this next ball. I didn't listen.
WHAMPF!

That was it. My anger exceeded my capacity to contain it. I
gripped my golf club like a sledgehammer and started beating it on
the ground.

"I GIVE UP! THAT'S IT! NO MORE! I SURRENDER!
THROWING IN THE TOWEL! WAVING THE WHITE FLAG!
THIS IS IT! I'M DONE! I QUIT!"

I fell back on the bench, completely drained. Everything I
perceived a golf swing to be had absolutely, positively,
unquestionably gone right out the window.

Chapter 27

"Well, John, I guess now we can get started."

Josh's voice startled me, and I jumped up. "Where did you come from?" I half yelled.

Josh just grinned. "Come with me," he said.

I followed him, grumbling under my breath, as he headed toward the small storage building. *What now? Is he going to take me behind the shed and whip me?* We walked around the shed to where he kept the John Deere. Next to it, a green tarp was covering a large "something." Josh threw it off all the while looking at me with raised his eyebrows.

What the hell? Had there not been a set of clubs in the back of this incredibly strange vehicle, I might never have guessed it was a golf cart.

"You've got to be kidding," I said.

The sleek body was custom-molded fiberglass, painted red, with flaming decals down each side. The body sat high over the wheels, like a customized four by four pickup truck. Diamond plated aluminum running boards ran down each side. Two chrome tailpipes protruded from the rear.

"Get in," he said.

I slid under the black vinyl roof and into a padded bucket seat that had adjustable arms. "This is unbelievable," I said.

Josh reached over and pushed one of the many buttons that lined the solid wood dashboard. The vinyl roof retracted and folded behind us. When he turned the key, a low rumble spewed from the tailpipes. He shifted, popped the clutch and gravel blasted the walls of the shed. I glanced back at the shed and then gave him a strange look as he said: "that shed needs painting anyway." He shifted again, and we flew across the parking lot onto the range. Within five feet of my bag, he hit the brakes, and we skidded the remaining four.

"Grab your clubs and put them in the back," he said.

"Okaaay," was all I could say. While fastening my bag next to Josh's, I grabbed a quick look at his clubs. It was a decidedly mixed collection — a few weathered Tourneys and Titleists, a couple of Wilson staffs, and some irons that looked like they came from a garage sale.

Apparently, the cart was incapable of going slow. It spun rubber leaving the tee area, sailed back across the lot, and dove into the woods. The only time Josh eased off the pedal was to swerve around trees — something he didn't do when we reached the riverbank. I shut my eyes as we plunged into the water. Thank goodness it was shallow all the way across. On the other side, the cart sprung from the water like a mating salmon heading upstream.

"Damn, Josh!"

We hit dry land with wheels still spinning and scooted up the vertical bank. All four wheels left the ground when we cleared the top. He downshifted again, and we coasted out of the woods into a small clearing, which I realized was a tee area. It lay in front of the most beautiful, perfectly manicured fairway I had ever seen. It was nestled in among elegant old trees, various plants, and wild grasses, giving the impression that the fairway was built in harmony with its environment, rather than an interruption. In the distance was a large green, bordered on both sides by bunkers.

"Where are we?" I asked.

"We're right here," he answered, laughing. "Why? Where did you think we were?"

Josh's question had me shaking my head and wondering why I ever asked him anything.

"Actually," he said. "I've brought us in on the back side of a golf course."

"What golf course?" I asked as we got out of the cart. "Where's the clubhouse? Shouldn't we check in?"

"No, we're fine," he said while reaching for his driver. "Grab a tee and a ball and let's play some holes.

If there were more holes to this golf course, they were not visible from where we stood. There were no buildings, posts, or human activity anywhere nearby. While Josh rooted through his bag for some tees and a ball, I scanned the tee area for a marker sign that might indicate what hole we were playing. Nothing. No sign, no ball washer, no trash can, yardage marker, or any other sign anywhere. At least there were two golden stones, marking the tee area. *Two golden stones?* I swiveled around, scanning the bushes and thickets that surrounded the tee.

"You or me, John?" Josh asked.

"Why don't you go ahead and show me the way."

After he had placed his ball on the tee, I glanced back towards the foliage and then back to his ball. Josh was grinning at me as if he knew what I was thinking. I closed my eyes and let out a deep sigh. What the heck was I thinking? That a real live fox would steal his golf ball?

When he turned his attention back to setting up over his ball, my focus quickly enlivened. I could now witness his swing up close — I would see what this True Swing was all about.

He drew his club back smoothly and naturally and when it reached parallel, his weight shifted forward, and his club followed. The ball flew from the tee as his body and club swung around to a natural, relaxed finish. The ball sailed out about as far as I could see. His movement was natural and free. But there was no slow motion or hyper speed like I had witnessed before.

"Did you change your swing?" I asked.

"No. Why do you ask?"

"It seemed different from the last time I saw it."

"Perhaps you're just seeing it differently from the last time you saw it." His eyes twinkled, and he pointed to the tee area. "You're up."

Maybe something *was* different in the way I was seeing things. When I set the ball on the tee, it looked bigger and whiter than usual, the dimples more pronounced. The grass around the ball was extraordinarily green, every blade sharp and distinct. As I stood over the ball, my mind didn't automatically run me through the usual "setup" information. I just drew that club back and swung.

WHASK!

To my amazement, the ball flew a long ways, but the elation quickly dissipated as I watched it slice into the woods.

"Damn. All that beautiful fairway and I hit into the woods," I grumbled.

"The woods are quite beautiful too," Josh said.

"Well, yeah. I suppose."

"You take the cart," Josh said. "I'll walk up to my ball."

It turns out that the cart did have a normal speed and I drove it up to the edge of the woods where my ball had disappeared. I found it quickly, but the only playable shot was to hit through a narrow opening back onto the fairway. I chose a low iron, positioned myself, and swung. It sliced again, flying laterally through the trees. *Oh, man. I'll never find it.* But then…

SMACK!

It hit a tree, sending it flying out of the woods and across the trap, rolling onto the green about five feet from the cup.

"Great shot," Josh yelled.

"Yeah, right!" I shouted back.

Josh was sniffing the air, and scanning the fairway when I drove up. "No wind," he said as he grabbed an old beat up eight iron from his bag. "And I say about a hundred and sixty-one yards, give or take a foot." With a smooth, powerful swing, he sent the ball to within eight feet of the cup.

"Wow. What a great shot."

"Not quite as good as yours," he said.

"What are you talking about?"

"You're ball is closer to the pin than mine, and look where you hit from."

When we reached the green, I marked my ball and waited for Josh to putt. He studied his line carefully and with one smooth stroke, sent the ball directly to the hole. But at the last instant, it turned slightly and rimmed the cup. He tapped it in for a par.

"Good par," I said.

Taking note of what his ball had done, I aimed my ball a little more to the left. The adjustment worked — the ball dropped into the cup.

"Nice birdie," he said.

"C'mon," I said in frustration. "By all rights, I should have been deeper in the woods, not laying on the green."

"You should have been? But you weren't. And you beat me on the hole."

"But it would have been better to play it like you did."

"But you got a birdie, John. I got a par. You know, if you would consider enjoying each shot for what it is, it makes the game a lot more fun."

"Well, yeah…I guess you're right." *Hold on. Did I just agree? It isn't like me to accept playing badly as being okay. Am I playing badly? What's going on here?*

My mind was working overtime, trying to sort this out as I walked to the cart. Josh was already behind the wheel. The tires spun just as I jumped in, and the cart dove back into the woods, flew over a shallow ridge and came to rest at the bottom of a small hill. We hiked up the incline to the tee area, from which a clear lake revealed itself between the tee and the green. It was a par three, with the pin placement in front of the deep green, guarded by a sand trap just over the lake. Huge sycamores, oaks, and elms lined the back. It reminded me of one of those "most spectacular holes" you might find in a golf magazine. Again, there was no yardage sign.

"How far do you think?" Josh asked.

"About one fifty, I'd guess."

"Good," Josh beamed.

We climbed back down the rise to the cart — me, for my seven iron, Josh, for his nine. When we trudged back to the tee, Josh said, "Birdies are up."

I reached into my pocket for my ball, and I found it empty. "Damn, I must have left my ball down in the cart."

"Here," Josh said as he tossed me a ball.

"What's this?" I asked while examining it. The ball had a brilliant white cover with hints of gold flake throughout. It glimmered in the sunlight. On one side, in gold lettering, was inscribed *Golden River.* On the other side was a Chinese symbol also inscribed in gold. It was certainly unique and probably expensive.

"This is beautiful, Josh. But on a lake hole — are you nuts? You must not want it back very bad."

"Consider it a gift, John."

"Really?" I said and put it back in my pocket. As I started walking back towards the cart, Josh said, "No sense in going all the way back to the cart. Go ahead and use it on this hole.

"Well, okay," I said with uncertainty.

With reluctance, I placed the ball on the tee and tried to pretend the lake wasn't there.

WHAMPF!

SPLASH!

"Damn, damn, damn," I repeated as Josh tossed me another ball — an old beat-up range ball. *So why didn't he give me that the first time?* Without hesitating and with a lot of anger, I placed it on the tee and swung at it while cursing myself.

WHACK!

The ball sailed straight toward the flag, landed ten feet behind it, spun backward, and dropped into the cup.

A hole in one! My first hole it one! No, it wasn't a hole in one because I had a two-stroke penalty for hitting the first ball into the lake.

"Nice par," Josh said.

I didn't know how to answer or how to feel — angry, exhilarated, disappointed, what?

"Why couldn't I do that the first time!?" I grumbled.

"Maybe your mind told you that you had too much to lose."

"But it's true; I didn't want to lose it."

"What difference does it make, John? You didn't even know it existed a few moments ago. Wanting to hold onto things that will eventually disappear can certainly take the fun out of things while they're here, don't you think?"

For some reason, his words came easy as if they were bypassing my normal listening system. And on the next three holes, Josh went to work on my swing. "Try this," he would say, and then he'd watch. "Good, now consider this," and it would work. At the end of five holes, my slice was gone, and my distance had increased dramatically. After playing another four holes, Josh was ahead of me by only one stroke. It didn't seem possible. As I watched, listened, and absorbed every word, my respect for him grew dramatically along with a deep gratification.

"It's time to head out," Josh said as we climbed into the cart. He drove more sanely on the way back, which allowed me to reflect on my lesson, rather than on whether I would survive. *Why did I learn so easily today after all the struggling with all my instructors? What happened that was different? Why did he wait so long before working on my swing?* Something had changed. I felt it, and I needed to confront him.

"Josh, what changed today that made you finally decide to coach me?

"You weren't ready until today."

"I don't understand. What made you decide I was ready?"

"Because of what happened to you on the practice tee. You gave up and questioned everything you thought to be true. You were ready to be shown new possibilities."

What he said made sense, but then again it didn't, and we drove the rest of the way in silence. After he parked at the side of the shed, I helped him cover the cart with the tarp. There was so much I wanted to ask him but all that came out was, "thanks for today, Josh."

"You're welcome," he said, then headed for his tractor.

I dropped my clubs at my car and headed to the building to give Bobbie the thirty-five dollars for the lesson. Bobbie took it and said, "Well, I see your lessons have started."

"You can't even imagine."

"By the way, Josh asked me to tell you that there is a two-week break in lessons after today, but if you want to come to the range and practice any day, or every day, you are welcome."

"Are you here every day?" I asked.

"Yep."

Great. With more than four weeks' vacation due me, what better way to spend two of them hanging out with Bobbie and practicing golf?

"I'll take him up on the offer," I said excitedly. "So I'll see you tomorrow?"

"I'll be here."

On the way to my car, I smiled. *When your thoughts vanish, your True Swing will appear.*

Chapter 28

Sleep that night was sparse, at best. The success of my first official golf lesson and the anticipation of seeing Bobbie every day for the next three weeks kept me awake deep into the night. Still, I was up early — no way could I sleep in, even if it was my first day of vacation. By nine, my clubs were out of the trunk, and I was strolling towards the range, anxious to see if my improvements hung in there overnight. But as I rounded the corner of the building, I stopped just short of the back window. A decision had to be made. Should I see Bobbie first? Or test out my new improved swing? I was feeling a twinge of guilt for even considering the latter.

"Anybody home?" I asked, sticking my head in the back window.

Bobbie's smiling face appeared at the window, her blue eyes sparkling in the morning sun. No question, I had made the right decision.

"Hi, Johnny," she said cheerfully. "Hot out there?"

"It's already eighty degrees," I answered, and then smiled. "Isn't it great?"

"I think you and I are the only ones who think so."

"I'm glad we have that in common," I said.

"Johnny, before you get started, I'd like to ask you something."

"Sure, as long as the question isn't over my head."

She chuckled. "Would you like to take me to a party?"

She's asking me out again? To a party? A real sure-fire date?

"Sure," I said. "When is it?"

"In two weeks. It's on July 29th, a Saturday."

"A little far off, isn't it?" *Two weeks sounded like forever.*

"Yeah, but something has come up. While Josh is on break, I need to run down to Raleigh, North Carolina. I won't get back until the morning of the party." My heart sunk, and she must have noticed. She quickly added, "Hey, I would love to hang around with you here, but at least we have the party to look forward to."

"Yeah, I guess," I answered while waiting for some explanation why she'd be in Raleigh for two weeks. When she didn't offer, I decided not to pry, "So who's giving the party?"

"One of Josh's students. They give him a party once every two years and take turns hosting it."

"Are you trying to tell me that Josh has more students than just me?"

She laughed heartily. "Of course," she said. "But it's not just current students that will be there. All his students from over the years are invited."

"No kidding." My interest jumped to an eight on the Richter scale. "How many years would that be?"

"Quite a few. Anyway, I'll be back in town that morning. The party is at seven. If you could come by my place about six thirty, I'll be ready." She handed me a card. "Those are the directions and my telephone number."

Gee, I got her address and phone number without even asking. "When are you leaving?"

"Tonight. My flight is at eight fifteen, so I'll be leaving here shortly. Have to pack."

I was tempted to offer her a ride — maybe find out what she was planning to do in Raleigh. But it didn't feel right.

She took my hand and squeezed it. "I'll look forward to seeing you when I get back."

"Me too," I said, allowing her hand to linger on mine. "By the way, what's the dress code?"

"Most anything, but I'd suggest nice casual.

She withdrew her hand, and I reluctantly reached down for my clubs. "Guess I'll see you in two weeks, then," I said offhandedly, trying to hide my disappointment. As she disappeared into the darkened room, I stared after her, not wanting to let go. But a voice interrupted.

"John, are you going to hang out at that window all morning?" Josh was standing on one of the tees with a bucket of balls.

"What are you doing here? I thought you were on break."

"I *am* on break," he said as I approached. "But we can't let that 'new and improved' swing of yours disappear, now can we? Do you think it hung in there overnight?"

"I don't know, what do you think?" I asked timidly.

"I think 'I don't know' is a good answer," he said, smiling as he handed me the bucket of balls. "So let's find out. Grab your pitching wedge and hit a few."

He watched intently as I hit about ten shots out to a flag he had set up over the hundred yard marker — all of which were very respectable. It was hard to keep from grinning when I stepped back off the tee.

"Well, what do you think, Josh?" I said, pausing in hopes of a compliment.

"Let me see your club, John."

"My club?" I said as I handed it over.

He took it gently into his hands as if he were accepting a newborn baby. After holding it a few moments, he let club slide down through his fingers until the club face rested on the ground. He then lightly placed it in his grip. Ever so slowly, he scanned the entire club while allowing his hand to slide along the shaft to the hosel and across the face. "Hmm," he murmured and flipped the club over. His attention was so focused that somehow I felt its residual, like an invisible force-field pulling me. *But pulling me where?* That's when I noticed that the club appeared different somehow as if I were seeing it for the very first time. *Gee. Could I be that unaware?*

Josh glanced up at me. "Don't go away," he said and picked up my golf bag. "I'll be right back."

"What's going on?" I called out, but he was already around the corner of the building. How long he was gone, I didn't know, nor did I care. A peacefulness had dropped over me, suggesting that at that moment, there was just nothing I needed to do — no place I needed to be. Life was right here, and so was I.

"Try these," Josh said from behind me, and I jumped.

"Gee, Josh. You sure know how to sneak up on a guy."

I took the wedge from my bag — the one Josh had eyed so carefully and pitched a shot at the hundred-yard flag.

CLANG.

The ball hit the pin and dropped on the marker. I was stunned.

"What did you do to this club?"

"It needed some adjustment. I hope you don't mind. I did a little work on the others as well."

"Mind? Are you kidding? It feels great!"

As I proceeded to work with my wedge, he began offering suggestions such as how I might approach a shot or adjust my alignment for different results. He gave me his thoughts on grip pressure, stance, and ball placement. The adjustments came easily and each shot achieved remarkable precision.

"Try one of your long irons," Josh said.

I slid my wedge back in the bag and took out my three iron. Josh let me hit a few balls in silence before suggesting some slight modification to the swing plane. Each ball went further, and the direction was more accurate. Before long, the ball was doing things I had not thought possible, at least for me. But the truly amazing thing; it was effortless, and my excitement quickly grew as I thought about testing this swing with my driver.

Josh must have sensed my anticipation. He had already taken the driver from my bag and was grinning as he handed it to me. As I set up over the ball, I felt my confidence surging, yet my mind was quiet. There was no mental checklist of postures and movements, no critical voice predicting failure. Only one thought popped into my head. *You are the True Swing. Rely on your self.*

WHAAACK!

The slice was gone, the wimpy-ness had disappeared, and a smile spread across my face as I took my time watching the ball sail long, very long, straight out over the meadow. Josh was smiling too as he said, "Okay. Let's try a few more things, shall we?" Within the next half hour, I could not only affect a slight draw; I could hit a fade. And that's how it went for the next two weeks. Each day, I arrived at nine, immersing myself in fun-filled, effortless practice until dusk. Every shot seemed better than the last. The improvement was miraculous, and my gratitude to Josh deepened more with each lesson.

On the final day of my two-week vacation, Josh watched me practicing in silence. After I had hit the last ball into the midday sun, he said, "Well, you seem to have a little different perspective on your swing than when you first came here."

"A little different?" I asked, grinning. "I think you're underplaying your incredible ability to teach."

"An instructor is only as good as his student," he countered.

"So you're giving me all the credit?"

"Of course."

As we walked off the tee, I beamed at his compliment. *If this is what the True Swing feels like, it certainly feels good… but wait a second. I remembered something Josh had said in our first meeting.*

"Josh, when we first met, didn't you tell me that I would not find a true swing here?"

"Yes," Josh answered.

"I don't understand. Why did you tell me that?"

"Because you will not find the True Swing here."

"So my swing is not the True Swing?" I asked, somewhat taken back.

"It's truly a good swing."

Here we go again. "So what is the True Swing?"

"When you are ready, it will show itself. And you will know instantly."

"Know what?"

"Nothing. Everything."

"That certainly narrows it down."

Josh laughed and said, "The mind cannot comprehend That which is incomprehensible."

"What was that again?" I asked?"

"The True Swing does not exist in the mind. The mind exists within the True Swing."

With a half-smile and a shake of my head, I asked, "Could you at least try somehow to explain it?"

"If I were to explain it…"

"I know, I know. It would not be the True Swing. But how can something not be explained?"

"Do you think you could adequately explain a sunset to one who can't see?

His question caught me off guard, and it took a moment to sink in. "I kind of get what you're saying," I finally said. "But then, when might I know what the True Swing is?

"It can happen anytime, John. Right now, the next instant, next week, or perhaps in some future lifetime."

"Well, that certainly pins it down."

Josh raised his eyebrows and with that familiar playful twinkle in his eyes, changed the subject, "John, have you considered entering any local tournaments?"

"Tournaments?"

"Yes, have you thought about it?"

"Funny you should mention that. One of my golf buddies called last night to remind me of the Cavendish Cup, a tournament put on by the county park district. We usually enter it every year."

"How's it structured?" Josh asked.

"It's a flighted tournament, where they take your first day's score and match you up to those who have equal scores. Then you play against them on the second day and total both days' scores. This gives you a chance to compete against those in your same scoring range. It's a lot of fun."

"Good. It will be interesting to see how you do." As we strolled back towards the building, Josh said, "I guess I'll see you at the party tonight."

"You bet," I said with a twinge of guilt. With all my attention diverted to golf rather than Bobbie, the last two weeks went by a lot quicker than perhaps they should have.

Chapter 29

Funny how one sets goals, makes plans, and then life does what it pleases. Eight weeks ago, Bobbie wasn't in my life, nor was Josh. And my golf game was in the crapper. *Now look at me.*

I was heading east on I-275 and had just crossed over I-75 when I glanced again at Bobbie's directions. It was interesting that she lived on the east side. The interstate cut straight through Cincinnati, literally and symbolically dividing it in two. If the west side was Willie Nelson, pickup trucks, and Budweiser beer, the east side was Tony Bennett, Mercedes, and Hendrix gin. *So Bobbie lives on the east side.*

Another ten minutes of driving took me to Milford, where I exited, and drove four miles to a condominium development called Eagle Chase. The entrance was a private road with a gate, but it was open. Once inside, my directions said to turn at the first stop sign.

Very nice. Two-car garages, wood siding, tall windows, cedar shake roofs, quaint porches, wide sidewalks, street lamps, large trees — it looked more like a Norman Rockwell version of a small-town neighborhood than a condo development.

As I neared the right street number, I spotted Bobbie sitting on her porch and instantly wondered how she could not have constantly been on my mind the last two weeks. As I pulled in front of her condo, she ran down the sidewalk, jumped in the car, and kissed me on the cheek. The sudden kiss, her short white skirt, the pale pink blouse, a hint of perfume — it all rushed at me so fast that my face flushed, and I fumbled for words. If that wasn't embarrassing enough, my foot slipped from the clutch; the car lurched forward, and the engine died.

But Bobbie laughed, and said, "That's exactly why I drive an automatic."

It was amazing how quickly she could put me at ease. But my witty remarks were still not forthcoming, so I just decided to tell her the truth. "Seeing you again, Bobbie, after not seeing you for three weeks…well, what can I say? My brain has turned to mush."

Her blue eyes lit up as she beamed me a smile and gave me another quick kiss. Funny how the truth can be just the right thing to say.

After starting the car and backing out of her driveway, I said, "Nice condo, by the way."

"Thanks," she said. "If you're not too tired when we get back, I'd be glad to show it to you."

Did she just invite me "up to her place" later? "If I'm not too tired? Are you planning to keep me out all night?"

"No, no. It's just that Josh said you had spent every day at the range for the last two weeks and I figured my job tonight might be to keep you awake."

" I feel pretty good, actually. The last two weeks went by quickly. *Too* quickly. Did he tell you how much I've improved?"

"You have? That's wonderful."

"He didn't say anything about my progress?"

"All he said was that you were 'most certainly on a path where there was no turning back.'"

"What do you suppose he means by that?"

"I don't know. Sometimes with Josh, you just have to accept what he says at the time, and see if it makes sense later."

"Where are we headed, by the way?" I asked after we turned onto the main road.

"We'll get back on the freeway and go two exits west. I'll tell you as we go."

When the freeway sign came into view, I turned onto the entrance ramp, settled back, and decided to do a little fishing.

"So, how was your trip to Raleigh?"

"It was a nice flight down and back," she said but didn't continue.

"Did you have a good time?

"Yes," she answered, and again offered no more. But I didn't let go.

"Do you like Raleigh?"

"Oh, yes," she answered, and then proceeded to talk about her favorite Raleigh restaurants. I didn't push it any further.

"Get off here and turn right," she said as we approached the Indian Hill exit. "Then take the first left."

"One of Josh's students lives in Indian Hill?" I asked, surprised.

The name Indian Hill was synonymous with affluence. Just minutes from Cincinnati, the beautiful woods, and rolling hills provided an exquisite setting for large country estates and mini horse farms — the perfect dwelling place for CEOs, wealthy business owners, and the social elite.

"Oh, you're in for an interesting evening," she said with a wry smile.

"Is the party always at the same place?" I asked while glancing at a mausoleum-sized Victorian home off to our left.

"No. The last party was an afternoon barbecue out on the west side, near Harrison. One of Josh's students has a nice double wide on two acres. Horseshoes, some banjo picking, lots of food. It was a great time. These parties are always…well, you'll see."

The winding narrow roads of Indian Hill were part of its mystique. We passed estate after estate and countless miles of fencing, from four-board oak to bedrock, from white vinyl to brick.

"Turn right up ahead," she said.

There was no sign, but the road improved and widened considerably. "What road is this?" I asked.

"Oh, this isn't a road. It's a driveway."

"A driveway? We're here?"

The driveway took us about a quarter mile through perfectly manicured pastures before we came to the house — a huge two-story country home of classic design. It sat among large leafy maples, on a sprawling stretch of rich green lawn. The driveway circled the front of the house, and at least fifty cars took up every available space. I looked at Bobbie and said, "Gee."

After parking a considerable distance from the house, we strolled up the long driveway. Bobbie was watching me, but was suspiciously quiet. Perhaps she was waiting to see my reaction to the variety of automobiles we were passing. It was quite an assortment of both old and new, which included two Mercedes Coupes, a Ford Mustang, a Porsche Carrera, a Ford Taurus, a restored Austin Healey 3000, a slightly rusted Studebaker Commander, two Rolls-Royces, a bunch of Lexuses, and a VW bus with a hand-painted peace sign on the side.

"Whose place is this?" I asked.

"His name is Mike Blair. He owns a catalog company in Cincinnati called Bentwood Fence."

"Isn't that the very expensive 'I must have that gadget' catalog?"

"That's the one."

His catalogs used full-color photos and top notch ad copy to entice people to buy all sorts of stupid things they didn't need and probably would never use — things like a hand-polished stainless steel dustpan, twice the size of an ordinary one, at the quality price of $59.95. *Who in their right mind would pay fifty-nine, ninety-five for a dustpan?*

"I bought a dustpan from one of his catalogs," I mumbled.

"What?"

"Oh, nothing. So you're saying that this Mike guy is one of Josh's students?"

"Yep."

I was impressed.

Chapter 30

The sun had sunk well below the trees behind us, spraying the sky in crimson and purple, dropping the front of the house into the first shades of night. We heard chatter and laughter drift out from the open windows and from the screen door that glowed in soft amber against the twilight. As we climbed the porch, the sound of gayety from inside had me liking the owner already.

A tall, well-dressed, good-looking man in his mid-thirties met us at the door. "Hi Bobbie," he said and gave her a big hug that I thought lasted a little *too* long. Finally, he let her go and noticed me. After a quick up-and-down glance, he said, "And who is this?"

Suddenly, I didn't like him anymore.

"This is John," Bobbie said.

He threw out his hand, and we shook. "My name's Mike. I'm so glad you could come." Just then, a stunning blond, impeccably dressed in a blue-yellow summer dress, appeared behind him.

"Hi, Joy," Bobbie said.

"Oh," Mike said and looked at me. "This is my wife, Joy."

Suddenly, I liked him again.

"This is John," he continued. I caught him raising his eyebrows as he glanced back at his wife. "He came with Bobbie."

"Really?" Joy said as she moved towards me for a closer look. "Is he a date or a student?"

"Both," she said with enthusiasm.

It's official. Date number two. I shrugged my shoulders at Joy, noticing that both she and Mike were surprised. *I wonder what that's about.* But before I could ask, Bobbie grabbed my arm and pulled me into the great room, which was already filled with guests. *Well, I guess I'm not Josh's only student.*

Josh was amidst a crowd of guests across the room but was easy to spot. He stood out among the smartly cut sport coats and silk shirts in his bright orange golf shirt, khaki pants, and sandals. Since my outfit was more in line with those around him, I suspect he didn't see me.

"Would you like something to drink?" Bobbie asked.

"Yes," I said while taking in my surroundings. Most of the guests were embracing glasses of wine or drink glasses filled with a clear or amber substance — martinis and scotch, I guessed, and I wondered if they were closet beer drinkers. After all, a cold beer on a hot summer night — what could be better. "A Bombay martini with an olive would be nice," I said, and she scurried off.

Just off the great room was a sitting area with numerous floor-to-ceiling windows. In the center of the room were two oversized couches and a matching chair. A number of guests were standing, clustered in small groups while two women were sitting on one of the couches, chatting away. The adjacent couch and chair were vacant.

The chair beckoned me — it had a good vantage point to observe Josh's guests. As I casually wandered over and sat down, one of the women on the couch glanced at me and smiled. I smiled back and looked away, but as she returned to her conversation, my ears perked up. She mentioned playing a round of golf with Patty Sheehan. Patty Sheehan had been a dominant figure in the LPGA and had won the Women's US Open championship a few years back. I snuck a closer look at the women who was talking. She did look familiar. *Who the heck is she — hob knobbing on the golf course with one of the most successful women golfers in history?* "Here's your martini, John," Bobbie said from off to my side.

"Oh, thanks," I said and started to get up.

"No, stay seated. I'm going to run to the powder room."

"Before you go…" I started to say while motioning her to lean over. But as her face came close to mine, her breath brushed my cheek, and the faint hint of perfume filled my head, and my mind went blank.

"Yes?"

"Oh," I finally said. "Do you know that lady on the couch, in the pink dress? I overheard her say that she had played golf with Patty Sheehan."

"That wouldn't surprise me?" she said with a sly smile.

"Why?" I said. "Who is she?"

"That's Laura Davies."

"Laura Davies? *The* Laura Davies who won the Women's US Open in 1987 and has dominated the LPGA ever since? Laura Davies is one of Josh's students?"

"Fascinating, huh?" she said playfully. "Johnny, are you sure you'll be okay by yourself for a few minutes?"

"Sure, go ahead," I said, and meant it. With Bobbie gone, it would give me a chance to absorb what she just told me and to scan the room to see who else might be here.

There! A face I know. It was Jim Scout, a local radio and TV celebrity. He was conversing with someone else who looked familiar. *Holy cow! Johnny Bench, Hall of Famer — catcher for the Cincinnati Reds! This is incredible!* Was it my imagination or is every face starting to appear familiar?

"Excuse me," a voice said over my shoulder. "Would you hand me that glass of wine there on the coffee table?" I picked up the glass, stood up, and handed it to a lanky fellow with bushy red hair.

"I hope I didn't take your seat," I said apologetically.

"No, you didn't. I just misplaced my wine."

"You look familiar," I said, even though he didn't. The way things were going, he had to be somebody.

"I'm Fred Biner," he said with a grin.

"Have we met somewhere before?" I asked, fishing.

"Maybe I've done work for you. I'm a mechanic at Joe's garage, over in the tri-county area."

"I'm John Arbor," I said, trying not to sound disappointed.

"And this is Frank Dolens," he said turning to a fellow next to him. "If you ever want a really good meal, stop over and see him at the Vine Street Pizza House."

Ah ha. The Vine Street Pizza House. There are at least five of those throughout the city and more in the works. "You have quite a franchise operation there," I offered.

"Oh no, I'm the cook at the one on Vine Street," he replied. Just then, Bobbie arrived and saved me.

"I see you've met Fred," she said. "He keeps my Jetta running. And Frank makes the best pizza in town."

"I like pizza," was all I could think of to say as I glanced around the room. Another familiar face caught my eye "Hey, there's Jim Weller."

"Oh, yeah," Bobbie said, "the one who got you your job at Waisting Away."

"Wait a minute," I said, both surprised and suspicious. "Jim is one of Josh's students?" It was the first time I saw guilt in Bobbie's face. She didn't answer so I continued. "Obviously, you must know him. Why didn't you say so the night I told you about him?"

"When you mentioned him that night, I thought about this party, and that's when I decided to ask you to come. I guess I wanted you to be surprised when you saw him here. I'm sorry. Can you forgive me?"

How could I not? Her blue eyes were penetrating and her smile, well, it dissolved away any suspicions or irritation. Glancing back over at Jim Weller, I was surprised to see another recognizable face. "Isn't that Carl Lindstrom that Jim is chatting with — the president of American Credential?" Suddenly, more pieces fell into place. "Then you know Carl Lindstrom as well?"

"Yes," she said. "I told you this would be an interesting evening."

"So could it be that R.J. Richards and his son Robert are here — are you hobnobbing with the multimillionaire American Credential people too? Are they also Josh's students?"

"If R.J. Richards were here, who would know? You said yourself he was a recluse." She paused. "By the way, have you seen Josh yet?"

"Yeah, I saw him when we came in. Listen, why don't you go find him while I say hi to Jim."

"Sure," she said and headed off. With Bobbie out of the way, and with a little luck, perhaps Jim could enlighten me as to what was really going on here. As I approached him, a waiter handed me another martini. "From Bobbie," he said.

When Jim saw me, he grinned with surprise. "Hi, John."

"It's good to see you again, Jim," I said.

"A small world, isn't it?" He said as he shook my hand. "So you're a student of Josh's?"

"I'm taking lessons from him now," I said, feeling like a member of an elite fan club "By the way, wasn't that Carl Lindstrom you were just talking to?"

"Yeah, it was. He's quite a character."

"So, is he one of Josh's students?"

"He is — has been for quite some time."

"This is amazing," I said.

"I know how you feel. I remember the first time I went to one of these parties."

"By the way," I said, leaning into him, "is there any chance that R.J. Richards and his son are students of Josh's?"

"Now that's something I had never considered. But I doubt it. I've never heard anyone mention them being at one of these parties. And I've been to the last five. Of course, if Richards himself stood in front of me, I wouldn't know him. Nobody seems to know what he looks like. I guess if you're worth close to a billion dollars, you can afford to be private."

"It's a wonder to me that all these people have found their way to Josh's range," I said, half to myself.

"You know, John, I've thought about that. It does appear that there's a common theme with everyone here. We're all searching for something."

"How do you mean?"

"Well, why are you here?"

"Good point."

"And remember that old adage? When a student is ready, a teacher will appear?"

"So you're saying that Josh is the teacher that appeared for all these people?"

"What do you think?"

"Well, I guess that's pretty much how it happened to me."

"By the way, I take it you've met Bobbie. Have you seen her around tonight? Rumor has it that she's with someone."

His statement startled me, and for a moment, I didn't know what to say. "She *is* with somebody tonight," I finally said. "She's with me."

"You're with Bobbie?" he said with genuine surprise. "You two are here together?"

"Yes," I said, somewhat irritated. "Is there a problem?"

"No! Not at all. It's just that…wow. You're sure a lucky devil."

"What do you mean?"

"As long as I have known Bobbie, she's never dated any of Josh's students, let alone brought any of them to one of his parties. And Lord knows, a lot of them have asked her, including me."

"Really?" I said, feeling my ego swell.

"You should feel good, John. She's one great lady."

"Yeah, I know, and she's some golfer, too."

"She plays golf?" Jim asked, surprised.

"You didn't know? She's a great golfer, as a matter of fact. She shot a 76 when we played."

"I guess I should have figured her a golfer."

Perhaps it was the martinis, or the party, or what Jim had just said, but it suddenly struck me how special Bobbie was. *Obviously, she can have anyone she wants. Yet, she's with me. Have I neglected to let her know how I feel?* Right then, I needed to see her, to be with her, to tell her how I feel.

"Good talking with you, Jim," I said as a passing waiter traded me a beer for my empty martini glass

Bobbie was easy to find in a crowded room. It wasn't just her beauty that pulled all eyes towards her, Bobbie's presence was commanding. She spotted me and waved. I hurried over and boldly grabbed her hand. "Let's go find a quiet, cozy spot in a back room. We need to talk."

"What's this about?" she asked, taking my arm. "Is everything okay?"

I led her out of the room and down a corridor. From the end of the hall, a rendition of "Margaritaville" floated out from one of the rooms. *Ah, perfect. There's nothing like a Jimmy Buffett song to set the right mood.*

We walked through double wood doors into a candle-lit library richly adorned with wood wainscoting and wall-to-wall bookcases. By lucky chance, there happened to be an empty loveseat near the wall. Across the room, occupying two facing couches, a guitarist was entertaining two women. As we sat down, the guitarist began crooning another Jimmy Buffett song, "Son of a Son of a Sailor." The two women waved to Bobbie and then turned their attention back to the entertainer.

Suddenly, I was nervous. *What am I doing? What if I'm misreading how she feels? What if I'm misreading how I feel? Why tell her now?* But I couldn't help myself. The music, the candlelight, the setting — it all felt right. With her hand held tightly in mine, I stared directly into those blue eyes. *Bobbie, you don't know it, but I'm about to tell you just how very special you've become to me.* "Bobbie…" I paused. "This is a great party. I'm really having a good time."

"Well, now that you're one of Josh's students, you have a standing invitation."

Damn. Let's try this again. What I need to tell her is that I don't remember ever feeling this way about any other woman. "Bobbie…" I hesitated again. "It's just that, well, I'm grateful that you asked me to come."

"I'm very glad that you came with me."

Geez. I know I can do this.

"Johnny, what are you trying to tell me?"

The singer had just started another song, and it was one of my favorites. "Come Monday it'll be all right, come Monday I'll be holding you tight..." *It's now or never.* I took Bobbie's other hand, squeezed it, and felt myself dissolve. Allowing all my attention to focus on her smiling face, I said, "Bobbie, Bobbie..."

"Yes?"

"You are, well, you need to know that, that...that fellow over there is singing those songs every bit as good as Jimmy Buffett." *Damn it!*

Bobbie smiled and squeezed both my hands hard as if she knew what I was trying to say.

"John," she said with a long, loving look.

"Yes?"

"That *is* Jimmy Buffett."

Chapter 31

"What?"

Bobbie didn't answer — she just grinned.

"What?" I asked again.

"That *is* Jimmy Buffett," she said, smiling from ear to ear. Then she peered into my eyes, which I'm sure were stuck wide-open. "Are you okay, Johnny? Maybe you need some air." She grabbed my arm to get me up. I resisted. *She wants me to get air when Jimmy Buffett is singing his greatest hits across the room?*

"I was hoping you would recognize him on your own but you seemed to be preoccupied with something else," she said as she dragged me across the hall and onto the back porch. The air helped, but it still took a moment for my voice to kick in.

"Jimmy-Buffett-is-one-of-Josh's-students?"

"Yep."

I drew a long breath and let it out slowly, then gave Bobbie a long searching look. Her eyes were wide and full of mischief. "You're getting a kick out of this, aren't you?" I asked.

"Aren't you?" she said with a chuckle.

"Hey Bobbie, over here!"

We both swiveled around at the same time.

Now, what?

In the faint amber glow of the porch light, three figures were standing at the other end of the deck. One of them was motioning for Bobbie to come over.

Don't worry, just some girlfriends," she said.

"You go ahead; I'm going to catch my breath here for a few minutes."

"Are you sure?"

"Yeah, I'm fine."

The hot night air sent a warm shiver up my spine. The August moon was struggling to cast its light through the tepid night haze, but it was another part of what I loved about the Ohio Valley, and it relaxed me into my thoughts.

"Hrumph."

Someone clearing their throat drew my attention to the opposite end of the porch. Silhouetted by the faint glow from the back window, stood a man, alone. Part of me wanted to stay with my thoughts, but another part had me heading in his direction to seek out *his* story if he had one. He was leaning with both hands on the railing, staring out into the night. As I approached, he said. "Hello."

"Hi," I said, and as discreetly as possible, I leaned into him to see his face. But in the faint moonlight, all I could tell is that he was old, so I struck up a conversation. "Beautiful night, isn't it?"

"That it is," he replied.

He started to withdraw his gaze from me but then stopped and gave me a closer look. He must have sensed I was anxious. "Are you okay?" he asked.

"Oh, yeah. It's just…this party. It's been full of surprises."

"Ah, this must be your first 'Josh' reunion."

"Yes, it is," I admitted.

"So I guess you haven't been a student of Josh's for very long."

"About two months now," I said.

"He's a Master Instructor, you know."

My attention jumped a notch. *He knows about Master Instructors. And he's saying that Josh is a Master Instructor. Maybe this guy can give me some answers.*

"So Josh is a Master Instructor?" I stated casually as if I knew what that actually was.

"Yes, he truly is." There was a long pause in which he was apparently waiting for my response. The problem was I had none, except to just come out with the truth.

"You know, I'm not exactly sure what a Master Instructor is."

"You're not alone. Not many do. But I *can* tell you this. A Master Instructor is one who has realized the True Swing."

Aha. So he also knows about the True Swing.

"Have you realized the True Swing?" I asked hesitantly.

"No," he answered wistfully. "But I hope to realize it before I run out of time." There was such sadness in his voice; I was almost sorry I had asked.

"Do you know what the True Swing is?" I continued.

"From what I know, there is no description that would be accurate. Only those who have realized the True Swing seem to understand what the True Swing is."

Now there's an answer I would expect from Josh

"I've heard it said, however, that it's like trying to describe the taste of a peach to someone who has never tasted fruit."

"So how do you know Josh is a Master Instructor? I mean, how can you tell a Master Instructor from a regular instructor?"

"Well, one way to tell is by what they want from you."

"I'm not sure what you mean."

"Have you had other instructors besides Josh?" he asked.

"Have I had other instructors? Boy, let me tell you about my other instructors."

"And what is it that they have wanted from you?"

"Well, one teacher wanted me to believe that my butt was the center of my swing. Another wanted me to spit on myself. Another had me in a pretzel position, and one said that I had two brains and that they were fighting with each other.

"Hmm, ah, no kidding," he said with an askance look. There was a long pause in which I figured my instructor stories might have killed our conversation. But then he asked, "And what has Josh expected of you?"

"Well, Josh has wanted me to…He has asked me to… He says I should…" Suddenly I realized that Josh had never asked or expected anything from me. Even in my lessons, he had only made suggestions. "I don't recall Josh wanting or expecting anything from me," I said.

"Exactly!" he said. "You see, a Master Instructor doesn't ask you to follow his ways or insist that you believe what he believes. A Master Instructor will just point the way in hopes that you will discover the True Swing for yourself."

His last remark brought the story of Golda to mind. "I guess you can also tell a Master Instructor by whether he has a Master Instructor's Handbook."

"Yes," I suppose that's true," he said and paused. "If there is such a thing."

His statement startled me. "What do you mean, 'if there is such a thing'?"

My question genuinely surprised him. "Are you telling me that you've seen one?"

"I've not only seen one, I've read from one."

"You've read from a Master Instructor's Handbook?" He asked with surprise. "I've only met a few people who even admit the possibility that such a book exists." He paused in thought for a moment, and then asked, "Can you tell me what was in it?"

"Sure." I started to tell him about Golda and the mysterious white nuts, but my words tumbled over each other. I tried telling him about the three students and their strange test, and the cryptic definition of the True Swing, but my explanation was vague at best as if something was blocking me from giving up its contents.

"I'm sorry," I finally said. "It seems to make sense in my head, but it just isn't coming out right. Perhaps it's the martinis and beer." As I thought about the book, all the flashes of light came to mind. "Very peculiar, that book."

"You're telling me," he said, sounding disappointed.

"So what do you think it all means?" I asked.

"Perhaps you were ready to read whatever was in the book."

"Hey, Johnny, is that you?" Bobbie called from the other side of the porch. "Come on over. I want you to meet some friends."

"Ah, my date calls," I said lightheartedly. "I'd better see what she wants."

"You're here with Bobbie?" he asked, surprised. *Boy. I must have truly accomplished something here.*

"Yeah," I said with a bit of ego. "My name's John, by the way" and offered my hand "It was fun chatting with you."

"My name's Ben. Good luck on the path you're heading down."

As he walked back inside, I proceeded towards Bobbie but stopped as something clicked in my mind. *Ben? No, it couldn't be.*

Bobbie took my arm, and when she introduced me to her girlfriends, they all fell silent. Since "surprise" was the general reaction to me being Bobbie's date, I figured they were probably checking me out. But while they were assessing me, I assessed them to see who might look familiar. No one did, but I gave them my best smile anyway. After exchanging pleasantries for a few minutes, I pulled Bobbie aside. "Do you know the fellow I was talking to over there?"

"Over where?" She asked while eyeing the other side of the porch.

"He went back inside."

"What did he look like?"

"I couldn't tell in the dark. But he was older, and his first name was Ben."

"Oh," she said, and half grinned. "It might have been Ben …"

"Stop! Don't tell me. I don't want to know."

"Why?" she said.

"Because if it's who I think it is — I just don't want to know."

"What did you talk about?"

"Master Instructors and their handbooks."

"Hmmm," was all that she said.

Bobbie's friends drew her back into their conversation. She shrugged her shoulders at me as if to say, "What can I do?"

"You go ahead," I said. "I'm going to find Josh."

Chapter 32

Maneuvering back through the house without being sidetracked wasn't easy. I exchanged introductions with a few guests and chatted with others as I moved from room to room, all the while scanning the crowd for Josh. On my way into the dining room, Jim Weller pulled me aside. He was with a guy wearing an old tie-dyed T-shirt, jeans, and sandals. It didn't take a lot of thought to guess he must be the owner of the VW bus parked out front with the hand-painted peace sign.

"This is RT," Jim said. "He owns the VW bus parked out front with the hand painted peace sign."

"Glad to meet you, Artie," I said while grinning from my insight.

"No, not Artie," RT said. "It's RT."

"Oh," I said, and continued, "I noticed your VW bus on the way in. Those things must last forever."

"They do," he said, and then asked, "Hey, is it true that you and Bobbie came here together?" There it was again, that look of surprise.

"Yes," I said. "But she gave me no clue what to expect at this party."

"That sounds like something she would do," RT said. "She is a lot of fun. You know, you, Bobbie and I ought to get together sometime — maybe come out to my place. Bobbie knows where to find me."

"I appreciated the invite," I said a bit hesitantly, wondering what kind of relationship RT and Bobbie might have. But then again, being invited somewhere together meant that others are seeing us as a real couple. "I'll work it out with Bobbie," I said and got back to my search for Josh.

He was not in the adjoining dining room, but I did find a beer and a full spread of food. I wolfed down a ham on rye and topped it off with the remains of my beer. As I was looking for a place to set down the empty bottle, a flash of light caught the corner of my eye and I spun in that direction.

Geez. Now, what? A dimly lit hallway was directly in front of me. At the end of the hall was an open door. *Perhaps it came from there.* As I walked down the hallway, I listened for music, thinking that maybe Paul Simon was playing the East Wing. With some apprehension, I stuck my head in the door.

It was a large room, lit with candles that flickered like fireflies — probably the explanation for the light that had caught my eye. Some overhead lighting together with the candles gave the room and ethereal glow but was enough that I could discern its contents. The floors were hardwood partially hidden by a very expensive looking Persian rug. Floor to ceiling bookshelves took up two of the walls. Looking across the room, I spied a small couch with a high-back chair on each side. One of the chairs was occupied.

"Oh," I said. "I didn't realize anyone was in here."

An elderly man was sitting rather still, staring blankly towards the bookcase. On second glance, it appeared that he was looking at nothing in particular. His body was frail, his hair thin, and he had a full grayish beard. His deeply lined face appeared serene and wise, and also familiar.

I was about to leave when his head turned in my direction. His eyes, which a moment ago were distant, came alive in a smile, glistening in the candlelight and the years fell from his face. He didn't speak, but I felt drawn to him, so I stepped into the room. "Hi, I said. "I didn't mean to disturb you. I was just looking for Josh. Have you seen him?"

"Yes," he answered softly. "He was here, and he will be back shortly."

Ah. A good excuse to sit down and see what his story is.

"May I join you until he arrives?"

"Please," he said, gesturing to the chair.

"Are you a student of Josh's?" I asked as I sat down.

"Most certainly," he answered. "And are you as well?"

"Yes. I met Josh about two and a half months ago," I said, while noticing that something about him was different from the others at the party — he was very much like Josh.

"Has he taken you out to the course, by any chance?" he asked.

"Yes, as a matter of fact. About three weeks ago."

"Ah, excellent. So he's giving you firsthand instruction."

"Yes, but it took quite a few meetings before we finally got to the lessons. Does he do that with everybody?"

"Master Instructors often begin only when the student is ready. Whereas most teachers expect you to adopt their teachings as your own, Master Instructors tend to suggest so that you might find your own way. They are to be listened to as one listens to a babbling brook or the song of a mourning dove."

"You've mastered the True Swing, haven't you?" I blurted out. His eyes widened, and he smiled.

"And who wants to know?" he asked.

A Josh answer. He must know.

"I don't get it," I said with frustration. "Can I master the True Swing? Do I need to become a Master Instructor first? Is it actually possible?"

He gave me a long searching look, leaned into me and said, "That's quite a lot of questions for an old guy like me to handle, don't you think?"

I laughed out loud and studied him more closely. "I think not," I said. He sat silently for a moment, studying me, then locked onto my eyes with such intensity that I reeled back.

"To seek the True Swing is itself the greatest obstruction. You see, what you are seeking you already have."

His words rifled into me, exploding my thoughts into a billion pieces. In that split second, I saw. *But what am I seeing?* The next instant, my thoughts kicked back in, and the recognition was gone.

Whatever just happened hadn't gone unnoticed by my elderly friend, for he said, "To see what is right in front of you, even to glimpse it for a moment, is to realize the Truth about what you seek. But to believe that someone is there to see it is a mistake. Only when you recognize this will you know what you are, and what you are not."

My head was still spinning, but I managed to ask, "And what is it that I really am?"

"*Who* wants to know?" he answered, or asked, for the second time.

Who wants to know!? Why does the answer to that question keep coming back as a question?

Just then I felt the energy in the room jump. With wide eyes, I looked to my new friend for a reason. His gaze had been drawn past me, to something over my shoulder.

"Hello, Josh," he said.

"Well, John, I see you've met my teacher, Lester," Josh said as I stood to greet him. Just then I knew why the old man looked familiar. He was the bearded man in the picture at Josh's shop.

"Well, we haven't officially met," I said while offering Lester my hand. "Hey, wait a minute. I thought you said you were Josh's student. Why is he saying that you're his teacher?"

"Lester doesn't see a difference between the two," Josh explained with a chuckle. "What have you two been up to?"

Lester looked at me. "I believe John wants to be a Master Instructor."

Just hearing him say it, I got excited. Turning to Josh, I asked, "Is that possible? Could I become a Master Instructor?"

As soon as I asked the question, I knew that whatever being a Master Instructor meant, it was what I truly wanted — to have whatever it was that Lester and Josh had — to be whatever it was that they were. They both possessed some deep rooted peace and joy. But how? Josh was doing what he loved; perhaps that was the key.

Josh's answer cut through my thoughts. "Nope," he said. "You can't become a Master Instructor."

"What?"

Lester, seeing my reaction, and on Josh's cue, quickly stated, "John, you can't aspire to be that which you already are."

"What?"

Josh added, "Which is why I told you that you would not find the True Swing at the Golden River Driving Range. How could you possibly find something that you already have?"

"What?"

Chapter 33

"There you are," Bobbie said, sticking her head into the room. She lowered her eyebrows in suspicion at Josh and Lester. "Are they ganging up on you in here?"

Josh and Lester gave each other an innocent shrug. "Yeah, I bet," she said, taking my hand. "Come on John, consider yourself rescued." She clutched my arm tightly and guided me to the front porch.

"Where is everybody?" I asked, noticing that there were a lot fewer guests.

"Many have left," she said.

I glanced at my watch — one-thirty. "Wow! I didn't realize it was so late."

"Yeah. We should get going as well."

Bobbie continued holding onto my arm as we walked out into the night. She had a little jig in her walk and was grinning widely. Me? I felt a little dizzy, not being sure if it was the booze or how tight Bobbie was holding onto me.

"Why don't you let me drive, John, if that's okay?"

"Sure," I said, surprising myself. My ego didn't usually relinquish control of my Mustang so easily, but then again, my head was spinning. I handed her the keys.

Before I had a chance to tell her how to find reverse on a standard transmission, she shifted, backed out, and eased my Mustang GT down the driveway. I shook my head, smiling, and settled back into the seat.

Neither of us spoke until we reached the main road when I finally broke the silence. "Bobbie, do you know what Josh and Lester meant when they said, 'What you are seeking you already have?'"

There was a long pause as if she were considering her answer very carefully. "Not really," she finally said. "Well, sort of. But I don't think I could put it into words."

"Now you sound like Josh," I said. "I'll tell you, this stuff about Master Instructors and the True Swing has got me thoroughly baffled."

"Josh would tell you that it's simple."

"Is that what you think?"

Again she paused as if giving this question even more due diligence. "Have you ever had an incident where for some reason, you became aware — so aware that it was like seeing everything for the first time only you weren't sure who or what was seeing it?"

"Why yes," I said. "It happened when I got clunked with a golf club a while back and then a number of times since I've been around Josh. It's like I stepped out of what was going on around me and just observed but I didn't seem to be the one who was doing the observing. Is that what you mean?"

"Something like that."

"So how do you explain this?"

"Josh says that who we are, exists between our thoughts and when our mind grows silent, our True Nature will appear.

"Huh?"

"Well, I'm not sure what that means, but I believe that Josh is suggesting that if we can truly drop into the present moment, Truth will show itself. And like you, I too, have occasionally glimpsed this."

"Do you realize you said 'Truth' instead of 'True Swing?'"

"I did? I guess I get that from Josh. He talks about them as being one and the same — that one cannot be without the other."

Up ahead, the freeway entrance came into view. She downshifted into third and scooted up the ramp. I was impressed.

"To answer your earlier question, "she continued, "Josh sees the mind as a useful tool when it comes to everyday living and very useful when learning, practicing and developing a good golf swing. But when it comes to what he calls the True Swing, he says the mind and thoughts get in the way — taking you out of the moment. On one of your index cards, he wrote 'when your thoughts vanish, your True Swing will appear.' I believe he's suggesting that the Truth, the True Swing, is always there, hidden behind our thoughts. So when thoughts drop away, well, the True Swing appears."

"So what he's saying is that we are all Masters and we all possess the True Swing, but we don't know it?"

"Something like that."

Now that's just too much to think about after two martinis and five beers.

"So how do we realize this True Swing? And please don't say, 'Who wants to know?'"

When Bobbie didn't answer, I looked at her. The frail light of the dashboard gauges gently bathed her in a soft glow. At that moment, she was all that I saw and all that I cared about, and it occurred to me that thanks to Jimmy Buffett's rude interruption, I had never gotten around to telling her. *Perhaps I should tell her now.* But with that thought, a strange feeling cropped up, and something started gnawing at me in the far corners of my mind, and I said nothing.

The Eagle Chase sign came into view. We were silent as she drove to her condo, and parked.

She handed me the keys, and said, "Are you doing anything tomorrow?"

"Nothing planned," I said, instantly enthused that she might be suggesting a third date.

"Then come on up."

Did she just say what I think she said? My heart skipped a beat, and like an excited but woozy puppy, I followed her into the condo.

"Make yourself at home, and I'll be right back," she said after flicking on the lights. "I need to freshen up."

"Okay," I said, glad to have a moment to check her place out. The kitchen and great room merged into one with a cathedral ceiling sloping out from the kitchen to give the appearance of separate rooms. An assortment of impressive watercolor prints hung on light yellow walls with bookshelves spaced evenly between. The shelves were filled with books and knickknacks lit by directional ceiling lights, which also lit the entire room. Two lamps, sitting on end tables, bordered a designer couch and love seat in the center of the room. It was as neat, tidy, and clean as my place but with a lot more taste. From what I *didn't* know about decorating, the place seemed to be well thought out.

I slowly meandered over to the couch while wondering how she could afford this on a golf range attendant's income. *Perhaps Josh helps her out.* But no, she had said she didn't need any financial help from him. *Maybe she owns part of the range. That would be good. With my belt rep job, we could have a nice income together.*

Wait a minute. A nice income together? Am I getting that serious? Instantly that same nagging feeling that had bothered me in the car came back. *What is going on? Why would the idea of Bobbie and me being together bother me?*

"Let me get you a beer," Bobbie said, entering the room.

It was hard not to stare at her as she walked into the kitchen. As she opened the refrigerator door, I slipped behind her. When she turned, I was right there, staring into those blue eyes, my face drifting toward hers. When our lips met, her arms gently moved up around my waist and met in the small of my back. I trembled at the feel of our bodies together, and so did she. A moment later, my mind let go, and we disappeared into the night.

Chapter 34

The early morning sunlight struck my face with a vengeance. I yanked the comforter and sheets over my head and rolled over.

THUD!

My bed was narrower than I remembered and I hit the floor all twisted up in some sort of huge puffy blanket. I frantically clawed my way out until my head emerged into the open air.

Nothing looked familiar. Then slowly it all started coming back — Jimmy Buffett, Johnny Bench, Carl Lindstrom, Josh, Lester, and being with Bobbie…*Wait a minute! Not just being with Bobbie, spending the night with her!*

Peeking over the edge of the bed, I scanned the room. The bathroom door was open, and the light was off. The bedroom was also empty. *Where is she?*

As if to answer my question, the aroma of fresh brewing coffee wafted into the room, leading me to believe that a long, leisurely, romantic breakfast was in the making. I drew in another whiff, trying to smell bacon and eggs, or pancakes, or fresh baked cinnamon rolls, or something that might hint at what was to come, but there was just coffee.

It took me a bit of time to find my pants and shirt and to use the bathroom. Doing the best I could with what I had, I spruced up and headed to the kitchen. Bobbie was fully dressed, pouring coffee for two.

"Going somewhere?" I asked.

"I'm sorry, Johnny. I just have time for coffee. Sunday mornings are the best times for me to get bookwork done at the range, and prepare for the following week."

We both sat down before our steaming mugs. A bit hurt, I said, "After last night, you're leaving me to go work on a Sunday morning?" But even with disappointment clouding my thoughts, I saw an opportunity to steer this conversation into some subtle prying. "Wait a minute. Only owners work on Sunday mornings. Now I know who the *real* owner of the range is."

I raised my coffee mug, waiting for her reply.

"Careful, Johnny, it's hot!"

I cringed at seeing an image of myself spurting coffee all over her kitchen table. *Amazing.* While *my* mind was plotting how to find out more about her, she was right here, attentive to the moment, saving me from making a fool of myself — not to mention sparing me a burned mouth.

"Thanks for warning me," I said.

She reached over and squeezed my hand affectionately. I squeezed back.

"To answer your question, the range is Josh's thing. It's what he does — what he loves."

"I guess he does extremely well with it," I said, fishing for more information. "I mean, with a clientele that includes the likes of Jimmy Buffett, and Johnny Bench, and Carl Lindstrom, and all those other business owners."

"Actually, Josh charges the same for everyone."

"Really?" I lifted my cup with both hands and blew over the rim. "You're saying he only charges *them* thirty-five dollars a lesson?"

"That's all I record on the books."

"Oh, I get it. He probably gets some incredible cash tips."

"Well, I know that some have offered. But as far as I know, he's never accepted."

"Bonuses, then, at Christmas time?" I asked. She wrinkled her brow as if confused why I was asking the question, but she answered anyway.

"Nope. Not that I'm aware of."

Why I was getting pushy, I wasn't sure. It wasn't like me and feeling a bit embarrassed about it; I changed the subject." I appreciate the coffee."

"Your quite welcome," she said and took a sip of hers. "By the way, did I understand Josh to say that you were playing in a tournament next weekend?"

"Oh, yeah, the Cavendish. My friends and I play in it every year. Have you heard of it?"

"I *have* heard of it. It's held over at Sharon Woods Park, isn't it?"

"That's the one. It's a flighted tournament with about seven divisions. They take your first-day scores and match you up to those with similar scores for the second day and put you in that flight."

"So you're playing against people in your same scoring range?" She asked.

"Well, it's kind of funny how the 'flight' thing works. A one-stroke difference could put you at the bottom of one division or the top of the next. Last year I shot a ninety-five and was the leader in my division. Had I shot a better score of ninety-four, I would have been last in the next division. So you never know where you're going to end up."

"Sounds like fun."

"It really is. I can hardly wait."

Bobbie took one last swallow of her coffee, picked up her keychain, and removed a key. "Here, Johnny."

Geez. I still haven't asked her out, and already I've spent the night with her and now getting a key to her place? She put it in my hand and said, "Why don't you hang here for a while if you like, and come over to the range later?"

"Thanks. I'd love to, but…" *I'd love to, but?* "I've been away from my office for two weeks, and I probably should take the day to get caught up." A moment of disappointment shown in her eyes but quickly merged into a smile of understanding. It was me who didn't understand. *Why on earth did I put a "but" on the end of "I'd love to…," messing up my chances of seeing her later?*

"I'll call you tonight," I said. But I didn't, and had no idea why.

After arriving at my office, I tidied up my desk, emptied my "in" box, and sorted out which clients to call the following week. In no time at all, I was caught up. There was nothing keeping me from seeing Bobbie, but for some unknown reason, I was unwilling. I was also begrudging my work — something I hadn't done before. It was a great job and always thought myself lucky to have it — easy hours, minimal work, and large commissions. Now, my heart just wasn't in it.

Later that day when I got home, I went to pick up the phone to call Bobbie, but grabbed a beer instead, and sank onto the sofa in front of the TV. Whatever was bothering me wasn't showing itself. Monday and Tuesday came and went, and still, I hadn't called her and still didn't know why. But when Wednesday morning came around, the urge to be with her was so overpowering, I broke speed limits getting to the range. By the time I reached the parking lot, my mind was so cluttered and confused about not calling her that I leaped from my car and rushed to the building. The screen door slapped behind me, and I impatiently waited for my eyes to adjust.

The wait was worth it. What a welcome sight she was. Even in the dim light, and across the room behind the counter, I could see the rich blue color of her eyes, which lit up when she saw me. I felt like a heel but offered no apologies or excuses for not calling. The truth is, I had none.

"Johnny, hi! Did you get all caught up with your work?" She asked as she moved towards me.

"Yep. Thanks to me, the people of this country can wear their pants again in confidence."

She laughed as I grabbed her and gave her a big hug. She held me tight, and my body went limp. I gave into it completely and at that moment, whatever had been gnawing at me was gone, at least for now.

"Enough of that," Josh said from outside the back window. "We've got work to do."

I let go of Bobbie, suddenly wondering what Josh might think of me, hugging and kissing his little girl.

"Be right there," I said with a sheepish grin while searching Josh's face for some sign of disapproval. But there was none. *Of course not.* Josh's manner never gave any indication of him being judgmental or of having any hidden agenda — as if somehow he knew that all was right with the world, and who was he to disagree?

I gave Bobbie a quick kiss, went to the car for my clubs, and headed to the range. When I got to the tee area, Josh was waiting with a full bucket of balls, smiling as usual.

"So, Josh, what's on the schedule for today? Is it time to learn…No, I mean, is it time to *realize* the True Swing?"

"Do you believe that you are ready to *realize* it?" he asked with a twinkle in his eye.

"Absolutely!"

"Then no. It's probably not time."

"Damn," I said with a half-smile and waited, expecting a riddle.

"John, when the True Swing appears who do you think might be there to realize it?

"My guess would be 'me' of course."

"Then your guess would be wrong."

"Then who *is* there when it happens? Or should I ask, who is not there when it happens?"

"*Who* wants to know?"

"I knew you were going to say that," I said and laughed. "But seriously, what advice can you give me if ever this is going to happen."

"Great doubt. Great faith. Great determination."

It surprised me that he actually gave an answer and I said: "Say again?"

"Great Faith — have absolute trust in the moment as it is, in the True Swing as it is, in life as it is. Great Doubt — look deeply and question everything. Great Determination — know what the most important thing is and act on it as your number one priority.

"Okaaay," I said, and not sure how to respond, I continued, "then I guess if it's not going to happen now, the next question is: what are we going to do in the meantime?"

"Work on fine-tuning your swing, of course."

The next three mornings, I gave to Josh. In return, he honed my swing into a seemingly effortless work of art. The afternoons, I reluctantly gave to Waisting Away, not forgetting from where my paycheck came. And the nights, I surrendered to Bobbie — attentive, intelligent, wonderful, fun Bobbie.

The evenings consisted of candlelight dinners and wine. On the first night, she had even baked a cake. But we never made it to dessert — that is, depending on how one defines dessert.

With the tournament being on the weekend, my plans for Friday were to stay home and rest, taking a break from the practicing, my job, the home-cooked meals, and even the long romantic nights. But Friday afternoon I found myself at Bobbie's door, brimming over with energy and excitement.

"Boy, you seem wired tonight," Bobbie said.

"How can I not be after spending the week with you and Josh? And the next two days I'll be playing in the Cavendish Cup with my best friends — two great days of nothing but golf."

"This tournament ought to be interesting with your new, improved swing."

"You know, I've been so busy with everything, I hadn't given it much thought. I haven't played a round of golf since my lessons with Josh officially started."

"Uh-oh,'" She said. "I hope I didn't give you cause to be nervous."

"Gosh, no, not the way the division thing is set up. But it just dawned on me that I might finally win some money from Larry, BJ, and Tom for a change instead of vice versa."

"Well, at least you've got your priorities straight," she said and laughed.

"Speaking of priorities…"

"Yes?"

I grabbed both her hands and said, "Tonight I intend to treat you to dinner and dessert at my favorite eateries."

"Eateries? Does that mean restaurants?"

"Well, I guess that depends on how you define Skyline Chili Parlor and Graeter's Ice Cream Shop."

Her big blue eyes widened as she said, "Three-way cheese dogs and Cincinnati's best mint chocolate chip ice cream? Life is good."

Chapter 35

After eating a leftover chili dog in the morning (breakfast would have made me late), I left Bobbie's with "all smiles," not just because I spent another remarkable evening with her, or because the temperature was already in the high eighties, or because I could see patches of blue showing through the chalky white sky, but because the Cavendish tournament was truly a "no stress, great time, enjoy your buddies" golf event. I was excited at the prospect of playing thirty-six holes of golf, and of course, the chance to be on the receiving end of our wagers.

After driving into the Sharon Woods Course parking lot, I jumped from the car, grabbed my clubs, and headed towards the Pro shop. A makeshift sign saying "Cavendish Cup" came into view with a hand-drawn arrow pointing to the rear of the clubhouse. I already knew where to go and what to expect. Sure enough, when I rounded the corner of the pro shop, there they were — countless golfers milling around an endless parade of shiny white golf carts. As I strolled along the line of the carts looking for my name, I heard Larry's voice.

"Hey, Arbor! Over here!"

"Hey," I answered, grinning. BJ and Larry were standing next to one of the carts while Tom was sitting in the other studying some papers. He, being a bit more responsible of the three, was probably reading the tournament rules.

"I see we're all together in the same foursome," I said, spotting our names on the two carts.

"Yeah," Larry answered as he took my clubs and fastened them to the cart. "That's because I entered us at the same time and our handicaps weren't all that much different, which reminds me, you owe me seventy-five dollars for the entry fee."

"Boy, it doesn't take long for you guys to start taking my money."

"That's the way it's supposed to be," Larry said as he put his arm around my shoulder.

"Well, if I have to fork over my cash, I guess I'd rather give it to one of you."

"That's the spirit," BJ said.

"But I've got to warn you. A lot has happened since we last

played."

BJ's eyebrows shot up. "A new instructor maybe?"

"Well, actually, yes."

"All right!" he said excitedly. "How about upping our regular bet from a dollar to two dollars a hole?"

"I guess you didn't hear me. I said I've got a new instructor."

"I heard you. Why do you think I'm upping the bet?"

"Gee, that's not very nice," I said, acting hurt.

BJ looked over at Larry and asked, "So what do you think this new instructor has taught him? He's already mastered slobbering on himself. Not to mention the 'butt and pretzel' stance. The only thing left would be for him to stick his thumb up his…"

"Now, now, BJ," said Larry. "Let's not get nasty."

"Okay, okay."

"I'll take your bet," I said, trying not to show enthusiasm. "But don't say I didn't warn you." I paused a moment, then added casually, "And, by the way, I've also found a girl.

That got Tom's attention — his eyes shot up from his rules sheet. "What was that?"

"I found a girl."

"You *found* a girl?" Larry asked. "What, did someone throw one away?"

"Very funny."

"Are you saying, like, a 'repeated dating' kind of thing?" Tom asked.

"Yes. Why?"

Tom looked at BJ. "I want in on the wager. A new instructor plus a new girlfriend? His golf game has undoubtedly turned to crap."

"How can his game turn into something it already was?" Larry countered.

I laughed out loud, thinking that sounded like something Josh might say.

"So who is she?" Larry asked while I counted out his seventy-five dollars.

I paused, considering how much to tell them about Bobbie, and Josh, and the party, and Jimmy Buffett, and everything else that has happened since I last saw them. *They'd never believe me — at least not yet.* So all I said was, "You've met her at Great Oak Golf course, the last time we played, where I slid off the bench. The three of them said almost in unison, "You're kidding!"

"Does she have a sister?" asked Tom.

"You're married, remember?"

"Oh, yeah, that's right."

"Well I'm not," BJ said. "So, does she have a sister?"

"No," I said but then paused. "At least I don't think so."

"What do you mean, you don't think so?"

It suddenly struck me that as much time as Bobbie and I had spent together, there was a lot I didn't know about her.

"I would think if it were a serious relationship, you'd know by now if she has a sister," BJ continued.

"Is this a serious relationship?" Tom asked.

I didn't answer. His question brought that nagging feeling back to haunt me. *Crap. What is this feeling all about?*

"Possibly," I finally answered.

My golf buddies looked stunned. But before they could think of what to say, a voice came over the loudspeaker. *"***Welcome to the sixth annual Cavendish Cup golf tournament***."* He then explained the rules and bade us good luck.

"Well," I said, grateful for the interruption. "I guess it's time to end this trivial chat and play some golf." As all the golfers headed out to their assigned starting holes, I asked, "Where do we start?"

Larry pointed to the tee area right next to us and said, "Believe it or not, hole number one."

The first hole had three hundred and sixty-five yards of gently sloping fairway. It doglegged to the right around a large cluster of trees that effectively hid the green from the tee. We all agreed that the trees had some magnetic pull on golf balls because that's where they usually ended up.

"I guess I'm up," Tom said as he strode onto the tee area.

To determine the order for teeing off, most golfers go through a ritual of tossing a coin, or flipping a tee, or courteously offering each other "honors." Not us; we'd been together too long.

Tom always hit first. He needed to get his drive, and his nervousness out of the way quickly. Larry took second because it made him feel better knowing that no matter how awful his drive, it probably wouldn't be as bad as Tom's. BJ hit third because he hated going first, and hated going last, and Larry would never let him go second. That left me bringing up the rear.

"Well, is everyone ready?" Tom asked as he stepped over his ball.

"We're always ready to watch your magnificent form," Larry said.

In actuality, it was Tom's feet that we watched. They'd roll around, shifting back and forth, go up on his toes, then back on his heels. When that stopped, his toes would quiver, and the tips of his shoes would vibrate up and down. Larry always said he looked like an elf with the DTs.

WHIP!

His club swung under the ball, popping it sky high. It seemed that five minutes had passed before it finally landed.

"If that had gone any higher," Larry said, "it would have landed in back of us."

"Well, I guess the pressure's off you," Tom said.

"As always," Larry said, grinning.

In one swift motion, Larry stepped up, placed his ball on the tee, and swung. He never wasted time over the ball — afraid he might think himself into miss-hitting it. Often it worked in his favor, but not this time. His ball sliced about two hundred yards, landing in front of the trees, proving once again that those trees had some magnetic force.

"Did you swing?" I asked. "If so, I must have blinked and missed it." That always got a laugh out of Tom, but I don't know why — it's the same line I always say to Larry on his first drive.

BJ shot Tom and me a sharp glance as he stepped onto the tee that warned us to quiet down. It wasn't smart to give BJ an excuse for hitting a bad drive so we stood there quiet and still, and accepted we would be that way for a while.

WHOOSH!

I rolled my eyes at Larry and Tom and shook my head. But as I stood there with the three of them, my mind drifted to thoughts of the three golfers in the *Handbook of a Master Instructor.*

WHOOSH!

What was it that Ben "whoever" said to me at the party — that perhaps I was ready to read what was in the book? Do the three golfers in the story relate to me somehow discovering the True Swing?

WHOOSH!

If I had taken the test on hole number nine, how would I have handled it? Would I have approached it with a narrow focus, like golfer number one? Or would I have hit the ball long and far like golfer number two and wonder why I failed the test? And what about golfer number three? It was as if he wasn't participating in the test at all, and yet…

WHACK!

The sound of ball meeting club snapped me back to the present just in time to see the aftermath of BJs swing. He had corkscrewed himself so far around that he was facing the opposite direction. The ball went right, then left, rose a little, then dipped down.

"Good grief," Larry said. "He hit a knuckleball with a golf club."

"Where'd it go?" BJ asked.

"To the right, out by mine in front of those trees," Larry said.

"Crap," BJ said, and slammed his club on the ground. I ducked, remembering the last time he had lost control of his club. BJ saw it and said, "Don't worry. I've learned my lesson."

"Thanks," I said. "But you know what? I'm starting to believe that hit on the head may have been the best thing that ever happened to me."

"Well, in that case…" BJ pulled his club back as if to throw it at me.

"No, no, that's okay. One whack was enough."

"John," Larry interrupted, "quit fooling around and get onto the tee," He shot a "this ought to be good" glance at BJ and Tom. "And hurry up. We're anxious to see what your new instructor has done for you. Or should I say *to* you?"

Chapter 36

As I walked to the tee area, it occurred to me that I had no idea what to expect from my game; I hadn't played a round since Josh's teachings. It also occurred to me that I really didn't care and wasn't the least bit anxious. How could I be? Here I was with my best friends, driver in hand, doing what I loved most, with nothing to lose. A smile spread across my face.

"What are you grinning about?" Larry asked. "Is this part of your new technique?"

As they chuckled, my attention shifted to the ball in my hand. I sensed its heft and seemed aware every dimple on its surface. "The precious white nut," I said to myself. While pushing the ball and tee into the ground, I saw the grass give way and almost felt the dirt take hold. The ball was whiter than I had remembered, framed against the deep green grass, but maybe it was just how I was seeing it. My gaze shifted to the fairway while I drifted back about ten feet behind the ball, taking in the entire landscape. *Amazing.* The trees to the right were much closer than I remembered. And the dogleg past the trees that I thought unreachable now seemed within distance and would accept an easy fade. I could see my ball rolling up towards the green. "Simple," I said to myself and stepped up to the ball.

My hands moved effortlessly to their rightful place on the club. Gripping it with a light firmness, my hands pressed slightly forward, which started the backswing. My arms, hips and shoulders all moved back at the same time, coiling as a spring being tightly wound until my club came over my shoulder, and stopped. A beat, and then my hips turned, my weight transferred, my shoulders and arms followed, propelling the club toward the ball in a powerful downward thrust.

WHAAAACK!

The ball shot off the tee as my body swept around and stopped in a relaxed arch, facing the fairway.

"Damn!" Larry said.

"Did that fade into the trees?" BJ asked hopefully. "It looked like it was drifting right." With money on the hole, BJ wasn't about to accept that I might have indeed hit a good drive.

"It was drifting right," Tom said. "I suspect it did go into the trees unless it went past them."

"Not possible," BJ said. "Those trees are two hundred and fifty yards out."

Tom stared at me silently as we both hopped into the cart. He wasn't so sure BJ was right. It was hard to keep from grinning as we drove to his ball.

While BJ and Larry lined up their shots, Tom hit a respectable four iron that put his ball past the trees and about a hundred and ten yards from the green. We drove to his ball for his third shot and waited for Larry and BJ to hit up. While standing there, I scanned the front of the fairway ahead of us. About twenty yards in front of the green, a round white spot stood out in the short green grass. Tom saw it too.

"Is that a ball up there?" I asked.

"I think it is," Tom said. "That couldn't be yours, could it?" I tried to look surprised.

It took two shots for BJ to hit up near the green, only one for Larry. Then Tom hit his onto the green's fringe. Larry and BJ drove over to us to say that they hadn't seen my ball anywhere down in the trees and wondered why I wasn't down there helping.

"I think it's up there," I said, pointing towards the green.

He looked to where I was pointing. "I don't think so," BJ said with sarcasm.

Tom drove me up close the green, where the white spot lay. Sure enough, it was a ball, and it was mine. Tom waited while I pulled my putter and eight iron from my bag then drove to the side of the green where BJ and Larry were parked. As Larry headed to his ball, he crossed in front of me.

"Damn, John. That was one hell of a drive. What did you have for breakfast? Chili dogs?" My burst of laughter surprised him, and he gave me a strange look.

BJ pitched his ball to about ten feet past the hole; then Larry chipped to about five feet short. His ball was in my line, so he marked it and stepped back. But already he was slipping from my peripheral vision, as was everything else around me. My attention was seeing the line that my ball would take to the hole. The grain of the green almost jumped out at me, as did a slight ridge that would cause my ball to break to the right. Without giving it any more thought, I took my eight iron, chipped onto the green, and watched my ball roll to the pin. Right before it hit the bottom of the cup, a thought flashed through my mind. *Is there more than just me playing this hole?*

"Crap, John!" BJ said. "You just birdied the first hole of the tournament, not to mention the fact that you've just taken our money. It's not supposed to work that way."

"Try Eagle," Larry said.

BJ's expression went blank for a moment as he realized his counting mistake. "Damn! You're right. It *was* an eagle. He just eagled a par four!"

They all stared at me silently, waiting for an explanation. I shrugged my shoulders. "Hey," I said. "You can't say I didn't warn you."

Chapter 37

BJ must have already spent the money he was planning on winning from me — he grumbled when he climbed into his cart and was still grumbling when he got out of it on the next hole. "His ball must have ricocheted off one of those trees," he muttered loud enough for all of us to hear.

"Maybe Larry found it in the trees and tossed it up near the green when you weren't looking," Tom suggested. BJ stopped to consider it and shot Larry a hard stare.

"Come on," Larry said. "I wouldn't do that in a tournament? Besides, I've got money riding on this, too."

While the three of them continued arguing, I turned my attention to the next hole. It was a short par three — one hundred and fifty-two yards, open in front, with a sand trap on the left. The three of us often hit our balls onto the green from the tee — but then again, we often didn't.

"Eagles are up, John," Larry said, making an exaggerated bow towards the tee. He then furrowed his eyebrows. "Hey, I don't think I've ever said that before."

A six iron had always been my club of choice on this hole. But while rummaging through my bag, a nine iron found its way into my hand. It was the right club — I knew it in my gut. After pulling it from my bag, I walked directly to the tee, surveyed the hole, set up, and swung.

WHAAACK!

The ball shot off the tee and headed right at the pin. It dropped beyond it, then spun backward, coming to rest about six feet in front of the hole.

"Lucky shot," BJ said with more sarcasm than usual.

"I don't know," Tom said. "That looked like a pretty good swing to me. And did you see the backspin on that ball?"

"What iron did you use?" BJ growled. He always chose one iron higher, believing that he could hit farther than anyone else.

"I'm not telling," I said, and walked over to Larry who was sitting on a bench at the edge of the tee. "What does it matter, anyway?"

But BJ wouldn't let it go. He marched over and lifted the end of my club. "I thought so. A six iron. I guess I should use a seven."

Larry, who was watching the drama unfold, casually said, "Try again, BJ."

"What?"

"I said, try again. You looked at the number upside down. He used a nine iron."

BJ's face scrunched up with a mixture of doubt and confusion.

"A nine iron?" He looked at the green for a few moments, and then glanced at the hole marker to verify the yardage. "It does look closer than the yardage indicates," he said with uncertainty. He exchanged the seven for a nine, walked to the tee, took seven practice swings, and swung.

THUD!

WHUMP!

He swung about as hard as I'd ever seen, but his club hit the turf a good foot behind the ball. It was truly remarkable that his ball carried a hundred yards. But even more remarkable was the size of his divot.

"My God!" Larry said. "That's not a divot it's a patch of sod. It would cover that bare spot in my back yard.

Tom's eyebrows raised and said, "Larry, do you still carry that camera with you?" "Yes."

"Go get it."

While Larry got his camera, Tom picked up the divot and made BJ hold it out like a ten-pound bass.

Larry took the picture while Tom said, "Too bad we don't have a scale."

"Very funny," said BJ. "Let's see you do better." He replaced the divot and then stepped aside as Larry teed up his ball.

"I do think you're right about one thing," said Larry. "The green does look closer. And if John can get there with a nine, I surely can."

WHACK!

It headed to the left of the pin but fell about forty yards short of the green.

"Well," Tom said. "You guys can play the macho game if you want, but I'm hitting my six iron."

WHACK!

His nice easy swing sent the ball right at the pin. It hit the green on the front side and rolled up just behind mine.

"Nice shot," I said.

"Thanks, John," he said and looked around to see if BJ and Larry were out of hearing range. "Was that really a nine iron or were you and Larry just screwing with BJ's head?"

"What do you think?" I said.

"I think that you and Larry wouldn't give a second thought to screwing with BJ's head."

"You're right about that," I said as I headed towards our cart.

The four of us drove to the green and parked. Tom and I grabbed our putters and watched Larry and BJ chip onto the green. Larry two-putted for a bogie, and while BJ's putt was a bit strong, it hit the center of the cup and dropped.

"Nice par," Tom said.

Since Tom's ball was behind mine, I marked my ball and watched intently. His putt would show me exactly how my ball would travel to the hole. His putt broke off to the right about three inches and came to rest about two feet past the hole. He easily sank it for a par.

Just as I was ready to putt, the jangle of keys in someone's pocket caught my attention. I looked up, surprised. *Gamesmanship already?* Gamesmanship — tampering with another player's mind under the guise of not being aware, or with the pretense of giving helpful advice. It was something we often did to each other when we wagered, and BJ always initiated it, but he usually waited until things got truly desperate.

It may have bothered me in the past, but the jangling keys didn't faze me at all. In fact, I found it amusing and was grinning on the inside. But for appearance's sake, I shot BJ a frown. After stepping back up to my ball, I paused, knowing there was more to come.

"Remember now," BJ said with feigned concern, "this is for a birdie, and there're two bucks riding on it. It's an easy putt. You can do it. Just don't choke."

"Thanks, BJ," I said. "I do appreciate you pulling for me," and putted it straight to the hole.

CLINK.

"Damn, John," Larry said. "Three under par for the game and were only on the second hole. How long do you think this will hold up?"

I had no answer to his question, so I just shrugged.

On the following tee, BJ raised the gamesmanship to the next level. "John, don't forget about the 'out of bounds' on the left. It would cost you two strokes." He paused to let me step up to my ball. "Yep. Two strokes. It'd be a real shame with such a good score going."

"Thanks, BJ. I'll aim a little right and draw the ball back into the fairway."

WHAAAAAACK!

The ball shot out a little right, and drew back to the middle of the fairway, traveling about two hundred and eighty yards before it landed on a downward ridge. It rolled another thirty yards before coming to a stop. While walking off the tee, BJ held out a handful of bills while Tom and Larry reached into their pockets.

"We give," BJ said sarcastically. "Just take our money now and save us from this."

Knowing they wouldn't really hand it over, I reached for it. They jerked it away and stuffed it back into their pockets.

"That's what I thought," I said.

The rest of the game went the same way, with me easily winning every hole despite BJ's gamesmanship. But on the last hole, while Tom and Larry had taken bogies, BJ and I were putting for pars. BJ had an easy short two-foot putt, while mine was an eight-footer. Since each hole was a separate bet, if I miss my putt, BJ would win making his.

As I stood over my putt, BJ said, "You know, John. That putt may look straight, but I think it has some break in it. Are you sure you have it lined up right?"

CLINK!

It dropped for a par.

BJ was hoping his last attempt at gamesmanship would cause me to miss, but he knew that he could at least tie me on the last hole. The way the wagering system worked is if anyone of the four of us would tie on any hole, no money would change hands on that particular hole. So he would at least shut me out for a clean sweep of their money. While BJ was lining up his putt, Tom walked over to me and said, "Do you know that you just shot a sixty-seven?"

"What?" I said.

"You shot a sixty-seven — five under par."

I knew I was playing well, but in tournaments each partner keeps the other's score, so I hadn't paid attention, except to the bets.

"You're kidding? Are you sure?"

"Yep, I added it three times. A sixty-seven. And not only that, you would have ended up with all our money, if BJ here wasn't going to save us with a tie on this last hole."

As BJ stepped over his short two-foot putt, my focus came back to what the real victory would be here. "BJ," I said "I'm curious. Do you look at your ball or your putter when you stroke the ball?"

He missed the putt.

Chapter 38

Seventy-two dollars sat in the middle of our table in the snack bar area. It should have been a hundred and eight. But BJ had disappeared when Tom and Larry started digging into their wallets to count out their losses.

"Typical BJ," I said with a smile.

"Don't be hard on him," Tom said. "After all, he *is* off buying us a pitcher of beer."

"That's just like BJ," Larry said. "Risking four dollars for the beer, thinking we might forget about the thirty-six. I'll bet when you ask him for it, he'll subtract the four dollars from what he owes."

"You're on," Tom said. "I'll bet you two dollars he won't subtract four bucks from the total."

Larry's eyebrows shot up, as did mine. It wasn't like Tom to come to BJ's defense.

"Here he comes," Larry said.

BJ passed a plastic cup to each of us and poured himself a beer. We did the same.

"So, what are you guys talking about?" He asked.

"Well," Larry said, nodding towards the money on the table. "We've counted out John's winnings, and it's thirty-six bucks short."

BJ swallowed hard. "Oh, that's right. I forgot." He pulled out three tens and a one. "Thirty-six bucks — minus five for the beer, of course, since John was the big winner."

Larry smiled and held out his hand to Tom, palm up.

"Wait a minute, Larry," Tom said with a sly grin. "BJ, you did say *five* for the beer, didn't you — not four?"

"Yeah, that's right. Why?"

Tom grinned even more broadly and held out *his* hand to Larry, palm up.

"The bar will remain open awhile if you'd like to stick around," the pro announced over the loudspeaker. **"All scores will be tallied later tonight and will be posted tomorrow morning. Thanks for joining us today and we'll see you all tomorrow."**

"So," Larry said, "are you going to tell us what's going on with you?"

"What are you talking about?" I asked.

"C'mon. A sixty-seven?"

Tom and BJ also turned their eyes on me. I took a generous gulp of beer, fumbling for an answer they would believe.

"Well, I'd rule out the girl," Tom said. "He can't be all that serious about her."

His remark caught me off guard. "Why do you say that?" I asked, somewhat miffed.

"Well, we finished our game an hour ago, and you still haven't called her about your outstanding day on the course."

His words stung. *Should I have called her?*

"I'm heading there from here," I said defensively. "I want to surprise her — see her reaction in person."

"Then you're saying she *is* a part of what's going on?"

They were boxing me into a corner. But what could I possibly tell them that would make any sense. After downing my beer, I slowly poured another, buying myself some time to think. Perhaps mentally sorting through the events of the last few months, I could pick and choose what to say or not to say. But then I recalled something that had been working for me lately — the truth.

"Okay," I said, "if you have to know the truth, I'll tell you." I paused. "But..."

"But what?" Larry asked.

"But you're not going to believe it."

"Of course we'll believe it," Larry said. "Why wouldn't we?"

"Well, then," I said and took another gulp of beer. "I guess I'd better start at the beginning. Remember that napkin Irma gave me over at Winton Woods back in the spring?"

Larry glanced at Tom and BJ, and they all shrugged their shoulders.

"I guess not," Larry said. "But go on."

So I took them on the wild ride, starting with the flash of light that had streaked through my car and the glimmering sign that had appeared out of nowhere. I described Josh, and his index cards with their cryptic messages, and the high-powered golf cart, and the mysterious golf course with no hole markers. I fumbled for words, trying to explain the supposedly magical appearance and reappearance of the *Handbook of a Master Instructor*. I explain about Bobbie — that Josh was her stepfather — that she was an excellent golfer and that when I wasn't at work, or with Josh, I was with her. Finally, I told them about the party with Jimmy Buffett, Johnny Bench, Carl Lindstrom, and all the others, ending with how Josh had helped me fine-tune my game all last week. My mouth was so dry when I finished I downed another beer in one gulp. That's when I noticed the blank stares. "Well? Aren't you going to say anything?" I asked.

"If you don't want to tell us what's really going on," Tom finally said, "why not just say so?"

I sighed.

"Are you sure you're not leaving something out?" Larry asked. "Something that we *might* believe?"

I thought for a moment. "Oh yes. I had a chili dog for breakfast."

"Aha!" Larry said, slamming his palm down on the table. "I knew there was a logical explanation."

* * *

On the way to Bobbie's, Larry's remark about the chili dogs had me laughing out loud. But my mood quickly shifted as I recalled Tom's offhand remark about my relationship with Bobbie. *Should I have called her?* If it weren't for that unidentifiable nagging feeling in the back of my mind, which must have something to do with her, I wouldn't have given Tom's remark a second thought. But there it was again.

And there she is. She was sitting on the porch when I drove up. When she saw me, she jumped up and ran to the car. Before I had chance close the car door, we were hugging each other tightly. When I let go, I held her at arm's length, looking for signs that she might be hurt or upset about not calling. To my relief, her eyes were untroubled, though they did seem to hold a question.

"Well?" she finally asked.

"I took all three of them to the cleaners," I said with a grin.

"You won every hole?"

"Everyone."

"Wow, Johnny! I bet they were surprised!"

"You can't even imagine."

As we slowly walked hand in hand to the porch, I gave her a play by play recap of the game, all the way down to BJ's last putt, and why he missed it.

"So, what was your final score?" she asked.

"Sixty-seven."

"Sixty-seven?" she repeated. "Wow! I didn't realize you had improved that much."

"Yeah, me either. I might even be able to beat *you*."

"Let's not get unrealistic," she said, and we both laughed. "Well, you must be hungry. Let me whip something up." I followed her inside, and into the kitchen. While she rummaged through the refrigerator, I pulled up a stool behind the counter and watched.

"Tuna fish okay?" she asked.

"Sure," I said and paused for a moment. "You know, it's been some time since I've had someone ask about my day, or was interested in what I did, or even cared whether I ate or not."

She stopped making the sandwich and stared at me.

"What?" I asked.

She rushed over and threw her arms around me. I held her as if I never wanted to let go. Our hug lingered until it led to a kiss. The sandwich was quickly forgotten as I swept her in my arms and whisked her off to the bedroom. The little energy I had left I surrendered to her totally and then collapsed into a deep sleep.

* * *

A whippoorwill called out from somewhere in the night. It woke me, drawing my gaze to the opened window. A faint yellow glow from the street lamp illuminated the sheer lace curtains, and they gently fluttered in the sultry night air. Bobbie was asleep under my arm, her head resting gently on my chest. I drew in a deep breath, and when I exhaled, my body trembled and my arm tightened around her back. She shifted, slightly, and nestled closer. It was fortunate she didn't wake up — she would have asked me about the tears.

Chapter 39

My mind kept me from falling back to sleep. It spun through all that had happened to me over the summer — from BJ whacking me in the head with his golf club to my shooting a sixty-seven just a few short hours ago. It was an incredible, almost unbelievable set of events, and only at this moment, lying with Bobbie in my arms, did I realize how well life had been treating me. But for some reason, there was still that underlying irritation, a nagging worry I couldn't shake off that was keeping me from enjoying it.

I slipped out of bed feeling agitated and depressed. As quietly as possible, I showered, shaved, dressed, and tiptoed into the living room. My plan was to leave before Bobbie woke up - no way did I want to talk to her while feeling this way. But just as I was about to leave, she came out of the bedroom.

"John, are you leaving already?" I turned slowly and our eyes locked. She was too attentive, too aware, not to see that something was troubling me. "Is anything wrong?" she asked.

"No," I said hastily and without conviction.

Tears formed in her eyes.

Crap! It was the first time that I had seen her feelings hurt and I caused it. It was so typical of me to hide my feelings — something I have always done. But now I can see no good can ever come of it. *Not this time, damn it.* I swallowed hard, and said, "Well, maybe."

She stared at me for a moment, not sure what to say. Nor did I know what to say. Or was I even sure what I felt? I was on new ground here, but then it occurred to me — why not tell her just that?

"Bobbie, I'm sorry. For some reason, I *am* feeling glum."

Her hurt look gave way to a slight smile. *Geez. Telling the truth can't be this easy.*

"Do you want to talk about it?" she asked, coming closer.

"I would if I knew what to talk *about.* Strange, isn't it? Yesterday morning I was on top of the world, looking forward to the weekend. I shot my best score ever, had a great time with my friends, spent a wonderful night with you, and today I'm feeling down. Who can figure?"

Bobbie reached out, gently touched my cheek and kissed me. "Thank you, Johnny, for trusting me enough to share that with me."

What is it about her that brings out the best in me? "I feel like I should be thanking *you*," I said. "It's amazing how much better I feel just having talked about it." I gathered her up in my arms. "Even if the rest of the day turns to crap," I said, "you've already made it better than I could have ever hoped." And I meant it.

Once I was out the door and in my car that unexplainable nagging irritation came back in full force. By the time I reached the freeway, my mind was working overtime, trying to figure it out. *Is it some hidden fear? Am I worried that things are just too good to be true?* The feeling hung on as I drove into Sharon Wood's lot, and continued as I headed towards the snack area of the clubhouse. Finding that the place was deserted, I glanced at my watch. No wonder. It was only nine. The tournament wouldn't start for another two hours.

The smell of coffee and bacon drew me to the counter and having missed breakfast, I ordered a bacon and egg sandwich and a large coffee. As I scanned the room for a suitable place to eat, a familiar face came into view at a corner table.

"Want some company?" I asked.

"John," Tom said, looking up from his newspaper. "How come you're here so early?"

"I could ask you the same question," I said.

"This is my day to be out playing golf, away from the wife and kids. I wanted to take full advantage of it. So what's your excuse?"

"I couldn't sleep."

"Couldn't sleep? Or *didn't* sleep?" he asked with a wry smile.

"Well…both, I guess."

"Have you checked the scoreboard yet?"

"No. How'd we all do?"

"Well, BJ's second in his flight with a ninety-seven. If Larry had shot one stroke worse, he would have been first in his flight. But he's dead last in my flight with a ninety-five. And I'm first with a ninety."

"Well, it sounds like we're in for an interesting day," I said.

"Don't you want to know where *you* stand?"

"Well, sure."

"You're leading the whole damn thing."

"Geez," I said, and let out a long drawn out sigh. "Who would have thought?"

"Now that's a strange reaction."

"Huh?"

Tom gave me a hard look and then glanced at my sandwich. "You look like you've either just lost your best friend, or you hate the food here." He paused. "Is something bothering you?"

I was about to say no but caught myself again hiding my feelings. "Yeah, there is something troubling me, but I can't put my finger on it. With everything going so well in my life right now, I should be ecstatic, but..." I paused, and then asked, "Tom, are you happy?"

"I love you, honey," he replied.

"What?"

"Oh, I'm sorry. That's the programmed response I give to my wife when she asks me that question."

"C'mon. I'm serious. Are you happy? Are you *really* happy?"

"Well, yeah. I'm pretty happy. My kids are great. My wife loves me. My job is fun. I play golf on the weekends. How can I not be happy?"

"Doesn't it seem like there should be something more?"

"What are you getting at?"

"I'm not sure. That day that BJ's club knocked me out, I felt there was more going on around us than what appears to be. But this nagging, irritable feeling that's bothering me is something different. You know, everything in my life is so perfect right now, maybe things are just *too* good. Maybe I'm worried it won't last. Could that be it?"

"John, you already know that everything changes and that you have to adapt. That's life. And you know who told me that?"

"Yeah, I do."

"Who?"

"I did," I admitted.

"Which is why I know for sure that whatever is eating at you, it isn't *that.*"

"Well, then, what could it be?" I asked.

Tom gave me a thoughtful stare, and I waited. When he wanted to, he had an uncanny knack for approaching a problem pragmatically, and coming up with an insightful solution. But he often hid this ability behind his quick wit, and I never knew which side of his personality was going to show. His next question would be telling

"When did you first notice this feeling?" he asked.

"I'm not sure," I said and paused, searching my memory for the past few weeks. "I believe it was the night of that party I told you about."

"The alleged party with Jimmy Buffet?"

"Yeah," that's the one.

"Okay, assuming you did go to a party, was there anything special or unusual about that night?"

"Are you kidding? Jimmy Buffett and Johnny Bench and..."

"No. I mean did anything unusual or special happen between you and Bobbie?"

"Well, yeah. It was at the party that I realized how much I truly cared for her. In fact, I was planning to tell her but got side tracked. It was also that night that she invited me to stay over and well, you can figure the rest. Why?"

He didn't immediately answer, so I waited, allowing him to sort it out.

"Are you having any problems at work?" he asked.

"No. Business is better than ever."

"Are you enjoying it?"

"Well, it's a job selling belts — what can I say?"

"Would you rather be doing something else?"

"Like what?"

"What do you think, for Chrissake? You shot a sixty-seven yesterday, and from what you've told me, you're spending all your time at that golf range with this new instructor."

"If you're asking me if I'd rather be spending my time golfing, instead of selling belts, of course, I would."

"Then why don't you?"

"What would I do for money?"

"With the way you're playing, you could become a pro at one of the city or county courses."

"Do you know how many pros in this town alone are on a list for those jobs?"

"You could teach."

"That's what the out-of-work pros are doing," I pointed out.

"Maybe you could get good enough to be a touring pro."

"Tom, even if I gave that shot, do you know how much it costs just to support yourself on the tour? Entry fees, travel, food, hotels.

And if you're not winning? I can't leave the security of a good job for some pipe dream."

Tom let my words hang in the air for a few minutes before continuing. "John, I've known you a long time, and you're one of the most positive guys I know. And when you've really wanted something, you've never, ever let anything as mundane as job security stand in your way.

His words struck hard. They were absolutely true. Why was I being so negative? Why was I fighting him?

"Except once," he added.

"What?"

"Except once."

"When was that?"

"When you were married."

He was right. Risk versus security, opportunity versus responsibility — these choices had taken on a whole different slant when someone else was depending on me.

"But I'm not married now," I said.

With eyebrows raised, Tom gazed intently into my eyes, waiting for me to make the connection. My shoulders abruptly slumped, and my eyes closed.

"Bobbie," I said.

Chapter 40

"The winner of flight eight is Phil Saunders," the Tournament Director announced. About a hundred half-drunk golfers, packed tightly in the snack area, let out a whoop and started clapping.

With a finger in one ear and a phone receiver pressed to the other, I hunched over a pay phone and waited for Bobbie to pick up at the other end. As soon as she answered, I gave her a quick summary of my day on the course.

"Well, I'd think you'd be feeling pretty satisfied right now," Bobbie said. "After all, you went into the weekend not sure how you would shoot."

"What?"

"I said, I'd think you'd be feeling…"

"I'm sorry, I can't hear you."

"WHAT'S GOING ON OVER THERE? IT SOUNDS LIKE A FREE-FOR-ALL."

"The place is packed. Everyone's been drinking the last two hours while the scores were being tallied. They've just begun calling out the winners now."

"And the winner of flight seven is Doug Courtney."

"Listen, Bobbie, Bobbie…Are you there?"

"Yes."

"Hello?"

"YES, I'M HERE!"

"If it's okay with you, I think I'll head home from here so I can get an early start on work tomorrow. But I'd like to see you tomorrow night and talk about some things."

"Has something happened?"

"What?"

"HAS SOMETHING HAPPENED?"

"I've figured some things out. It's hard to talk with all the noise here."

"The winner of flight six is Sonny Baylor."

"JOHN, SOMETHING HAS COME UP, AND I HAVE TO GO

TO RALEIGH TOMORROW. I WON'T BE BACK UNTIL THURSDAY. CAN IT WAIT 'TILL THEN?"

Her news caught me off guard.

"JOHN, DID YOU HEAR ME?"

"Yes, I did. Is everything okay with you?"

"Sure."

"What?

"YES, EVERYTHING'S ALL RIGHT. I'LL TELL YOU ABOUT IT WHEN I GET BACK."

"I'll tell you what. Let me take you out Thursday night for a real dinner. Wine, steak, seafood, the works."

"That sounds wonderful."

"What?"

"SOUNDS GREAT. AND BY THE WAY, IF YOU WANT TO CATCH UP WITH JOSH, HE WILL BE AT THE RANGE ALL DAY WEDNESDAY."

"That's good. I will. See you Thursday about five."

Good thing I stopped for another pitcher of beer on the way back to the table. Larry, Tom, and BJ had sucked the last one dry without my help.

"Where have you been?" Larry asked. "They're about to announce the winner of flight five."

"The winner of flight five is Tom Jenkins."

We all clapped and hooted as Tom stumbled his way around the tables to get to the makeshift podium. Being the more intellectual member of our group (not to mention an incredible optimist), he had planned ahead and brought along an empty bag for his winnings. Good thing he had. Besides the one hundred dollars in cash, he collected a small trophy, a golf shirt, a golf glove, a set of club head covers, and a dozen balls. With his bag of prizes in one hand, he gave us a "thumbs up" and a huge grin on his way back. It was good to see him smiling. He had become quite worried this morning during our chat, thinking that by zeroing in on my problem might have ruined my game

"And the winner of flight four is Jamey Decker."

But I had assured him that the clarity of knowing what was bothering me was better than the confusion of not. And that yesterday's sixty-seven had been my best score ever, so however I played today, it really didn't matter. And I had meant it.

"The winner of flight three is Darryl Carver."

Besides, Tom had been right on target. If not for my involvement with Bobbie, I'd dump my job in a minute and pursue golf full-time. Thanks to Josh's instructions and seeing the way he lived, I could see that what matters most in life was doing what one loves, whatever the cost. *"Who are you?"* was Josh's continual question. He knew who *he* was, and was doing exactly what he loved, seemingly without worry.

But then again, he wasn't married. But then again, neither am I. So, the question is, do I want to be?

"And the winner of flight two is RT Smith."

"Did he say, RT Smith?" I asked, snapping out of my thoughts. They were too busy whooping and clapping to hear me. I strained to look. Sure enough, it was the fellow from Josh's party who had the old VW bus with the peace sign. *He must be a pretty good golfer to win the second flight.*

"And finally, the winner of the Cavendish Cup and two thousand cash is John Arbor."

I was surprised at how loudly BJ, Larry, and Tom cheered when my name was announced, especially since just two hours earlier they had been ruthlessly interrogating me about my sixty-five. But what could I have said that made sense? The truth was that it had felt as if something, — or someone else was playing my shots and I was just going along for the ride.

At the podium, the pro shook my hand and handed me the trophy. Next came the envelope of cash, three golf shirts, a new Titleist driver, two dozen golf balls, a Ping putter, and a Wilson golf bag.

"Would you like to say a few words?" he suddenly asked, then shoved the microphone in my face.

"Yes. Do you have a bag to put this stuff in?" I said.

A wave of laughter spread through the room

"I meant do you want to say a few words about your win here today?"

I shook my head, but he pushed the microphone at me again and waited. To my amazement, the hundred or so golfers abruptly went quiet.

Here it was, my first tournament win, with everyone staring at me, and I was completely at a loss for words. Should I say something humble, or witty? Should I be grateful, or confident, or aim for something profound? Suddenly it hit me. Just tell them exactly how I was feeling. After all, that strategy had been working so far.

"It's not the trophy or the win that is the important thing here," I finally said, and paused a beat to scan the faces in the room. I was about to say, "It's doing what you love in the companionship of fellow golfers and good friends." But the beer took over, and I found myself saying, *"***It's getting all the cash and prizes***."* Thank goodness I was playing to a drunken audience. They all cheered.

As I headed off with my prizes, the pro grabbed my arm. **"Hang on a second,"** he said. He unfolded a piece of paper and read into the mike, **"The final prize for this year's Cavendish Cup winner, John Arbor, is an invitation to play next weekend in the Greater Ohio Challenge. And the winner of the Greater Ohio Challenge will receive a one-year, fully paid sponsorship while qualifying for the PGA tour. This year's sponsorship has been generously provided by American Credential. Good luck, John."**

His announcement left me stunned. For the first time ever, I felt as if I were being played — that life was playing me, moving me around like a pawn on a chessboard. Yes, it had introduced me to the woman of my dreams. Yes, it had provided me with a teacher who showed me the possibility of pursuing my life's passion. *But then it paints me into a corner where I feel I have to choose between the two. And if that isn't enough, it drops in my lap a chance, however remote, to resolve the conflict.* All I had to do was win a major statewide tournament.

Chapter 41

Three days without Bobbie was a blessing and a curse: a curse because I would miss her terribly, but a blessing because it gave me time to figure out how to approach her with my dilemma. Our Thursday night date would be here soon enough.

There was no longer any doubt in my mind that pursuing golf was a must. How Josh lived and embraced life convinced me that following one's passion was a key to happiness. But it also probably meant eating beans and weenies for no telling how many years. Not a problem for me had I not met and fallen hopelessly in love with Bobbie. But at age thirty, how could I ask her to wait for something that might never financially pan out? A future with Bobbie meant a house, medical insurance, probably kids, schooling, vacations, saving for the future. Her income couldn't be much, but combined with what I was earning now, it would be more than enough for us to live a comfortable life. And with Waisting Away growing rapidly under the umbrella of American Credential, I'd grow right along with it. *American Credential. It's funny how it keeps popping up in my life.*

Helpless in love was my predicament. There had to be a resolution, but by Tuesday night, none had shown itself and my mind started grasping at straws. *How do I know Bobbie even wants to spend her life with me? We've never really talked about marriage. Maybe I'm not ready for a serious relationship. Look where my first marriage ended up. Maybe I don't love Bobbie as much as I think I do. Right. I don't love her, but she's on my mind every waking minute of the day.*

Clearly, there was only one real solution. If I wasn't willing to give up Bobbie, and I wasn't willing to give up golf, I needed to win the Greater Ohio Challenge. It would allow me a full year, with all expenses paid, to give golf my best shot. A simple task. All I had to do was beat all the top golfers in the entire state of Ohio. Was it possible? Josh would know. After all, he was directly responsible for creating the possibility in the first place.

* * *

Wednesday morning was another hot August day, but it rendered a dry stillness that warned of summer's end. A cloudless sky of powder blue hung over the harvested cornfield as I drove down the gravel road. If only my mind were as clear.

My mood was melancholy but uplifted somewhat as I drove along the river. The woods were surrendering their verdant color to a deeper green — another sign that a season was coming to a close. But when the white cinderblock building came into view, my spirits sank again, knowing that Bobbie wasn't inside. *At least Josh will be here.* If anyone could lift my spirits besides Bobbie, it was Josh.

When I rounded the building, I saw Josh sitting on one of the benches, but he wasn't alone. As I approached, the person with him turned toward me, and we both smiled at the same time.

"Ah, so the Guardians of the True Swing have met to conspire against me," I said.

Lester grinned as Josh greeted me, "Well if it isn't this year's winner of the famed Cavendish Cup."

"Hi, Josh," I said. "It's good to see you again, Lester — I think. You know, my mind's still spinning from our last meeting."

"Good," Lester said. "Better that it spin than wander off course."

I was starting to feel better already. "You can't think and hit at the same time. Is that it?"

"Why, yes," Lester said. "Sounds like you've learned a thing or two since our last conversation."

"Tell me, John," Josh asked, "what did it feel like, shooting a couple of rounds in the sixties?"

"Josh, I have to tell you that it was a little weird. It felt as if I had stepped out of my body, and was observing someone else playing my shots."

Lester put his hand on my shoulder and said, "And who do you think that 'someone else' might be?"

Ah. Here we go again. Another form of the ever-popular question, "Who are you?"

"I have no idea."

"Are you sure, John?" Lester said with a twinkle in his eye, and then let out a resounding laugh. For a brief instant, I felt his laugh deep in my body and the joy behind it. But just as quickly, the feeling vanished, and I dropped deeper into my gloom.

"Listen, you don't understand. If ever I've needed the True Swing, it's now."

They both looked at each other. "What's going on?" Josh asked.

"Well, I don't know if you know this, but winning the Cavendish Cup got me an invite to play in the Greater Ohio Challenge this weekend. And the winner of the Challenge gets a shot at the tour, with a full year's sponsorship while trying."

"Ah," Lester said. "So is that want you want?"

"Yes. I'm pretty sure I do. It would give me a shot at doing what I love, same as you, Josh."

Josh gave me one of his penetrating stares and asked, "Why not take a shot at the tour anyway, whether you win or not?"

"It's not that simple," I answered.

"Are you sure about that?" Josh asked.

"You don't understand. It's just too risky, trying to make a livelihood from anything that involves golf, especially since I already have a pretty secure job."

"John," Josh continued, "how can you count on a job being secure when you can never really be sure of your next breath?"

"Yes, you're right. I mean, no, I've got to have a plan. I mean, if it were only me..." I abruptly stopped, not wanting to reveal any more. But it was too late.

"Oh," Josh said. "I see." He smiled and looked me square in the eyes. "Have you talked to Bobbie about this?"

I was about to feign ignorance as to the meaning of his question, but instead, I gave a weary sigh. "I haven't yet because I haven't had a chance. But we've got a date tomorrow night."

"She might surprise you."

I smiled sadly. "She always surprises me, Josh. But I'm thirty, not twenty, and I don't have the time to build a financial future if the golf thing doesn't pan out. The only answer is to win the tournament this weekend. That's why I came out here, to see if you thought I had a chance, or if there was anything you could do to help me prepare."

"John, you've already got the ability to do whatever you decide. There's not anything else I can show you that would change that."

For a moment I was angry that he wasn't offering to help. After all, he was a Master Instructor. But underneath the anger, I saw the wisdom of his words." I guess you're right," I said halfheartedly. "Anyway, I suppose there's not much more I could learn in only three days."

He heard the disappointment in my voice and said. "John, the

True Swing is already always there."

"I'm not so sure, Josh. If it were, wouldn't I know it?"

"The True Swing is resting in the silent space between your thoughts," he said while tapping my forehead between my eyes. "When the time and place are right, it will seek you, and when that happens, your search and struggle will drop away."

"Well, it would be nice if it happened before this weekend."

"John, if the True Swing were to reveal itself to you before the tournament, it would not necessarily improve your ability, but the game would certainly be played from a whole different perspective."

His words gave me pause. "I don't get it, Josh. If grasping the true swing doesn't help me, then what's the point?"

"Exactly. What *is* the point? When there is no longer any point, what is left is a choice-less awareness of what you are doing right here, right now. Sort of like what you were feeling last weekend. Both the seer and the seen disappear, and all that remains is the seeing."

Josh and Lester had managed to put my head in a spin again. "You know, this isn't fair," I said. "I don't have Bobbie around to rescue me." They both chuckled.

"John, sometimes focusing on what you want keeps you from seeing what you already have."

"Well," I don't know if I fully understand any of this, but if there's nothing more to do, a rest could do me good. Not just for this weekend but for tomorrow night's date with Bobbie. I expect it's going to be an interesting evening."

"No question about that," Josh said as I shook Lester's hand and then headed towards my car. As I crossed the parking lot, a sound arose that I rarely heard at the range. It was an approaching vehicle.

Geez. What's going on today? There's never anyone here except for Josh and Bobbie. First Lester, and now this?

A sleek looking red car entered the parking. From the front, it looked like my Mustang but then again, not quite. The driver waved to me after he parked. "Hi, John," he said as he came toward me, offering his hand. "RT Smith," he said. "We met at Josh's party. It's good to see you again."

"Yes, I remember," I said, "And I saw you last weekend at the tournament. You won the second flight."

"Yeah, and you won it all. Great scores. Sixty-seven and sixty-five. Wow!"

"I guess you and I made a pretty good showing as Josh's students."

"Oh, I'm not one of Josh's students. As a matter of fact, I don't even know him all that well."

"But you were at his party. I just assumed you were one of his students."

"I was playing chauffeur for my Dad. My dad and Josh have known each other for quite some time."

"Oh," I said. "Then what brings you out this way, if you don't mind my asking?"

"Well, two things. Josh offered to show me this golf course I've heard about."

"Are you talking about the course across the river?"

"Yeah. My father said it's quite something."

"Well, maybe you can solve a mystery for me," I said. "I've been wondering what course it is. I've looked for signs every time I drive out this way, but there aren't any. And Josh is fairly secretive about it."

"It's Josh's course."

"It is? Are you sure?"

"Yeah, my father has been telling me about it for years."

"For years?"

"Yeah, ever since Josh started it. I think he's been working on it for over twelve years, doing all the work himself. He only has eleven holes done."

"Why does that not surprise me?" I said.

"Apparently he's not in any hurry. According to my dad, it's just something he likes to do. He plans each hole around the existing landscape, being careful not to disturb the animals that live there. And he only uses it for his students. Have you ever seen it?"

"Yes, he took me there to play some holes when my lessons first began."

"You should feel fortunate. From what I understand, very few students get to play on it."

"Wow," I said, half to myself. "Do you think he'll ever get it done, or open it up to the public?"

"The way it's going, I would doubt it, which is a shame. It could be a good source of income for him. I don't think he does anything other than teach." RT glanced at his watch. "Well, I'd better get going."

"Yeah, me too. Thanks for solving that mystery for me."

"Sure," he said.

While opening my car door, I said, "By the way, did you give up your VW van for that Mustang you're driving?

He smiled. "In actuality, it's an Aston Martin."

"Really?" I said, surprised. "That's got to be quite a change: a VW bus to an Aston Martin."

"My dad bought it for me since he doesn't drive and doesn't do well in my van, which is the other reason I'm here. I'm playing Chauffeur.

"For your dad?" I asked, and peered over at his Aston Martin. He saw me looking and said, "Oh, he's not in the car, I'm picking him up."

"He's here?"

"I'm sorry, I didn't realize you didn't know. My dad is over there talking to Josh."

It took me a moment to put it together.

"Lester?" I asked.

Chapter 42

My anxiety was significantly rising as I drove down Bobbie's street. *What am I going to say to her? If she is interested in a serious relationship, is it fair to pursue something that is so "iffy?" Will she understand how important it is to me? But then why do I want to risk hurting our relationship? She is the best thing that has ever happened to me.*

Bobbie was waiting for me on the front porch, again. When I saw her, my worries quickly retreated to the back of my mind. After all, I hadn't seen her for five long days. When she saw me, she jumped up and ran to the car. Before I had time to put on the parking brake, she was sitting next to me and giving me a big kiss, which I returned with equal enthusiasm.

"So Bobbie, did you miss me so much that you decided to camp out on your porch?"

She laughed. "I figured if you came in, we'd get distracted and never make it to the restaurant. And I'm not about to let you off the hook that easy."

"Are you saying that you don't have enough willpower to resist me?"

"That's exactly what I'm saying."

"Good thinking. I wouldn't be able to resist you either, and we've got reservations at Mike Fink's."

"The paddlewheel boat across the river?"

"That's the one."

"You must have missed me more than I thought," she teased.

As soon as we pulled out of her drive, she launched a lengthy interrogation, drilling me again for a complete shot-by-shot description of how I played every hole in the Cavendish tournament. I enthusiastically obliged, also telling her about my acceptance speech, and the Greater Ohio Challenge. Not until we had crossed the Ohio River into Kentucky and parked at Mike Fink's was she satisfied she had the whole story. I was glad to give her the detailed account — it kept my mind off the issue that was foremost on my mind — the issue I knew we'd be getting to soon enough.

The concrete lot sloped downwards to the Ohio River where the majestic riverboat was docked. It was a stately old paddle wheel and the perfect setting for fine dining. The entire riverboat made up the restaurant and had acquired quite a reputation for its superb seafood over the last seventeen years — quite a feat since it was five hundred miles from the nearest ocean.

While strolling hand in hand in the final moments of a hot August day, my anxiety eased a bit. Across the river, the setting sun was painting the Cincinnati skyline in a warm glow.

After crossing the narrow plank walkway that led to the deck, a hostess welcomed us, then seated us next to an open window overlooking the river. As we sat down, she handed us a wine list. While Bobbie studied it, I studied her. It was hard not to stare. *Is this what love is all about? Not being able to look at someone without feeling your insides turn to jelly?*

Bobbie must have felt my stare. She glanced up from the wine list and gave me a smile. My body trembled, and I smiled back.

"I missed you, Bobbie."

"I missed you too, John."

As her attention dropped back to the wine list, my gaze drifted to the river. My mind again started mulling over the questions that had gone unanswered all week and an idea of not bringing it up at all, suddenly made sense. *Why not wait to see what happens at the tournament this weekend.*

I sighed, perhaps a little too loudly and it caught Bobbie's attention.

"Something on your mind, John?" she asked.

"I was just thinking how great it would be to win this weekend. Could you imagine?"

She appeared somewhat surprised. "I didn't realize that winning this weekend was that important to you."

"You didn't?" How come?"

"Well, last weekend you were just interested in having a good time. Oh, and taking your friends to the cleaners."

"This tournament is a little different. With the money I have saved and a whole year's sponsorship paid for, I'd have a shot at getting on the tour."

"Is that what you've been thinking? That you might want to pursue being a tour player?"

Her question gave me pause because I wasn't sure how to read it. *Is she worried that if I said yes, it might make a difference in our relationship?*

My answer was slow and careful. "I'm not sure, Bobbie. All I know is that I love being around golf. And it seems to me that when one is lucky enough to discover one's true calling, it's important not to ignore it. I mean, look at Josh. I've never met anyone so alive, and so fascinated with life. And he's doing exactly what he wants to do, at whatever cost."

A low, distinguished voice interrupted us. "Good evening, my name is Leonardo. May I get you something to drink?"

Bobbie pointed to a selection on the wine list. "I'd like a glass of this Pinot Gris, please."

"And you, sir?"

"I'll have the same. As a matter of fact, why don't you bring us a whole bottle? And two glasses," I added, absently.

"Two glasses," he said with a hint of sarcasm. "Very good, sir." Bobbie covered her mouth with her hand to hide a chuckle as he bowed himself away.

"I guess I didn't need to tell him we needed two glasses - one of us isn't going to drink from the bottle. I guess that shows you what condition my mind is in."

"You do seem a bit perplexed," she said.

"Do I?" I said and glanced out the open window. A wash of colored lights from the Cincinnati skyline rippled on the water in the dusky twilight. When I turned my attention back to the table, a waitress had set a basket of assorted breads and dinner rolls on our table and was lighting our candle.

"You know, John," Bobbie said, "when you last talked to me, you mentioned that you had figured some things out."

The candle flickered in the warm air that drifted through the window. Her blue eyes glistened, diamond-like, in the flame's glow. My heart skipped a beat as I prepared myself for what I was about to say.

"Bobbie, I have figured out what's been bothering me, but I haven't figured out how to deal with it. It has to do with…what I mean is, I look at Josh and how happy he is… what I'm trying to say is that golf…"

Bobbie reached across the table and took my hand. "Why not just tell me exactly what's on your mind, John?"

Her direct question caught me off guard and the emotions that had been building over the last week began to rise uncontrollably. It was important to choose what to say, and how to say it, but the torrent of those feelings was unstoppable, and they abruptly exploded outward all at once.

"You," I blurted out. "You. That's what I want. I can't imagine being without you for a moment, let alone for my entire life. I've fallen head over heels in love with you, and have thought how wonderful it would be to have you as my wife. And of course, if you would marry me, there would be absolutely no question that I'd be the happiest guy in the world. But," I reached for her other hand and stared down at them to avoid her expression. "I've also fallen in love with golf. Besides you, it is the only thing I'm passionate about. I look at Josh's life and see him doing what he loves and figure if anyone knows the meaning of being alive, it's him. But to pursue a career in golf is so very risky and I would be turning my back on the security of a great job, and a promising future. If it were just me, it wouldn't matter, but with an 'us'... So you see, it all comes down to me winning this weekend. It would solve everything."

Chapter 43

There was silence after I finished — a long, still silence. My hands were still holding hers tightly, and I stared at them, afraid to look up — afraid to see the expression on her face. I looked anyway.

To my shock, she was grinning, and I have to admit, I was miffed. After pouring out all my heartfelt emotions, there she was, grinning. My immediate thought was to react, but the salesman in me said no. It was her turn now — it was time for me to shut up and listen. So quietly I waited.

"Yes," is what she finally said.

"Yes? Yes, what?"

"My answer is yes," she repeated with eyes wide and eyebrows raised.

"What are you talking about?"

"Yes. I will marry you. I can't imagine a life without you either."

Suddenly it struck me. In the middle of my ongoing ranting, I had asked her to marry me. And she had just said yes!

"You will?" I asked A feeling of joy surged through my body like nothing I'd ever known. *I'm getting married to Bobbie!* What had been a complicated mind-consuming dilemma for the last week abruptly vanished without a trace. There was no doubt in my mind that this was the right decision.

"You will?" I asked again, returning her grin.

"Yes. Yes, I will," she said excitedly, and laughed. "I love you, John, and knew it from the first time we met. But listen. What you said about following your path and pursuing golf — there's something you need to know."

"Bobbie, I know what you're going to say, and I don't want to hear it. I'm thirty years old. Even if I win the Greater Ohio Challenge, I'm not going to marry you and go off in pursuit of some pipe dream, not knowing if we'll make it financially. I just won't do it."

"But John, I already told you that I can take care of myself."

Crap. I don't have a ring. Here I've asked her to marry me, and I haven't even given her a ring. Where am I going to get one this time of night?

"John, are you listening to me?"

"Of course," I said. *Perhaps there's an all-night jeweler somewhere in Kentucky.*

"John," she said, with some impatience.

"Yes? I mean, no. Now that we're getting married, we have to think about more than just you and me. We're talking a possible family here. It's too risky to think I could make the kind of money I'm making now. Bobbie, I'm telling you it's okay."

Just then, the waiter appeared with our wine. "Wait a minute," I said as he set the glasses on the table. "Will you take the wine back and bring us a bottle of champagne? We just got engaged."

The waiter glanced at Bobbie's left hand, probably to see what size diamond I had given her. With a slight shake of his head and a deadpan look, he picked up the wine glasses and asked, "I presume you would like *two* champagne glasses?"

Great. First, he thinks I'm an idiot, and now he thinks I'm cheap. But he's right. I should have a ring, or flowers, or something. I'm getting married!

"John, will you settle down for a moment? There are some things you need to know."

"Okay, okay," I said. "I'm listening." *Maybe the waiter knows of a jeweler that might be open.*

"Remember at Josh's party when we were talking about Carl Lindstrom and you asked me about R.J. Richards?"

"Yeah," I said while selecting a dinner roll from the basket. "You said that he wasn't there, as I recall. Why? What does that have to do with anything?"

"In fact, what I said at the time was, 'Who would know since you said yourself he was a recluse?' Well, I didn't exactly tell you the truth about that, John, and I've been feeling bad about it ever since."

"You mean he *was* there?"

"Yes."

I was intrigued, but at the same time amazed that she had been worrying all this time about not being honest, especially since it was about something that really didn't matter.

"Bobbie, it's okay. But why *didn't* you tell me?" Before she could answer, it dawned on me. "Oh," I said. "Of course. He's one of Josh's students, isn't he? And you needed to guard his anonymity. So you were protecting him and worrying that you had to be dishonest with me to do it."

"Well, that's pretty close to the truth, John."

"Geez, Bobbie. That's really sweet that you've been fretting over this. But after all, you were protecting someone. That's a pretty good reason; I should think." I searched the room for the waiter. "Where is our champagne? We need to celebrate." I raised my hand to get his attention and then turned my gaze back to Bobbie.

"So, can you tell me who it is, now that I'm going to be family," I asked, while scanning my memory of the party, "or do you still have to keep it secret?" Before she could answer, another thought struck me. "Wait a minute. Was his son there too?"

"Well…"

"Wait. Don't tell me?" I said as my mind started piecing it together. *No. It couldn't be, could it? Lester and RT? There is no "Lester" in R.J. Richards, but Lester's son's name is RT. The "R" could stand for Robert, and they're both golfers — very good golfers, and now that I think about it, the name "Smith" seems awfully suspicious. And he drives an Aston Martin. Of course! What better way for Richards' son to conceal his identity — drive around in an old VW van with a peace sign and show up wearing jeans and a T-shirt? But Lester — an "almost" billionaire? Maybe RT is the one who's made all the family money.*

"I know who it is," I announced triumphantly.

"You figured it out?" she said, surprised.

"Yes. It was a simple matter of deduction. And it's brilliant."

"So?" she asked.

I paused to slather some butter on a roll. "Before I answer, am I allowed to know, or will it put you in a compromising position?"

"No. It's okay that you know now. No secrets between future husband and wife."

"It's Lester and RT," I said proudly, then bit into my dinner roll.

"That's interesting," she said. "What made you think that?"

"Hiding in plain sight wearing jeans and driving an old hippie van while secretly driving an Aston Martin. And using his initials "RT" instead of his first name which is probably Robert. The only thing is that there is no "L" for Lester in "RJ Richards.""

She smiled and shook her head. "RT's first name is Ronald, and the "R" in "RJ" stands for Randal. I assure you it's not them but your reasoning does make sense."

"Oh," I muttered through a mouthful of bread."

As I swallowed, my mind scanned who else was at the party. But before I could take another guess, Bobbie said, "Let me ask you this: do you know Josh's last name?"

"Sure. It's Atkinson. The same as yours, isn't it?"

"Atkinson is my real father's name, so most people assume that Josh's last name is the same."

"Oh," I said again and took another bite from the dinner roll. While diligently chewing, I asked, "So, if it isn't Atkinson, what is it?"

"Richards."

I started choking on the roll. Bobbie grabbed my water glass and thrust it into my hands as people around us started to stare. While still choking, I asked, "Are you telling me that Josh is somehow related to R.J. Richards?"

"Well, not exactly," she said. She waited until my choking ceased. "John, in all that you've read about R.J. Richards, have you ever read what the 'J' in R.J. stands for?" She stared into my eyes, watching, waiting, for a light to click on.

No, no! It couldn't be! "Josh? Josh is R.J. Richards!?" My jaw dropped, my eyes went wide in shock, and for a moment, all I could do was stare. "How could that possibly be?" I finally asked in disbelief. "Josh's life... it's...it's...I mean...how he lives, it's so..." I shook my head while fumbling for words.

"It's so what?" Bobbie asked.

"I don't know — it's so uncomplicated. The way he lives, the way he sees everything. Crap! He's got more money than God! I guess he can live any way he wants."

Bobbie's expression changed to one of concern.

"John, it's important that you understand that who Josh is, has little to do with how much or how little money he has. There is no doubt in my mind that if he lost it all, or gave it all away, it just wouldn't matter to him. But it just so happens that building successful companies is something he's good at,"

"Good at? I'd say half a billion dollars makes him damn good at it," I said, still in shock. "So what *does* Josh do with all that money? I mean, he's driving around in an old Chevy pickup, for God's sake. Is he a philanthropist? Or are you going to tell me he secretly owns a Ferrari and a large estate somewhere, and the free spirit thing is just a ruse."

"John, I told you that who Josh is, is not a ruse, but…"

"But what?

Well," she said with some hesitation, "he does have a rather large ranch in Montana, and he did have a Ferrari once, but gave it up for some Rolls-Royces."

"*Some* Rolls-Royces? How many does he have?

"Three."

My head was thrust back into a spin. Who I thought Josh was, was disintegrating rapidly, replaced by someone I no longer knew. While rubbing my forehead, trying to put this all in perspective, I mumbled to myself, "Why would anyone have three Rolls-Royces?"

"I asked him that."

"Asked him what?"

"Why he had three Rolls-Royces."

Not really expecting an answer, I looked at her soberly and waited.

"He said it didn't make sense to own any more."

For a few moments, I held her stare with a blank look but then a smile crept across my face, and we both broke out laughing. "Now that sounds like something Josh would say."

Bobbie's laughter was infectious, and as I settled down a bit, I asked, "Is there anything else about him that I might want to know?"

"Well, he has more houses around, and there's the boat."

"The boat? What kind of boat?"

"Well, 'boat' might be the wrong terminology for its size."

"It's size?" I asked, as another wave of disbelief hit me. "How big is it? Never mind. I don't want to know. Where the hell is the waiter with our champagne? I need a drink."

As Bobbie patiently watched and waited, I dropped my head in my hands, trying to think, trying to piece all this new information together, but my mind was still in shock. Finally, I looked up and said. "Okay Bobbie, you need to help me here. I guess I'm having trouble understanding how Josh can be the way he is and also be wealthy beyond comprehension. I mean, having all that money — what does he do with it?

"As you get to know Josh and hear him talk about his companies, you will quickly understand that it is not about the money."

"How can it not be about the money?"

Bobbie half smiled, leaned forward on the table and asked, "Have you ever heard the expression if you give someone some fish you feed him for a day but if you teach him to fish, you'll feed him for a lifetime?

"Yes," I answered. 'But what do "fish" have to do with his money?"

"Don't you see? You work for one of Josh's companies and the money you earn — what do you do with it? You are using it to buy this meal tonight, which helps those who work here and those who own this place. It helps those who have distributed the food to here and those who have grown the food and all those who supply the farm equipment to grow the food. And it helps those who manufacture the farm equipment and on and on. Multiply that times the thousands that work for Josh's companies, and you'll start to realize he contributes a great deal. And Josh vividly sees the interconnectedness of all of this.

As her words sunk in, the pieces started to come together, and I could see how they fit Josh's view of life, only on a much larger scale than I ever could have imagined. "So why does he teach?"

"Why do you think, John?"

I smiled at her answering my question with a question and wondered if the salesman in me was catching. "So others might see the Truth for what it is," I said without hesitation. "But still, this is all so unbelievable."

The waiter finally arrived, carrying a bottle of champagne. He popped the cork, and after pouring a small amount into Bobbie's glass, I grabbed the bottle out of his hand, poured my glass to the brim, and downed it in one gulp. He grabbed the bottle back and while giving Bobbie a sympathetic glance and a shake of his head, he finished filling her glass.

After he had left, I sat for a minute, waiting for the champagne to take effect when another startling realization burst into my mind: my future father-in-law was a multi-millionaire. *What are the implications of that? Would he have set up some kind of trust fund for Bobbie? Could her salary be one hell of a lot more than I thought? No, she said that she took care of herself financially, and she's not one to bend the truth. Maybe Bobbie has refused to take any of his money or be part of his corporate life. But that wouldn't make sense. They're family. Wait a minute. Family — R.J. has a son. Bobbie has a brother somewhere whose worth as much as Josh is.*

"Bobbie. What about Robert? You never mentioned about having a brother. Isn't he worth the other half billion dollars?"

She didn't answer, and it suddenly struck me why. "Oh, I get it. You couldn't say anything because you've been protecting him, too."

Bobbie inhaled deeply and let out a long breath. "That's the other thing I have to tell you, Johnny. That information is not exactly correct. First of all, it's not quite a half billion dollars. It's four hundred and eighty-four million and some change."

Gee, so I missed it by sixteen million.

"And it's not his son Robert — it's his daughter Roberta."

"So you have a sis...Roberta...Bobbie? YOU?!"

Section II

We shall not cease from exploration
And the end of all our exploring
Will be to arrive where we started
And know the place for the first time

Quick now, here, now, always
A condition of complete simplicity
(Costing not less than everything).

— TS Eliot, *The Four Quartets*

JUNE 2017

Chapter 44

It was difficult, finding myself crossing this same bridge and seeing the Golden River Sign again. Nineteen years had passed since it first revealed itself to me, and here it had hardly changed at all — the tall summer grass still keeping it well hidden from those who weren't meant to find it. Had it not reflected that glint of sunlight all those years ago I just might have passed it by.

Sunlight? Funny how I'm still trying to explain away that flash of light that drew me in, just as I've tried to explain away all the mysterious things that had happened around Josh and this place. So why did I come back here now? This too was a mystery. *Or maybe not.*

After pulling onto the gravel road, I slowed my BMW and parked just past the sign. With the convertible top down, the still, humid air went to work, creating beads of perspiration on my forehead. While wiping it off with the back of my hand, I glanced into the rearview mirror. The face staring back was unfamiliar. Wrinkles lined my forehead. Gray was seeping into the freshly cut crop of brown hair. Crow's feet were forming on the sides of my eyes. *How is it that I've aged so when this sign has hardly changed at all?* At least my eyes were no longer bloodshot, and the bags under them not so severe.

Has it truly been two years since…?

Out of habit, my mind instantly shut down, making sure no memory of *that* day would show itself. *That* day that cast me on a two-year path of self-destruction, where I spent all my waking hours in bars along the Carolina coast. Strange how time works. It didn't feel like two years had passed. But then a month went by, then two, then three — each month thinking I could muster up the courage to leave — to head back to our home in North Carolina. But then the memory of *that* day would start to surface, and only more alcohol would push it back down to where it belonged. When the memories started fighting their way back, the drinking came earlier, starting with beer, ending with bourbon, until I was never *not* drinking. Nothing short of a miracle could have pulled me from that drunken abyss. But fourteen days ago, that miracle happened, and I don't know how, or why.

I had been sitting alone in a hotel bar. It was late afternoon. The

TV was on — some sports show recapping the last five years of Major Golf Tournaments. The announcer had said my name and had mentioned the famous swing that had won me the PGA Championship two years ago. The infamous swing that I thought was the True Swing. I was well into a bottle of bourbon when the announcer continued, **"After finally winning his first major, the PGA Championship just two years ago, John Arbor was well on his way to winning The Tour Championship three weeks later. With a five-stroke lead on the sixteenth hole, he pretty well had it wrapped up, but as fate would have it…"**

"Turn that off, please," I said to the bartender.

He glanced at me, then back at the TV. As he reached for the knob, he said, "Hey, aren't you…?"

"Probably not," I interrupted and got unsteadily up off the stool and stumbled back to my room.

That night, the air outside my open motel window was still and thick. While lying there sweating on the sheets, trying not to think of what the announcer had been about to say, I must have passed out. What I remembered after that was waking up screaming. Crawling things, hundreds, were all over my body. I slapped and kicked at them while drawing myself back against the headboard. And then the light appeared. It flashed through the window, illuminating the room with a brilliant, fiery white glow. All those crawling things exploded in the light. Then the light got brighter and more intense until it crystallized and shot straight down into my forehead. A blaze of fire blasted through my body and then shot out in all directions, flashing the room like a Roman candle. Then everything went black.

Had it been a dream? A day passed or was it two that I awoke feeling amazingly calm and more rested than I could remember being in a long time. Rested, hungry, and thirsty — but incredibly, not thirsty for alcohol. That was the mystery, the miracle. The craving was incredulously gone. After a week of rest and reflection, feeling the sand under my feet and the sun warming my face, I found myself heading north — not to my home in North Carolina, but back to farmlands of Ohio where it had all started.

So here I am, but why? What am I searching for — another miracle?

An urge to turn around and go back kept arising, but to go back to what? I clenched the steering wheel, leaned back against the headrest, and stared up at the sky. It was so blue it hurt — the same brilliant blue sky that stretched above me the day Bobbie and I got married, a million years ago.

Chapter 45

"You lucky devil," Larry said with a slur. Bobbie had just appeared in the back of the covered pavilion, absolutely radiant in her wedding dress. Larry and I both stared at her as the minister settled into place.

An outdoor wedding in late October was risky in Cincinnati, but life had delivered us a seventy-degree day. Resting high above Cincinnati, Ault Park was drenched in deep crimson and bright yellow from the fall leaves. And yet the splendor of the backdrop paled in comparison to Bobbie's beauty. Of course, I was biased.

Larry squinted, then jutted his head forward as he stared at Bobbie.

"What's the problem now?" I asked.

He unsteadily moved his head close to my ear and asked, "Has Bobbie been drinking?"

"What on earth are you talking about?" I said in a harsh whisper. "Why would you think she's been drinking?"

"Because she's all out a' focus," he answered with a crooked smile.

After a quick jab with my elbow, my attention focused on Bobbie. Josh was now by her side, wearing a tux as if it were his everyday attire. Josh never ceased to amaze me. He could be the center of attention one minute — strong, confident, and full of life, and could all but disappear the next, blending into the surroundings so effectively that one might not notice he was even there. Perhaps that's why no one at this wedding, except for immediate family, had a clue that he and Bobbie were the multimillionaires behind American Credential.

The organist took her seat. As we waited for the guitarist to finish his final love ballad, Larry leaned into me, and said, "You should have let me usher instead of this best man business. Do you see what Tom 'n Bee Shay are doing?"

"Shhhhh! People will hear you," I warned as he fell against me.

None of us was sure why, but Larry detested weddings and proved it by drinking heavily. It was the reason he was chosen as my best man — so I could keep an eye on him. Larry was an usher at Tom's wedding, and at one point, had refused to take people down the aisle because it didn't have a net under it.

Larry nudged me again. "Did you hear me? Do you see what's going on?"

"Yeah, I see it."

Except for our immediate families, Tom and BJ had apparently decided to seat people by the way they looked instead of by their relationship to the bride and groom. All the unaccompanied good-looking women were seated together near the rear (I could somewhat see the logic in that), but they had placed all the bearded men together in one long row, with all the balding men right behind them (I guess to balance out the hair). Fortunately, it wasn't conspicuous unless one was up front, looking back. In fact, it surprised me that Larry had noticed.

The guitarist plucked out a strange chord at the end of the song, perhaps to grab everyone's attention for the main event. It worked because they all fell silent in anticipation. Then, in the still fall air, the Wedding March struck, and all eyes were drawn to Bobbie as she walked down the aisle with Josh at her side. Despite his drunken state, Larry was right. I was a lucky devil. Not just to be marrying Bobbie, but to have Josh as part of my new family. And, of course, there was the small matter of four hundred and eighty million dollars.

Josh winked at me after delivering his "little girl" to my side, and I'm sure he saw me choke up. It saddened me that my mother and father were not alive to meet Bobbie and Josh.

"Dearly beloved, we are gathered here today to…"

As the minister spun out the words, my heart soared. But there was still something shadowing my happiness. Perhaps it had to do with my not understanding the True Swing, even after all of Josh's lessons. What was it Josh had said? *"You will never find true joy in the game until you are outside of it, and see it for what it is."*

The minister's voice cut into my thoughts. **"Do you, John Arbor, take Roberta Atkinson to be your lawful wedded wife?"**

"I do," I answered emphatically.

"And do you, Roberta Atkinson, take John Arbor to be your lawful wedded husband?"

Bobbie stared right into my eyes with her baby blues and smiled. "I do."

"Do you have the ring?" the minister asked.

I looked at Larry.

"Aw Crap," Larry mumbled to himself while searching his pockets with clumsy hands. I froze but then remembered taking the rings from him earlier, not trusting his condition. Larry continued patting himself down, fumbling through his suit as I pulled the ring from my pocket. Finally, I elbowed him hard in the side.

"Ouch!"

"I now pronounce you man and wife," the minister said as Larry began to wobble. Bobbie and I quickly grabbed him by the arms, propped him up, and looked to the minister for help. The minister just shrugged his shoulders and said, **"You may now kiss the bride."**

Larry jerked his arm away from me, threw his arms around Bobbie, and gave her a big kiss. For years afterward, Larry insisted that *he* had married Bobbie instead of me, and demanded that I hand her over. I never did.

Chapter 46

The sweat from my brow dripped into my eyes, ripping me away from my wedding day and plunging me back into my BMW. I absently turned the ignition and slowly moved forward. There was no reason to hurry, and I didn't get far before stopping again. "How about that?" I said right out loud. The cornfield was still there.

The corn stalks crowded up to both sides of the gravel road — the sea of green stretching as far as the eye could see. I climbed out and leaned back against the car, recalling how often I had passed through this field on the way to the range. I suddenly realized how much I had missed it and wondered why I had never gotten back here after moving to North Carolina.

***

"I'm not sure we could have done this without you," I said to Josh as the empty moving van pulled away. We were sitting on the front porch of a spacious two-story home in the heart of Pinehurst, North Carolina. On both sides of us, and along the street, azaleas had burst into reddish pink and snow-white clusters. They appeared almost electric in the sun.

"Sure you could have," Josh said. "The movers did all the work."

"I meant your moral support. Giving me the confidence to leave everything I've ever known and move five hundred miles away."

"And look what you've moved to," Josh said as he swung his arm out.

"I have to admit," I said, "Bobbie sure picked a beautiful home. And, of course, it's better for her that she's closer to the Raleigh corporate office."

"And you can practice and play golf year-round, John. You're right in the heart of golf country, not to mention the famous Pinehurst Number Two course is right around the corner. It will be good for your career, now that you're playing with the big guns."

I grinned. "I'm still stunned that after losing the Ohio Challenge last September, I was able to get on the tour."

"Setting a course record on the last round didn't hurt."

"Well, it couldn't have happened without your insightful teaching, and of course, Bobbie's support."

"Where is Bobbie, by the way?" Josh asked.

"She's out getting us pizza and a bottle of champagne."

"Ah. Pizza and champagne," Josh exclaimed with satisfaction. "What better way to celebrate your new home?"

"She actually said that we were celebrating two things. But she hasn't told me what the second thing is yet." I took a swig of beer and leaned back on the step. "I wonder if the Pinehurst sky is always this clear and this blue," I said as I looked up at the towering green pines with their needles flashing silver in the sun.

"Do you hear that, Josh?" It was an unfamiliar sound — a steady whispering, high up in the branches.

"Yes," Josh said. "It's the sound of the wind slipping through the pines."

"It's very soothing," I said and let go a long sigh. "It's hard to believe all this."

"All what, John?"

"Being here, with Bobbie, in our new home, just eight short months after getting married, looking forward to a career as a pro golfer, having no financial worries whatsoever. How can any one guy be this lucky?" My voice cracked a bit. "I have to wonder how long it can all last."

Josh took a long swallow from his beer, and said, "John, isn't it fascinating that someone can have it all, yet still feel incomplete?"

I half laughed, waiting for him to continue. He didn't, and I realized he was waiting for an answer. "This has something to do with the True Swing, doesn't it?"

"John, you're lucky in a way that you don't realize. Not just because you've married the woman of your dreams, and are living the vocation you love and have more money than you could ever need. But because you've discovered that there's still something missing."

"The true swing," I said, and shook my head. "How do I know it's out there?"

"How do you know it isn't?"

"Good question, Josh, and I know you're right because I've glimpsed something that tells me it's there. But for you, it seems like it's always there. Your life seems to stem from some inner peace that never falters. Are you saying that it has nothing to do with your having everything you could ever want?"

"Once you fully awaken to the True Swing, it will never leave, whether you're at the bottom of the heap or at the top."

"I'm just not sure how that can be," I said.

Josh took a deep breath, then let it out slowly. "John, you've told me before that your best and most enjoyable golf games have been when you felt like something else took over — that you were just going along for the ride, watching it all unfold. So the question becomes: when you step aside, who is it that's actually playing the game?

"Is there, in fact, an answer to that question?" I asked.

"Yes, and no," Josh said, and laughed "If there were an answer to that question, it would be the question falling away.

"If... when that happens, will everything change drastically?"

"No. Nothing will change. Everything will be as it was, but..." Josh hesitated, "how you experience everything after that will be extraordinary."

My mind was spinning as it so often did during my chats with Josh. It was trying to grasp what was probably ungraspable, so it just gave up. At that very moment, a deep appreciation for having known Josh flooded into my body. During that same moment, my heart soared, and all that I felt was gratitude for being here, now, and the world around me was complete. But then my mind interrupted with a question; *how might I hold onto such a feeling*? And the feeling flitted away. "Josh," I said with amazement, "tell me I what I just saw wasn't imagined."

"What you just experienced was real, John," Josh said as he put his arm around my shoulder. "It's everything else that's imagined," and he laughed from a place that I had yet to find.

"Looks like you guys are working hard," Bobbie called out from the car as she pulled up the drive.

"It's not 'you guys' anymore," I called back. "'You guys' is Northern for 'y'all.'"

She giggled at my dry humor, and for the life of me, I never understood why. As she approached with the pizzas, my face contorted. "What's that awful smell?" I asked.

"Oh, it could be the extra anchovies, but then again I bought some Limburger at the store, and I persuaded them to shred some on the pizza."

Josh gave me a wrinkled brow look that I returned with

befuddlement and said, "You never told me anything about this before I married her. I might have reconsidered.

"This is the first I've heard about it," Josh said, surprised.

"Geez, Bobbie," I said, holding the pizza boxes at arm's length, "when did you take a liking to Limburger and anchovies?"

"When I became pregnant," she said, with as wide a smile as I'd ever seen.

Chapter 47

After one last but long look over the top of the cornstalks, I fell back into my car. *Why has nothing about this landscape changed except me? But have I changed all that much? Is my reluctance to go forward now the same as when I first came here? Am I afraid of what I might find at the end of this gravel road? Or am I afraid of what I might **not** find at the end of this gravel road? With all the magic and mystery that has surrounded this place, could Bobbie be waiting for me in that white block building?* The rearview mirror reflected a weary face staring back at me — a face of someone who was tired of running away. There was no turning back.

In fact, it was amazing I was here at all, that such grace existed that could expunge my addiction with one swift stroke — and in its place grant me the absolute proof that what I had spent a lifetime searching for did indeed exist.

But still, how can an addiction that is so all-consuming just vanish? Maybe it didn't. Maybe this is just a dream. Maybe I'm still lying in bed in the hotel room. Or just maybe it's not nineteen years later, and this has all been a dream. And Bobbie is waiting for me at the end of this gravel road. But if it's not a dream, then what happened fourteen days ago?

I recalled stumbling out of the bar and back to my room. As always, I was running away. This time it was from the voice of that TV sportscaster and the memory of that dreadful day two years ago.

But the rest of that night — it had to be a dream. No. Nightmare would be more accurate. It couldn't have been real — those hundreds of insects and bugs crawling on me. And that light, such a brilliant light materializing from nowhere, drenching the room in a blinding white glow.

Think, John.

What was it that I saw that night, squinting through drunken eyes? Did I imagine those crawling things dissolving to dust, unable to exist in such radiance? Or were they just part of the addiction? Did I imagine the vision of Josh somewhere nearby as that light gathered itself into a sphere the size of a marble, floating just above my eyes? The searing pain had certainly felt real when it dropped between my eyebrows, striking my face like a red-hot steel ball, burning its way into my forehead. And that blaze of fire that shot throughout my body, flashing the room like a Roman candle. *I couldn't possibly have imagined all that, could I?*

I fished a handkerchief from my glove compartment and wiped my forehead. What difference does it make, anyway? The truth is, dream or no dream, my addiction vanished, and I was here. The real question was "why?"

I suddenly remembered asking Josh the same question years ago.. "If you're going to ask why, John, you have to ask why not."

* * *

"Damn it. I can't believe I missed seeing her being born by only two hours," I said to Bobbie as I rushed into the hospital room. Her eyes lit up when she saw me — or maybe it was the dozen roses in my arms. I leaned over her bed and gave her a big kiss. The news that I was the father of a baby girl had arrived while I was doing a charity benefit with Jack Nicholson in Michigan. "You weren't supposed to have this baby for another week," I said. "That was the plan, remember?"

"Well, I guess we forgot to ask Billie Jo about that. It seems she had her own plans."

"I guess so," I said. "You know, I could have made it in time if we didn't live in a town two hours from the nearest major airport."

The door opened, and the nurse brought our new daughter into the room. As she handed her to Bobbie, I felt a hand on my shoulder.

"She's beautiful," Josh said.

I smiled from ear to ear. "I guess Bobbie told you that we named her Billie Jo. 'Billie' was my idea — it sounds good with Bobbie. And 'Jo' after you, Josh."

"Do you want to hold her, John?" Bobbie asked.

"Wow. Sure!" I said.

Ever so gently, I lifted her from Bobbie's arms, and suddenly my heart sank. "Oh my God! What's wrong with her hand?" I saw only three fingers. The fourth was malformed. "What happened? Did you know about this?"

Bobbie's smile vanished, and in its place was a look of hurt. I didn't know what to say. How else could I react as I saw my newborn daughter's future flash before my eyes? All the kids poking fun at her deformed hand. The difficulty she'd have doing simple things. And how would she ever be able to play golf?

"What are you seeing, John?" Josh asked.

"Her hand, of course," I said sadly. "And all the problems. Why do things like this have to happen?"

"John, if you're going to ask why you also have to ask why not."

"But…"

Josh cut me off. "There's nothing wrong with that hand as far as your daughter is concerned. And you don't have to see anything wrong, either. Where some see deformity, others see uniqueness. Where some see hindrance, others see opportunity."

His words sliced into me, as always, cutting away at my fear and anxiety. I closed my eyes for a moment and felt myself relax. When I opened them, I realized that my attention had been so riveted on Billie Jo's hand that I had yet to look at her face. When I did, it surprised me. It was so tiny, helpless, innocent, and beautiful. Tears of joy abruptly welled up along with a grin. Billie Jo scrunched her tiny face into a big smile and gurgled a laugh. Instantly, I fell in love.

"My God, Bobbie. Besides you, she is the most beautiful thing I've ever seen."

Tears were now flowing from Bobbie's eyes. Even Josh's were glistening a little more than usual.

"Thanks, Josh," I said.

"There's no need to thank me for pointing out that my granddaughter is perfect."

"A little biased, are we, Josh?" I asked.

"Of course," he said as he held out his finger to his new granddaughter.

Chapter 48

The bottle of water on the console of my car was hot, but I guzzled it down anyway. Strange how water could now satisfy my thirst when alcohol couldn't.

After flipping the empty bottle onto the passenger side floor, I continued on. But it was getting harder, driving down this road that was paved with so many memories. At the turn, I again stopped, hesitant to face what might lie ahead.

Looking for a fresh towel to wipe my face, I opened the console. Just inside was a photograph. I already knew what it was, but picked it up anyway. There was Billie Jo, all of seventeen, holding a golf trophy. What a great golfer she had become despite her hand. On the back of the photo, it said "Pinehurst Amateur, 2014". It was the tournament she had won the day before she left for college. As if it were yesterday, I could still hear Josh's words when I told him how hard it was to let go.

"She'll be fine," he had said.

"I know she will. It's me that's hurting here."

"The essence of life is change, John. If you can accept that, and you can celebrate her joy in heading off to new adventures. Clinging, however, just pulls you down into despair." I guess I was a clinger. As I recalled, that day had hit me pretty hard.

***

"I can't believe the time has passed this quickly," I said to Billie Jo as I lifted her suitcase into the trunk of her car. "Just yesterday I was holding you in my arms."

"That *was* yesterday, dad. Remember? You hugged me right after I scored an eagle on the eighteenth hole."

As I closed the trunk, I shook my head. She had inherited my dry sense of humor. "You know what I meant. Just a moment ago you were this tiny, helpless, little thing. And now look at you. Where does the time go?"

"Josh says it doesn't go anywhere," Billie Jo said. "We only think it does."

"He's right as usual but still, I should have had him talk you into choosing a college closer to home, scholarship or no scholarship. We certainly could afford it."

"Dad, we've been over this a million times. Oxford, Ohio is a peaceful, beautiful little town," she said. "And it's no more than twenty-five miles from Josh's range. You know he'll keep an eye on me, and my golf game."

"But who'll keep an eye on me?" I joked.

"I will," Bobbie said as she carried a cooler of drinks and sandwiches to the car. I took the cooler from her and set it on the floor behind the driver's seat. And then we all stood there, not sure what to do next.

Finally, Billie Jo said, "I guess this is it."

"Yeah," I said. "I wish we were going back up with you, but you know Josh will be there to help."

"I know."

I stared at her, desperately studying her every feature, trying to memorize every detail. But I finally I let go and held out my arms for a big hug, as did Bobbie.

"Well, you know we love you," I said. "And you'd better stay in touch."

A moment later, she was gone.

Bobbie put her arms around my waist and squeezed. She felt sadness about her little her girl leaving as well, but thanks to a lifetime of Josh's influence, she could feel these emotions and let them go while I held on to them like glue.

That evening, dinner was a subdued affair. Bobbie tried to cheer me up, mostly by reminiscing about Billie Jo, but it just made me miss her all that much more. As I got up to help her with the dishes, she said, "I'll take care of this. Why don't you go hang out in the den for a while?"

The den was my unofficial haven. Tournament jitters, post-tournament letdowns, frustrations, doubts, worries, sadness — all seemed easier to handle from the comfort of my large, overstuffed leather recliner. On late summer afternoons, the den didn't get the sun as did the far side of the house, so I clicked on the small table lamp and sunk into the chair. The dim glow of the lamp was not quite enough to light the room, but it was enough to keep the room from falling into darkness, allowing my mind to drift somewhere in between.

The den was not doing its job. The shelf with my golf trophies and mementos now seemed to be just a reminder of a time passed. Without Billie Jo rushing in to share her latest adventure or accomplishment, the den became an empty room. If only Josh could be here now, he would know what to say to chip away this hollowness.

Bobbie stuck her head in the room. "Are you coming to bed?"

"I think I'll sit here for a while,"

"I miss her, too," she said sadly, coming closer. "I wish there were something I could do to make you feel better."

"I'll be okay."

"I know," she said with a wan smile. She walked in, gave me a quick kiss, and left.

My reminiscing dropped me deeper in despair and deeper into the night. Memories both happy and sad crowded my mind causing the emptiness to expand. *Why is it we take for granted those we love until they're not around?* As I drew in a long breath, I felt my body shake from the loneliness and wondered what words of wisdom Josh might have offered had he been here.

Suddenly, my thoughts were interrupted by shadows leaping about the room. The light bulb in the lamp was flickering. When I reached for it, the flickering intensified and sparks of light danced on the walls as if reflected from a mirrored ball.

FLASH!

The room lit up in a burst of light, then vanished.

BOOM!

"What the hell was that?" I yelled.

"Thunder in the distance," Josh said.

"Josh? Am I dreaming? Where are we?"

"Where do you think we are?" he asked, nodding past me.

I spun around. We were both standing up high, on a hill, looking down over a valley.

FLASH!

BOOM!

In the distance, thick black clouds were unleashing torrents of rain, moving quickly toward the valley.

"I don't understand. How'd I get here?" What is this place?"

"Take a look," he said, smiling.

A long, winding river stretched through woods that lay below. As I followed its path, I noticed a clearing among the trees, and a small white building. On the other side of the river were long oval patches of green.

"Is that the Golden River range, and your golf course?" I asked.

"Yep. Quite a view, isn't it?"

There were a lot of fairways, and I counted them quickly. Eighteen. "You've finished it," I said excitedly.

FLASH!

CRACK!

BOOM!

The storm was now over the valley. We could hear the sound of rushing water as the river tore over its banks and swept across the fairways. Moments later, a huge funnel cloud touched down and swept over the course tearing up everything in its path.

But just as quickly as it had come, it was gone. But so too was Josh's golf course. I was beside myself with grief, knowing how long it took Josh to complete it. In utter disbelief, I said, "I'm so sorry!"

"Sorry?" he repeated. "About what?"

"What do you mean, 'about what'? Didn't you see what just happened?"

"Of course," he said, his eyes sparkling with delight. "Have you ever witnessed so grand a spectacle from nature such as that? It was magnificent."

"How can you say that, Josh? All your years of effort, gone in seconds."

He started laughing from the depth of his being.

"Josh, why are you laughing? How can you see humor in this?"

"But John, it's all new again. Think of the possibilities."

"Boom!"

A loud crack of thunder bolted me straight up in my chair. The lamp flickered a few times and settled into its previous dim glow.

What had happened, I wasn't sure, but all was as it had been in my den. Except for the words — the desperately needed words at that time. "It's all new again. Think of the possibilities."

Chapter 49

"It's all new again. Think of the possibilities." Dream or not, those words had etched themselves into my mind. Standing on the cliff, conversing with Josh seemed so real that I had to confront him. My plan was to do so the coming week when I hooked up with him in Illinois for the PGA Championship, but I didn't. Since that night, an incredible exhilaration had befallen me, and I was afraid that talking about it might cause it to slip away.

It was a strange feeling as if *I* had dropped out of the picture altogether, yet amazing because everything was taking care of itself all on its own. The experience reminded me of how I had felt in 1995 when playing the Cavendish Cup, the first tournament I had ever won.

When Josh met me on the practice range, as always, he sensed something was up. His usual coaching advice was replaced by a silent smile — and somehow we shared an understanding of what was happening. It was as if we both were watching me practice from the same place. And my swing was taking care of itself, sending the ball right where it should go. After about thirty minutes, I put my clubs back in my bag and shrugged my shoulders. "What do you think, Josh?"

"Nothing to think about, John," he said. "Just let it be. See what happens." So that's what I did.

On the final day of the tournament, Davis Love III and I, stood in the middle of the seventeenth fairway. We were the last two players on the course, I was leading by one stroke — or rather, *whoever* was playing me was leading by one stroke — and Davis Love III, my playing partner, was the one to beat. We had both just hit crushing drives off the tee. But mine was twenty yards longer. As Davis prepared to hit, my caddy leaned into me and whispered, "Your game has been right on today."

Ollie had been my caddie for the last fifteen years. Not only was he a good friend, he was my trusted advisor in the fairways and on the greens. It was uncanny how well he understood my game, always knowing exactly which club to use, where the ball would land, and how the putts would fall.

"I have to admit," I said in a low voice, "everything seems to be working."

"And here we are," he responded, "near the end of the PGA Championship, and you're up by one stroke." Ollie stopped talking as Davis swung at his ball. It flew straight towards the green, landing within eight feet of the pin — an easy birdie.

After handing me my eight iron, Ollie continued his encouragement. "The way you've been playing, John, you can easily put your ball inside of his and make him sweat for his birdie."

I smiled in agreement. But as I stepped up to the ball, he added one more statement. "Just hang in there this hole and the next, and the PGA Championship is yours."

His words struck me like a rock hitting a pane of glass...*the PGA Championship is yours.*

It felt as if my body had suddenly been invaded by an alien force — a force that no longer wanted this tournament left to fate. The stakes were too high — not only a first major win but the PGA Championship to boot. It suddenly felt as if I had come this far by accident and too much could go wrong if *I* didn't step in and take control. It was time to get serious.

Ollie must have sensed the change. "Are you okay?" he asked.

My smile was forced, and I didn't answer.

"A simple shot, John," Ollie said. "The eight iron will put you right on the stick."

In my heart, I knew he was right, but my mind wasn't so sure, so I put it through a drill of how to execute the shot. Still, something was dreadfully wrong. The club just didn't feel right.

WHAMPF!

The ball flew out of the grass much too hard and fast, and started fading.

"Oh, crap!" Ollie said, and so did I as we both watched in shock as the ball sailed off to the right of the green.

CLUNK.

Incredibly, it hit the temporary TV tower and kicked back to the edge of the green. Ollie and I shot each other a "God, that was lucky" glance, and proceeded to walk to my ball in silence. Behind us, someone in the crowd yelled, "Nice bank shot, John." At another time and place, I might have laughed.

My mind was struggling to focus on the shot when Ollie handed me my seven iron. It was the right club to hop the ball onto the green and let it roll to the cup. An easy shot. I had done it thousands of times. But my legs felt rubbery, and my arms trembled. As I drew the club back, it felt hurried, and I ended up forcing the club through the ball.

CHUNK!

To my horror, the bottom of my clubface caught the ball, shooting it out of the short grass, and rocketing it across the green.

CLANG!

By sheer luck, it hit the pin and dropped straight down into the cup.

"Nice birdie," Ollie said with trepidation.

"Yeah, right," I said with equal foreboding.

But his words and my response rang familiar. Then I remembered. It was the day Josh first took me onto his course. "Nice birdie," Josh had said after I drove into the woods, banked my ball off a tree, and sank a short putt. After complaining that I'd rather have played the hole with his form than with my butt and pretzel swing and dumb luck, he said, "But you won the hole, John."

My last two shots obviously weren't making Davis sweat. He sank his putt for a birdie. With my one stroke lead, there was still hope, but Ollie gave no advice as we slowly walked to the last tee. The eighteenth hole was a one-hundred-and-seventy-four-yard par three. Davis didn't give the hole much thought before he stepped up and swung. The ball sailed to the middle of the green, landing about thirty feet from the hole. As I watched it roll to a stop, I felt alone in the universe.

Chapter 50

Get a hold of yourself, John. It's just a game. There's nothing at stake here. Just the chance to win the PGA Championship, and your first major tournament.

"Oh man, I just don't know," I said to myself while staring blankly out over the eighteenth hole. It was an undemanding par three. No big deal, and unless Davis sank his thirty-foot putt, all that was needed was a par, and the championship was mine.

"Oh, man, I just don't know," I said to myself again.

The green was long and narrow with a lake that stretched from tee to the green. It was protected by a sand trap on the right. It *was* manageable in three shots, and that's all I needed. One good swing was all it would take. But if the ball landed in the water, it would cost me two strokes and cost me the tournament. "Not much riding on this swing," I said to myself with sarcasm.

Ollie slid a seven iron from my bag and held it out to me. I closed my eyes, drew a deep breath, and hesitated. The murmuring of the crowd increased. Were they getting impatient, or did they sense my panic? With reluctance, I took the club, but once it was in my hands, something felt wrong. In my mind, I heard a splash. And it was not the "finish-with-a-big-splash" I was looking for.

What on earth should I do?

"Trust your instinct," I heard Josh whisper in my ear.

"What?" I said, spinning around. Only Ollie was there.

Bewildered by my outburst, he checked behind him, then turned back to me. "I didn't say anything," he said.

"Trust your instinct" is what I had heard, and suddenly it was clear what had to be done. I handed the seven iron back to Ollie. He took it with raised eyebrows.

"Hand me my driver," I said.

His expression changed from surprise to shock. He didn't budge, so I repeated, "Hand me my driver, Ollie."

"You're kidding, right?"

"No, I'm not. Please hand me my driver."

"I don't think so," he said nervously.

"My driver, Ollie. Trust me."

"Are you nuts?" he finally said, frantic. "If you use your driver here, you'll send your ball straight over the clubhouse and into the parking lot."

I grabbed for the driver. He pulled the bag away.

"Ollie, I'm not kidding," I said sternly and lunged for the club.

He jerked the bag away again, but I managed to catch the end of the club head, and it slid from the bag. Ollie grabbed the other end and pulled back, and a game of tug-of-war ensued for a good minute before I wrenched it from his grip.

Someone in the gallery let out a hearty laugh. It was Josh. After calming Ollie down with a promise to pay him a big bonus no matter what the outcome, I shot Josh a hard look. Still laughing, he motioned me over. Reluctantly, I went.

"Driver, huh?" he said, chuckling. "This ought to be good."

Maybe it was clear what I had to do, but it didn't mean I wasn't panicking. And it certainly wasn't helping that he was relishing in my plight.

"What's going on here, Josh?" I whispered in exasperation. "What happened to my rhythm? Where did that feeling go?"

"Well, I suspect that the "whatever-is-going-to-happen self" got shoved to the background when the "I-want-to-control-this-tournament self" showed up to grab hold of the glory."

"What?" I said as I glared at him. "So what am I supposed to do now?"

Ollie called out, "John! They're waiting."

Josh glanced at the driver again and grinned. "It looks like you already know what you're going to do."

"Damn it, Josh," I said and spun around. As I started walking towards the tee, he called after me, "Just remember John; it's all new again. Think of the possibilities."

I stopped dead in my tracks but didn't look back. I'm not sure he needed to see the smile spreading across my face. "Darn him anyway," I murmured, and walked to the tee.

***

That night, the cable sports networks and national news replayed my performance on the final hole more than any other shot in the history of the game. And they all had the same footage.

"There's a skirmish going on at the eighteenth tee between John Arbor and his long-time caddie," the booth announcer said. "Let's go to our field announcer. Jane, can you tell us what's happening down there?"

"It seems they're fighting over what club to use," Jane said. "His caddie has given him a seven iron, but he wants to exchange it for another club, and I think it's his driver."

"A driver?" the booth announcer exclaimed. "Are you sure? He'll hit that over the clubhouse."

"That's what I would think, but it doesn't look like we'll find out. His caddie won't let him have it. Wait a minute — he's strong-armed it away, and now he's walking over to someone in the crowd."

"Can you hear what they're saying?

"No. They're too far away, but the fellow he's talking with seems to be grinning. Arbor looks worried. Now Arbor's heading to the tee. The fellow he was talking to called out something, but Arbor appears to be ignoring him. Wait, he stopped. Now he's smiling. You don't think he's going to hit his driver, do you?"

"It looks like it from here," the booth announcer chimed in. "He's approaching the tee... Wait a minute — what's he doing now?"

"This is unbelievable," Jane said. "He's lining up way left of the hole, and...holy cow!"

"What?" the booth announcer asked.

"His, uh, rear section is inching out..."

"His what?"

"Rear section. You know, rump. And he's changing his grip. Strange. Now he's dropping his right leg back, and sort of shriveling up into a contorted...Eeeeewwww."

"What?" the booth announcer asked.

"He just dropped a wad of spit on the back of his hands. And he hasn't wiped it off. Now he's going to swing...!

WHAMPF!

I swung with all I had. The ball shot out left and did a "banana" curve around the left side of the lake, completely avoiding the water. At a hundred and seventy yards it dove into a mound in front of the sand trap, shot straight up over the sand, landed softly on the green, and ran straight to the cup.

PLOP.

It dropped, and the crowd roared. Ollie and I just stood there, stunned. A hole in one. When the shock wore off, Ollie dove into my arms, knocking me straight to the ground.

"That was quite a shot, John," the announcer said while walking along with me towards the clubhouse. He put the microphone to my face and half laughed. "How long have you been saving it?"

"Longer than you might think," I said, not sure how else to explain it.

"Where did you learn such an unusual swing?"

"Well," I said, "it's more or less a culmination of techniques from every instructor I've ever had."

The announcer gave me a doubtful stare. "So you're saying that you were paying tribute to all the teachers that got you here today."

"Yeah. That's it," I said. "That's exactly what I was doing."

While the announcer considered how to respond, a tournament official handed me the trophy and check. After thanking him, I bolted to turn in my score and then to find Josh. It had occurred to me that maybe the "butt and pretzel" swing was the True Swing — and had been all along. After all, hadn't Josh said that it was always with me? And it just won me the championship.

Josh was waiting for me in the bar, and he was all smiles. Before I even sat down, I started drilling him. "Josh, was that the True Swing? Is that what you've been trying to tell me? Was that what you meant when you said it's always there, waiting to be recognized?"

"What do *you* think?" he asked.

"Hell, I don't know. That's why I'm asking you."

He burst out laughing. "John, I only wish that you had enjoyed those last two holes as much as I did. What great fun it was, watching you out there. And you've probably done more for the game of golf today than all the players in the last forty years combined."

"I'm glad you found my struggles amusing," I said. "But are you going to answer me? Was that the True Swing?"

"John, it's all the True Swing," he said and started laughing again.

I never did ask him about the dream.

Chapter 51

A sudden gust of wind swirled over the car and disappeared. The next moment, the air stilled, and I trembled.

Strange. The wind. The chill. The shiver. Just the way it happened two years ago on hole fourteen when...

I cranked the engine and shoved the shifter into drive while forcing *that* day from my mind. But getting rid of that memory was becoming more difficult the further I traveled this road.

As I peered ahead, the many shades of green gave way to the river that ambled along the road. Seeing it here, now, again, nestled in among the spreading oak and maple trees, flowing peacefully within its shallow banks, reminded me how it so easily had lifted my spirits, always preparing me for whatever was waiting at the range. Even now, I feel its energy reaching deep inside me as if searching for something it might recognize as itself. *What power, what love, could create such beauty? And yet...and yet allow it to be so...so temporary.*

Driving slowly along the riverbank, my mind drifted back through the years; to those long-ago treks down this winding, gravel road. It's staggering to think where this road had taken me and is still taking me, all of it wrapped around the insane idea of something called the True Swing. And yet with all that life has thrown at me, it will not let go. What was that question Josh had posed to me years before? "What you see here in front of you, John — is it really there at all?"

"Are you suggesting that it's not real?" I had asked. "That nothing is real? That it's all just an illusion?"

"Everything you see is as real as you are," he had said. "The question is how real are you?"

Ah, Josh. I've missed you. Can you ever forgive me for walking away, leaving you for the last two years without so much as much as a letter or a postcard? Or is all that I've been through really just a dream. Will everything be just as it was at the end of this road?

The drive was quickly becoming an internal struggle. Something hidden inside me was trying to show itself while another part was fighting it, terrified that to do so would destroy whatever was left of John Arbor. "The question is, how real are you?"

The river slipped into my rear view mirror as the road turned, depositing me under the grove of towering sycamore trees. The end of the road was near, but I could go no further. I knew now that my final destination was unreachable until *that* day was faced. But how? Just a mere thought of it brought torrents of unbearable pain.

I can't go through that day again! Why put myself through this!? Why does any of it matter!?

"It matters," a voice said from deep inside. "It's now or never."

***

Ollie glanced at my driver, smiled and said, "Just hang in there this hole, and the Tour Championship is yours."

I chuckled. It was a running joke because we both knew there was nothing he could say (short of telling me he had a better job offer) that would ever rattle me again. After all, how could anyone who had shown the "butt and pretzel" swing to thirty million people ever get rattled?

We were on the fourteenth tee at Pinehurst #2. I was excited. Not just because the sky was almost as blue as Bobbie's eyes, or because the temperature had climbed to the high-eighties, or because my six-stroke lead on the fourteenth hole would probably assure me a win. My excitement was in anticipation of the gala event planned for later that evening. Josh and Billie Jo had flown in from Ohio, and BJ, Larry, and Tom had accepted our invitation to come down for the festivities. It was going to be an old-fashioned picnic and barbecue, with family, friends, and neighbors — a perfect ending to a glorious summer day. As far as the tournament was concerned, I had long since realized that any wins I got, would be the *result* of doing what I loved to do, not the reason for doing it.

"I'm sorry I can't go to the course with you," Bobbie had said that morning over breakfast. "I've still got a lot of shopping to do for tonight." She had given me a quick kiss before I headed out the door and said, "I'll try to catch the last few holes."

As I leaned over to place my ball on the tee, Ollie said, "Put it just a little to the left, John; it will set you up for the best shot into the green."

"That's what I was thinking," I said, and stepped back behind the ball to scan the fairway. As I moved forward to the tee, a sudden chill struck my body as a gust of wind whipped the branches of a nearby tree. A moment later, all was still.

Something was terribly wrong. Ollie was scanning the surroundings as if he had felt it too. Our eyes met, reflecting our mutual uneasiness, but neither of us knew what to say. So he just shrugged his shoulders, and I stepped back over the ball and swung. The ball soared a good two hundred and eighty yards, landing on the left side of the fairway.

Ollie took my driver without a word as Freddy Couples, my playing partner, stepped up to the tee. Freddie hit his ball about the same distance, but to the other side of the fairway. Instead of bantering as we usually did, Ollie and I walked towards my ball in silence. When we reached it, he finally asked, "Everything okay?"

"Why do you ask?" I replied.

"'Don't know," he said and handed me a six iron.

A flock of birds abruptly bolted from a tree behind us sending another sharp chill up my spine. I spun quickly, watching the birds soar erratically upwards into the sky. Searching a reason for my trepidation, I let my eyes drift to the spectators and my sight settled on a golf cart that was racing towards us. On the side of the cart was a sign that said "official."

"What's happening, John?" asked Ollie with concern.

I said nothing — just stood there frozen, staring, waiting, dreading. When the cart reached me, the official said, "Mr. Arbor, you need to come with me right away." Without asking why I jumped into the cart. His face was grim, his eyes unfocused and I could see that it pained him when he finally spoke. "There's been an accident." My mind was reeling as the cart sped back towards the clubhouse.

"It's my wife, isn't it?" I asked.

He stared straight ahead as he drove. "A witness said she was struck by a pick-up truck as she was walking across the player's parking lot. One of the officials recognized her and radioed me immediately. An ambulance has been called and is on its way."

After what seemed like hours, we reached the lot. Before the cart stopped, I bolted from the seat and ran towards a gathered crowd. *Bobbie, please be all right.*

Sirens arose in the distance as I pushed my way through the onlookers and officials. When they saw me, they moved back, revealing Bobbie lying on her back on the ground. A blanket covered her body but not her face. It was drained of color, but she was conscious. "My God! This can't be happening," I cried as I knelt over her and took her hand.

Ever so softly, her hand squeezed back. "John?" she said in a whisper.

"Bobbie, I'm here. I'm holding your hand. Can you feel it?"

"Yes," she whispered.

"Hang on, Bobbie. An ambulance will be here any second. We'll get you to the hospital. You'll be all right. Just hang on."

"John…" she whispered again.

I leaned closer. "What is it, Bobbie?"

"John, I see. I see what Josh sees. I'm not afraid."

"Bobbie, please. Don't…"

She moved her fingers over my wedding band. "We are not separate, you and I," she whispered. "I see that now. Like two rings made from the same gold — we appear separate, but we are the same. We will never be apart."

"Bobbie, I love you."

A tear slid down the side of her cheek. "I'll miss you," she said, as she exhaled her last breath and the light faded from her blue eyes.

"NO!"

✱✱✱

An abrupt wind suddenly struck the top of the sycamores, violently whipping them from side to side. Shafts of sunlight scattered in all directions, streaking across the ground, flashing over my car.

"WHY!?" I cried.

My hands were clenching the steering wheel, bracing me against the pain that shook the very core of my being. And then came the tears, and for the first time since I left Bobbie's side, I wept.

Like two rings made from the same gold — we are separate, but we are the same. We will never be apart. *That's what she had said.* We will never be apart. *Could it be that this has all been a dream? Josh, with his magical book, mystical ways and topsy-turvy view of what is real and not real — could he have me entwined in some dream to find the True Swing? Is it possible that no time has passed, that nothing has happened? That I will awaken and find Bobbie at the end of this road?*

The question ignited a burning at the base of my spine as if I were sitting on a red-hot coal. As it rose upwards through my body, a sense of urgency gripped me. I cranked the engine, stomped the gas pedal, and spun forward. When I reached the lot, I slid to a stop and jumped out. *Incredible! Nothing has changed!* The trees, the bushes, the white cinderblock building, the screen door — they were all as I remembered! *Is it possible? Could it have all been just a dream?*

The burning heat was spreading through my body as I took off running towards the building. Whatever was happening had me shaking violently, so violently I wasn't sure I would make it. It was as if something was uprooting the very foundation of who I was, or who I thought I was. Panic set in as I felt myself slipping away, but there was also this indefinable feeling of excitement or joy somewhere underneath trying to break free — both fighting each other for survival. I pushed on, certain that all the answers were here, waiting inside the building. Tears were streaming down my face when I reached the screen door, but when I grabbed the handle, what was left of John Arbor shouted inside my head — *STOP! This is insane! How could you possibly believe that Bobbie and you could be together again as one? Don't delude yourself! Go back!*

NO! My heart knew that somehow she was here. Whoever or whatever that was telling me different was lying. Still, I hesitated. *What power could be so great as to keep me from seeing the Truth?*

Then I saw it clearly. The final obstacle. The only obstacle. Fear. Fear was the great power that had given life to who I thought myself to be. Somehow I knew that after entering this door, who I thought I was, would be no longer. A life of searching has brought me full circle, landing me here, now, arriving back at the beginning, arriving back to where it all began to face that one final question.

Who? Who is it that is afraid to face the Truth? Who am I?

"Only one way to find out," I said to myself. I grasped the handle and pulled.

Chapter 52

CREAK.

SLAP.

Darkness. My eyes squinted against the intense sunlight pouring in the back window.

Wait a minute. Did I see something move?

There, behind the counter, a silhouette framed by the window.

Could it be possible?

My eyes struggled to adjust.

I recognized something. The movement behind the counter was familiar. I remember the gentle sway of her hair as she turned.

Her eyes briefly caught the sunlight, and my heart leapt into my throat. My legs turned to jelly. There were no other eyes that clear, that blue. By the time her gaze fell upon me, my sight had adjusted enough to see her fully. Her eyes grew wide in recognition, and that unmistakable smile spread across her face. I reeled backward and froze in astonishment as the fire rising in through my body burst to the surface and took what was left of me, completely.

"Dad!" Billie Jo yelled.

The room exploded in a flash of white light as Billie Jo vaulted over the counter and threw herself into my arms. As I spun her around, I felt the whole universe dancing. So immense was the joy, my body seemed to melt into its vastness. All questions, all doubts, were gone. It wasn't just Billie Jo in my arms, it was Bobbie, and Josh, and BJ, and Larry, and Tom, and everyone I knew, and everyone I didn't know. It was everything! *Like two rings made from the same gold, we are both the same gold. We are* all *the same gold.* I laughed until I cried.

There it was — the Truth. There is no True Swing, and yet there is — it's all the True Swing, just as Josh had said. And it *has* always been there. But who, or what, now recognizes it, is anybody's guess.

Billie Jo finally let go, but I didn't.

"Don't worry, Dad," she finally said, wiping her tears away. "Now that you're back, I'm not letting you go."

"Billie Jo! If you only knew how wonderful you look right now."

"I've missed you so much," she said. "So often I've wanted to go hunt you up, but Josh said we had to be patient. So we just kept your bills paid, and your credit cards up, and waited."

As I cupped her cheek in my hand and brushed away the rest of her tears, she stared into my eyes for a long moment and wrinkled her brow.

"What?" I asked.

"The way you look, Dad."

"I know," I said. "Two years of what I've put myself through can do it to you."

"No, it's not that. The way you're looking at me — it's hard to explain. It's the same way Josh looks at me."

"Josh! Oh my gosh. Where is he? Is he here?"

"Right out back," she said. "Funny thing, he's usually not here on Wednesdays, but he came in early this morning and planted himself on the bench. Said he was waiting for someone. When I asked him who, he said, 'you'll see.'" She shook her head and laughed. "I'll tell you; he's something else."

Chapter 53

It is as if no time has passed at all. Josh is resting on the bench behind the tees, a driver and a half-bucket of balls sit next to him. On his other side lies the *Handbook of a Master Instructor.*

He looks at me. His penetrating stare recognizes something, and he grins big.

"Hi, Josh."

"Hi, John."

"Rumor has it you've been waiting for me."

"Who says?"

"A spy inside the building."

"Then you've got me."

"Sorry, Josh."

"Sorry? For what?"

"That you've been patiently waiting for me, and here, now we both know that *I* am never going to show up."

We stare deep into each other's eyes, and he sees there is no one looking back. A moment passes, and I say, "I had no idea." Another moment passes and uncontrollable laughter erupts from both of us simultaneously, the sound booming out across the meadow. When the laughter subsides, Josh asks, "So, do you think the search for the True Swing has been worth it?"

"*Who* wants to know?"

Josh bursts into renewed laughter, reigniting mine, and we laugh ourselves to tears.

***

A good while had passed before we settled into quiet conversation. Billie Jo joined us, and we all spent some time catching up. She then headed back to the building as Josh and I fell into a comfortable silence. After a few minutes, he said, "John, I'm leaving for a while — going out to the Montana ranch."

"What will you do there?"

"I've put in another range on the back side of it. 'Thought I'd hang out and teach a little. But I'll stay in touch with you and Billie Jo, and I'll be back often. You're always welcome to visit."

"Well, you know I'll miss you," I said, "When are you leaving?"

"Tomorrow. But I'm taking you and Billie Jo out tonight to

celebrate your homecoming."

With that, he stood, as did I, and we hugged. He picked up the *Handbook of a Master Instructor* and with a grin, handed it to me and walked off.

I sat down and opened the book. Just inside the front cover were numerous blank white index cards. I chuckled, closed the book and gazed out over the range. All that *is* was right in front of me. It had always been right in front of me. The only difference now is seeing the miracle behind it.

After a while, the sound of a car engine merged with the sounds of the range. Not long after, a young man carrying a bag of clubs came around the corner of the building. He was in his early twenties, with wavy brown hair, a slim build, and a weary expression. As he approached the tees he glanced at me and then his eyes darted quickly to the book lying on the bench as if something about it had grabbed his attention. He stared at it for a moment looking very much puzzled, but then shook his head and shrugged his bag off his shoulder. After rummaging through his clubs, he selected a driver and teed up a ball.

WHIFF!

His club just barely caught the ball and rolled it about five yards.

WHOMP!

The ball hit the heel of the club and bounced a little further into the range.

WHAMPF!

The ball started right but then sailed in a wide arc to the left. He stepped back off the tee and when he glanced at me again, I smiled.

"Some swing, huh?" he said.

When I didn't answer, his eyes caught mine directly, and he stared into them. He then glanced away. "There's got to be a way to develop a good, true swing," he mumbled.

"Where have you been looking?" I asked.

"Huh? For what?" he asked, a bit confused.

"For the True Swing."

"Where have I been looking? Well, I've been taking lessons at Blue Ash and Sharon Woods."

"Any luck?" I asked.

"Not even close."

"Do you believe you will find it here?"

There, in his eyes, for however brief the moment, he *saw*. But then his mind kicked back in.

"I don't know," he finally said. "Is it possible I will?"

"No. You will not find it here." I answered with a smile.

He looked stunned. "Are you an instructor?" he asked.

"Are you a student?" I asked back.

"Yeah, I guess I am. And I don't know where else to look."

"This is the end of your first lesson," I said as I picked up a ball and tossed it to him. "Tee this up and swing away." While he consumed himself in thought, working into position over the ball, I walked back to the building.

"Billie Jo, would you hand me a pen?"

She leaned out the back of the opening and as she handed me a felt-tipped marker, she said. "Josh left this for you."

"'Doesn't surprise me," I said as I took an index card from the book. While writing on it, Billie Jo glanced towards the tees. "Nice-looking guy, don't you think?"

THWOMPF!

"But could use some work on his swing," she added. "Think you could help him?"

I handed her the card and winked. She grinned and said, "I'll give it to him. By the way, you feel like raking up some of the range balls?" She nodded towards the tractor.

"Sure," I said and headed off. But just as I was about to climb on, a familiar sound rang out through the meadow.

WHAAAAACK!!!!

AWAKENING
IN
SURRY COUNTY

For an excerpt, turn the page.

Chapter 1

"Hey, Dad! Look at that!" Jimmy yelled from the passenger seat of his dad's pickup. He was pointing out the driver's side window. At the top of the mountain, right before I-77 dropped steeply into North Carolina, a fellow could see all the way to Pilot Mountain.

"No need to shout," Jake said. "I'm not in the next county." He smiled big at his son and glanced at the view. But only a quick glance. Flying along at seventy miles per hour, his attention didn't need to stray too far from the road.

When they neared the bottom of the hill, Jimmy shouted again, "There! 'Lots of rocks just ahead!"

"What did I just say about...?" Jake stopped. Why quash the kid's excitement? It was a good thing — his thirteen-year-old having such adventure in so simple an outing — helping his old man collect rocks for an outdoor grill. "It was just over that rise," Jake said, "where my dad used to take me fishing long before this freeway came along."

"I miss Grandpa Clayton," Jimmy said.

A lump caught in Jake's throat and he swallowed hard. Cancer had stolen his father from him three years ago and did it slowly. For reasons he couldn't explain, he felt responsible, watching him fade away without knowing how to fix it.

"Daddy, pull over before we pass them up!"

Jake shook free from his thoughts and glanced in the rear view mirror. No cars behind him and no cops that he could see, so he slowed to a near stop before pulling off the road. It probably wasn't safe, or even legal, taking rocks from the bottom of the huge cliffs that lined the Interstate, but ever since he struck out on his own as a mechanic, his income had been shaky at best. Why spend money on stones for his outdoor grill when all these rocks were just laying around going to waste.

The rocky ground was giving his four by four a workout, and his lower back was letting him know it. At age thirty-six, he was slim and kept in good shape but years of bending over hoods and sliding under cars were taking its toll on his back. On the other hand, those years also made him an exceptional mechanic.

He spotted a flat area, probably used for parking heavy highway equipment when the crews were working on the cliff, and headed towards it. As he was pulling to a stop, Jimmy bolted from the cab and sailed over the broken terrain as if it wasn't there.

"Hey! Jake shouted, but then shook his head and smiled. He couldn't help it, watching the way Jimmy moved. Being taller than most kids his age, he was what some might call lanky, but sure-footed and moved with a certain grace that reminded Jake of himself in his younger days. Since he was headed towards the bottom of the rock cliff rather than the expressway, he wasn't too concerned. Jimmy was always careful. But his wife Sarah was another matter. If she knew he had her oldest son out on the side of the Interstate, there would be hell to pay. If anything were to happen… he yelled after him, "Careful, Jimmy! And stay away from the road. You hear me?"

"Jake circled to the back of the truck and began lifting stones into the bed while keeping a watchful eye. But the when the rocks became more than his back could handle, his attention swayed. That's when Jimmy screamed.

Jake spun in panic. "Oh God!"

On a large flat rock near the cliff, his son was lying still, face-up. Despite his back pain, Jake sprinted across the huge broken boulders. But as he got closer, Jimmy stirred, and by the time Jake reached him, he had rolled onto his side and sat up.

"Jimmy! Are you okay!?"

"Yeah," he said. "Wow! That was something else!"

Jake kneeled down and looked his son square in the eye. "Look at me! Are you sure you're okay?"

"Yeah, dad," he said, as he stood up.

Jake put his hands on Jimmy's shoulders, gently shook him, and let go a long sigh. "Gees, Jimmy. Don't go scaring me like that."

"'Sorry dad. It's just that…"

"Holy Crap," Jake said. "Look at those scrapes." Jimmy tried to look, but the bruises were on the back sides of his elbows. "Your mom's going to be madder than a wet hen. What in tarnation happened?"

"It was that rock over there."

Jake looked to where he pointed. Embedded into the side of the cliff was an odd stone, shaped sort of like a cedar chest, and was reflecting a bluish-white color in the sunlight. The way it stuck out from the cliff gave the appearance that there was more to it.

"What about it? What did you do?"

"I didn't do anything. Honest. I just touched it and got thrown back here."

"What?" Jake eyed his son with skepticism and then proceeded to check him over. "Are you sure you just didn't slip and fall?"

"I don't think so."

"You don't really expect me to believe that a rock can throw you anywhere, do you?" Jake asked while examining the back of his head. A bit of blood was seeping through his thick brown hair and when he parted it, found a good sized bruise.

"It surely did Daddy. I swear it did."

"You got a fine looking lump on the back of your head, but I don't think it's anything to fret about."

"You believe me, don't you daddy?"

Jake rolled his eyes and glanced back at the stone. "Okay, son, I'll take a look."

Jake grimaced as he straightened and favoring his back, he made his way across the uneven rocks. As he got closer to the strangely shaped rock, he saw what attracted Jimmy to it. The bluish-white glow appeared liquid in the sunlight. Jake glanced over at his son and headed back towards the pick-up.

"Where are you going, Dad?"

"I'm going to get my pickaxe and see if I can dig it out."

"I don't think that's a good idea," Jimmy said.

"Don't be fretting, Jimmy. Nothing's going to happen."

Jake retrieved a rag and cooler from the cab and placed it on the open tailgate. After he soaked the rag in the half-melted ice, he grabbed the pickaxe from the bed and hurried back to his son. "Let me clean this up a bit first," Jake said as he gently wiped the scrapes on his arms and the back of his head.

"Daddy. Please don't go touching that thing."

"Hells bells, Jimmy. You can be such a worrier," Jake said. "Just stay put while I check it out."

The stone stuck out from the cliff about a foot and a half, just a little below Jake's waist. He swung the pickaxe high to avoid damaging it. "Crap!" he yelled and jumped back. Huge chunks of dirt and rock poured down over the stone, partially burying his work boots.

"Daddy? What happened?"

"Nothing, Jimmy. The cliff just doesn't' seem as hard as it looks." His next two swings did the same and exposed a lot more of the stone.

"Well I'll be," Jake said.

"What is it, dad?"

"I ain't sure, Jimmy. This rock is like nothing I've ever seen before. It's longer than it is wide and the shape ain't natural. It looks like a rectangular stone box. And the way the sunlight is making it glow is pretty weird."

Jake put more muscle into his next swing, only to feel a sharp sting shoot straight up his spine. "Damn it," he said to himself. Wincing in pain, he leaned heavily on his pickaxe and waited for it to pass. When he opened his eyes, the glow of the rock seemed brighter, but something was different. The sun — it had ducked behind a cloud, yet the stone was still shimmering in a bluish-white glow. Dropping the pickaxe, he moved in for a closer look.

"Daddy! Don't touch it!"

"Jimmy, quit being silly," Jake said. "Look here. I'll show you."

"No!" Jimmy shouted.

But Jake paid no attention and reached for the stone.

About the Author

"To be present is to see for the first time, the miracle that is continually unfolding around us. The good news is that the "Here and Now" is always there, waiting for us. Why not take the leap?

Tom Scheve, in his books *The True Swing* and *Awakening in Surry County,* uses fiction to show us the incredible power of being present, alive, and effortlessly aware. Awakening in Surry County, available in paperback and Kindle won an award for best fiction from a London Publisher. It is the first book in a series now available. Tom, also having had a history of classic migraine's, and discovering a way to free himself of the pain, is sharing his experience in the soon to be available book *Free Yourself From Migraine Pain*. He resides with his wife in Southern Pines, NC.

Made in the USA
Columbia, SC
24 April 2022

59310884R00154